death row

JON KATZ

death row

A Suburban Detective Mystery

DOUBLEDAY
New York
London
Toronto
Sydney
Auckland

Kat

PUBLISHED BY DOUBLEDAY
a division of Bantam Doubleday Dell Publishing Group, Inc.
1540 Broadway, New York, New York 10036

DOUBLEDAY and the portrayal of an anchor with a dolphin are trademarks of Doubleday, a division of Bantam Doubleday Dell Publishing Group, Inc.

Library of Congress Cataloging-in-Publication Data

Katz, Jon.
Death row: a suburban detective mystery/ Jon Katz.—1st ed.
    p. cm.
I. Title.
PS3561.A7558D43   1998
813'.54—dc21   98-5410
CIP

ISBN 0-385-47922-0

August 1998
First Edition

10 9 8 7 6 5 4 3 2 1

For Jane Richter

death row

one

EMILY'S HAMSTER committed suicide right before her eyes. It was the perfect cap to a day of misery and self-loathing brought on by the raw, exposed ganglia of the bright young adolescent woman.

Loathsome pet rats like Marissa adorned thousands of local dresser tops. Girls loved them because they were cute and cuddly. I hated them. They were the final, foul-smelling insult after years of grubby, drooled-on stuffed bears and glittery-maned plastic ponies.

Every rodent in suburbia is purchased with the usual exhortations about responsibility, the animals-aren't-just-for-cuddling lectures. But when the sun sets, it's Dad walking the dog, feeding the cat, or scraping hamster poop into garbage bags while holding his breath. Still, Marissa's death was bad news. I wouldn't mourn the hamster much, but the loss would only heighten the sense of tragedy and injustice that in recent weeks had come to loom over Emily like a dark cloud and would, I was reliably informed, remain for a year or so—if I was lucky.

I had listened for years to horror stories from unnerved par-

ents of teenagers. I'd always nodded sympathetically but chuckled inwardly with the self-righteous certainty that these ills
afflicted other families, not mine; other dads, not me. I was a
perceptive parent with an adorable—and adoring—daughter for
whom adolescence would be just a little speed bump on the
driveway of life.

After all, I was a new and sensitive male. I knew the names of
all Emily's friends and teachers and kept her schedule burned
into my brain. I knew precisely how brown her morning toast
ought to be, and which brand of mint–chocolate chip ice cream
was acceptable. I had never once left her standing abandoned at
the school bus stop or required some clucking SuperMom to
remind me that I'd forgotten to pick her up at Kimberly's house.

In fact, I basked in the glow of my own warm opinion of my
parenting skills. During my Wall Street years, I hadn't a clue
about what Em or her big brother Ben did all day. Now I was
their gatekeeper and schedule-maker, the all-purpose, pile-up-
the-mileage, yak-with-the-moms, shop-till-you-drop Master of
Ceremonies.

And yet one Monday morning just before Christmas this
changed instantly and forever. Ben had already left for his bus
stop. Emily had staggered downstairs to face another day. "Hey,
what's up?" I asked, as I always did. Instead of answering, she
stared at me in shock and revulsion, as if I was something that
had fallen from a horse's behind.

If I'd been arrogant enough to think I'd escape this fate, I was
at least realistic enough to recognize the awful truth instantly
when I saw it. Adolescence.

"What's wrong?" I wondered.

"Nothing," Emily hissed in exasperation. "Why do you keep
asking me that?" I raised my hands in surrender and backed
away.

"It'll just be a couple of years," my wife, Jane, soothed, with a
rueful laugh. She should know. She'd finally completed her
training to become a psychologist and was accepting her first

private patients. "This round is between you and Em," Jane said, wisely if cravenly. "I'm staying out of it."

I knew this was a phase. It was a phase Ben had already embarked on, with sometimes painful consequences. I also knew, therefore, that the sweet Dad-and-daughter days had vanished in the blink of a breakfast greeting.

Overnight, I had morphed into someone unspeakably stupid. Everything I said was ignorant or embarrassing. "Jeez, Daaaaaad!" became Em's new motto for everything I thought, cooked, said, did, or didn't do. I didn't understand the simplest thing about her life, a life I was in the process of ruining beyond repair. Sometimes I had the feeling it was all Em could do to avoid throwing up when I came into a room.

A kind of war had been declared in which much depended on my not fighting back. I had to keep repeating the mantra I'd gleaned from Jane and all the books I'd begun to ingest: This is a healthy way for a healthy child to separate. The more she's attached to you, the more she needs to do this. She'll need your love more than ever. You have to stay constant while she rockets up and down. Don't take the bait.

So I didn't. But it was tough, because no matter how much I read, a lot of the time I wanted to kill her. I found Emily just as annoying as she found me. She was thin-skinned, self-absorbed, whiny, obsessed with how she looked and—here was the sad part—so uncomfortable in her own skin that she often looked as if she might jump right out of it.

And Marissa had picked this point in history to end her life. I had just brought my sullen daughter home from her voice lesson. Although it was late in the day, I planned to get back to my office in the American Way, a dingy '50s mall a few miles outside our town. I had some overdue reports to finish up. I hadn't said a word in the car; since discovering that "How was your day?" had suddenly become a profoundly offensive question, I'd learned to keep my mouth shut.

"Dad. You better come up here! Please! Hurry!" When we heard the shrieks from Em's room, Percentage, our black Lab, and I both headed upstairs on the run. I beat him easily, though to be fair, his right rear leg was still game from his having been poisoned during one of my early cases. I would have beaten him up the stairs anyway, though. Percentage was the Ferdinand of Labradors, a deep thinker and flower sniffer, not really into running, hunting, fighting, or retrieving.

Em is no stranger to pet deaths. We've had tropical fish roasted alive by a malfunctioning aquarium heater, a cat run over, innumerable mice who succumbed to old age. We even have a Rodent Graveyard in a corner of our backyard where past casualties rest in peace. We used to put a flower on the grave, observe a moment of silence, and offer a few reflections on the dear departed. This sort of loopy ritual is widespread in Rochambeau, the child-centered New Jersey suburb we live in. But an unexpected benefit of adolescence was that these rites were no longer cool. And Emily's nearly twelve, after all. Much of life revolves around being cool.

But Marissa's death was not peaceful. The fat little brown hamster was backing up, charging across the cage at astonishing speed, and ramming her head into the glass wall. Over and over. Before I could get the top of the cage off, she took one last ferocious plunge, hit the wall with an impressive thump, keeled over, and lay still. Percentage, knowing he was a hunting dog of noble lineage and thus expected to *do* something, wagged his tail, then jumped onto Em's bed and went to sleep.

Emily was stunned, though not all that torn up. "Jeez," she said, forgetting for a moment what a repulsive slug I was and taking my hand. "Why do you suppose she did that?"

"Well, she gave birth to those dead babies"—I nearly gagged at the thought of that waste disposal operation. "Maybe Marissa was depressed about it." Good work, Deleeuw. A crackerjack detective. Solved that case in seconds, using your vast knowledge of hamster motivation.

I almost made some smart-ass crack about Marissa's never having learned to share her feelings when I realized this would be further evidence of my insensitivity. So I shut up quickly.

"Sorry, Em," I mumbled. "She was a . . . a good hamster." Talk about lame. Besides, I'd never known a good hamster.

All in all, I thought it was a smart move on Marissa's part. She shared a room with an adolescent girl. More than once, I'd thought of ramming my head into a wall myself.

It's tough to lose a pet, especially when one kills itself right before your eyes. But Em didn't seem traumatized, just sad. So I was sort of relieved when my pocket beeper went off. I peered at the number on the little screen. Evelyn, my secretary and the organizer of my existence, was calling from the office.

I picked up the hamster cage. "Sorry, Em. Gotta run. Mom should be home in time to make dinner. Don't be too blue. Love you. Bye."

She waved distractedly, then looked over at her computer. By the time I'd disposed of the remains and could back my ancient Volvo station wagon out of the driveway, she'd be on-line pouring her heart out to some guy named Flashy432Z.

I toted the cage downstairs, emptied Marissa and all those revolting cedar shavings into a garbage bag, and dumped the whole thing into the trash. Percentage was uncharacteristically alert, sniffing and panting. "Don't even think about it," I growled, fastening the lid firmly on the can. He'd brought home worse from walks, holding various dead creatures gently in his mouth, wagging with pride, expecting warm recognition.

"S'long, girl," I said by way of eulogy. I decided to skip the formal send-off that usually accompanied entry into the Rodent Graveyard. I decided to skip the Graveyard, too.

I called Evelyn, who was probably obsessing over some insurance report due a week ago. Evelyn, a forceful retired librarian, had a way of putting her foot down when things got out of hand. It was wise to respond instantly and compliantly.

"Kit," she said. "I have bad news for you." She paused to give me a chance to collect myself. Em was okay, more or less, but Ben wasn't home yet, and I hadn't talked to Jane since morning. My young associate Willie was supposed to be testifying in a fraud case.

"It isn't Ben or Jane or Willie," Evelyn said, anticipating me. "It's Benchley."

"Oh, Jesus," I said, assuming the worse. My friend was eighty-one.

"He's had a stroke, Kit. They called from the Garden Center. It happened two days ago. He didn't come to work, and when they checked his house, they found him."

Two days ago? And no one had called me? "He's at Rochambeau Memorial?"

Evelyn hesitated.

"No, Kit, that's the strange part. He was there, but as soon as he was stable, they sent him to Elston Manor, a private nursing home in Clifton. He was transferred there this morning. Benchley had apparently left instructions that he wanted to be taken there in the event of a serious illness. That's what Rose, his assistant, told me."

Benchley was my closest friend. He ran the Rochambeau Garden Center, amid whose flowers, shrubs, and trees he and I had spent countless hours, sipping lemonade in the summer, mulled cider in the winter, talking about life, work, movies, books—and sometimes death. Benchley was white-haired but lean and hearty. He had never stopped being handsome and carried himself with a natural grace and dignity that I'd come to associate with his being a Quaker.

The Garden Center was a haven not only for lawn- and garden-lovers, but for lots of people in town who just liked being around Benchley. He had provided me with some desperately needed encouragement during the scary times when my Wall Street career fell apart and I was struggling to keep my family intact, keep my house out of the bank's clutches, and find a new career. He was the first male I'd ever truly been close to. I had other friends—especially Luis Hebron, a onetime Havana defense attorney now managing a fast-food franchise called the Lightning Burger ("Food in a Flash"). But that was a more formal relationship. It was Benchley who taught me perhaps the single most difficult thing for men to learn: how to talk openly to another man.

I stood shaking at the news. Benchley's loss would leave an enormous hole. His suffering would be even more unbearable. Every day I seemed to hear more and more of these stories from friends and clients—older friends and parents suffering heart attacks or strokes, facing one kind of surgery or another, grappling with complex, expensive, and wrenching decisions.

"Evelyn," I asked. "Can you call Elston Manor? Find out where it is?" I hung up and decided to begin driving in the general direction of Clifton.

A stroke. I dreaded seeing the shape Benchley might be in. I prayed the stroke wasn't very serious. And if it was very serious, I prayed even harder that Benchley would die.

two

THE AFTERSHOCK hit me outside. Perhaps I didn't want to cry—that male reflex—where Emily might see me. But the minute I climbed into my venerable blue Volvo (115,000 miles and counting), the floodgates opened.

Not Benchley, I thought. Anybody but Benchley. His real religion was helping people. He hired the lost and afflicted souls of the world whenever he could, lobbied to find them better jobs, paid their medical expenses, intervened in their crises, and tried to raise them up by the sheer force of his fierce love. A childless widower, he poured much of his great heart and energy into creating the special space that was the Garden Center. He was a shrewd businessman, but it wasn't only a business. I suspect he gave away half as many plants and trees as he sold—no kid left the center without a posy or pack of seeds. Benchley advised on half the gardens in town, paying house calls to diagnose a fading rosebush or withering azalea. He loved reviving neglected or mismanaged gardens.

In the six years I'd known him, I'd never heard a harsh, critical, or cynical word from him. This stood in jarring contrast to most of the people I knew. But Benchley was an inspiration in that way: If he wasn't somebody I could be, he was someone I could struggle to be more like.

I realized I was delivering a eulogy, and a premature one at that. Swiping at my wet cheeks, I drove on, past the Rochambeau Municipal Park athletic field a few blocks away.

This aging stuff was in the air, but I had never imagined it would hit Benchley, whom I thought of as indomitable, vigorous, and eternal. I should have known better. In fact, reminders of old age kept going off around me like little bombs, or one of those ugly land mines I'd seen on the evening news.

I pushed the specter away as often as I could, but Jane and I, along with almost everyone our age, had entered a new phase. The older people in our lives were beginning to stagger and fall. As we headed deeper into our forties, we heard more frequent stories of parents and grandparents, crazy aunts and fondly remembered uncles, old and beloved teachers, figures from our past, getting cancer, having heart trouble, writing living wills.

We never quite got used to it. I winced whenever Jane picked up the phone and said, "Oh, God, when? How bad?" It had become a generational theme. Until recently, whenever we got together with friends and neighbors we swapped tales of schools, play dates, sports, and lessons. Now, more and more, the chatter was about assisted care, Medicaid payments, living independently versus being in a supportive environment. We worried over the dread question. What were we willing to do when the time came? Take them in? Visit every week? Pay for home care?

This preoccupation was typically boomer. Nothing in the world was real until we ourselves experienced it, at which point we invariably overreacted. Now we were approaching the first real consciousness of death.

Seeing it all as a warm-up for us, preparation for our own inevitable face-off with aging, was my way of finding a bright side. It didn't often help.

This had become more than an abstract worry in our own lives. Jane's father had died a year earlier. Her mother was, like many of our friends' parents, determined to stay in her own home "until they carry me out." Jane had flown to California twice in the past year to take her mother on a tour of apartment complexes and assisted-care facilities. Annette, despite her increasing frailty, wasn't buying any of it. Jane worried about her because any day, it seemed, they *would* have to carry her out.

My own mother had recently had knee surgery. My father—overweight, still drinking and smoking well into his seventies—was suffering from congestive heart failure. Or so I'd heard—I hadn't talked with him in twenty-five years. Jane, Ben, and Emily had never met him. He had never visited any home I'd ever lived in. But a favorite uncle who lived nearby had called recently, concerned because my father was going to need medical care and support. My mother, who'd divorced him years earlier and was remarried and living in North Carolina, had also gotten such a call. She had asked me to talk to my father about moving out of his decaying apartment house and into some sort of retirement community. So I called and he had instantly hung up. I'd have to go to Chicago to confront him; I was dreading it.

Benchley had seemed immune to all this. For his sake, I had to accept that this would not be true any longer. The last thing he would need was for me to be disappointed in him for being human. But this was going to be rough for both of us. Benchley would hate being patronized as much as he would hate being helpless. Careful, I cautioned myself. Lots of people have partial or full recoveries from strokes. I was already way ahead of any concrete information.

I pulled alongside the chain-link fence that surrounded the field. I wanted to get a grip before I drove the short distance to Elston Manor. I didn't want Benchley to see me red-eyed.

A long row of massive Chevy Suburbans was lined up in front of me, brawny workhorses, the wagons of choice for the athletically minded parents of suburbia who had to cart kids, balls, cones, nets, sticks, whistles, and other paraphernalia around to Rochambeau's many sports leagues. If it was early spring, it had to be soccer planning time.

When I looked out onto the field, I knew right away what was going on: the first ritual meeting of the coaches. I had been one myself for a few hours when Ben played, but I went berserk at our first game when some creep started screaming that his son was a sissy because he'd missed a goal.

"Get the fuck off my field," I shouted, hooting at him with a whistle, then actually giving chase, pursuing the guy—a dentist, I think—as he rushed off the field and jumped into his BMW. I stopped myself just short of pounding on his hood.

I was fired an hour later, causing considerable grief for me and my kids. My social standing was already diminished by having been run out of Wall Street bond trading by overzealous federal prosecutors pursuing an insider-trading investigation that destroyed my firm. I'd done nothing wrong, and knew nothing about anybody who had, but the FBI didn't believe that. Agents badgered me for months to testify against my friends and colleagues, which I wouldn't, then made their vengeful deal: They wouldn't charge me with anything if I agreed to leave Wall Street forever. I did.

After months of agonizing and watching our bank accounts empty, and with Benchley's unfailing encouragement, I returned to the only other work I'd ever done—investigations. For two years, way back, I'd been a U.S. Army criminal investigator. So I took a six-month course, applied for a New Jersey PI certificate, and rented the only office I could afford, a hole above the atmospheric but slightly seedy American Way Mall, forever eclipsed by the larger, more prosperous malls a few miles away. I bought a handgun, and immediately locked it in my office safe, where it has remained untouched.

PIs didn't have loads of social status in Rochambeau, it turned out, and as word of my outburst on the soccer field quickly made the rounds, people stayed even farther away from us.

Soccer politics are legendary in suburbia. The Democrats and Republicans and their dirty tricksters have nothing on the over-involved moms and dads who battle to get their kids onto the best team, scramble for the best fields and equipment, scope out the deficiencies of opponents. Parents maneuver to keep their kids off a team whose coach has a poor record or is known to be a softie—aka someone who thinks every kid on the team should get to play the game, ability notwithstanding. Soccer was not for the faint of heart, nor for people who thought childhood should be fun.

But I had no regrets. If I'd had to watch this guy abuse his boy every week, I might just have done something worse. I did, after all, own a gun.

On the field, this spring's coaches, male and female, stood around, arms folded like baseball umpires, feet pawing the dirt, pointing back and forth across the field, undoubtedly imagining the boundaries of the game, trading information about the most whacked-out parents, pledging to be sportsmanlike and cooperative (dream on). Two of the coaches already had whistles dangling from their necks, just in case they had to hoot at something.

In a few days, kids, moms, dads, dogs, siblings, grandparents, and friends would be standing along these sidelines as the first game of the year kicked off. Ben continued playing soccer after my expulsion, but after a while I'd stopped going, even as a spectator. There seemed nothing enjoyable about it. Nobody—not the coaches, the parents, or the kids—seemed able to relax or have a good time. I stayed away, another step in the disconnection I sometimes felt from other boomer parents.

The coaches exchanged hearty back pats and handshakes, then headed back to their Suburbans. I couldn't help contrasting this most vigorous of youthful springtime rituals with my worst fears for Benchley—that he was a vegetable lying comatose in a nursing home. I wiped my eyes, took a deep breath, and drove into Clifton. Evelyn called on my cell phone to give me directions.

Elston Manor looked like an upscale garden apartment complex, the kind sprinkled throughout Rochambeau, favored residences of young singles, couples starting out, and those whose charges had left the nest. It was set back off a busy street, its curved driveway marked with a discreet wooden sign that read "Elston Manor." Nothing would mark it as an institution or nursing facility—except there were no children, dogs, toys, bikes, lawn chairs, or other signs of everyday life. In fact, though it was a warm bright day, I saw hardly a soul outside.

Its only distinguishing characteristics were, to my surprise, a guardhouse with two men inside and a lowered security gate at the entrance.

I could see that the grounds were not only expansive but expensively landscaped and well tended. Trees shrouded the one-story building; the grass was emerald and precisely mowed. A dark-skinned gardener was on his knees, spading a tulip bed. There was nothing cheap or threadbare about this operation.

I expected the guard to wave me through, but he came out of his guardhouse and approached the car, gesturing at me to roll down the window. He carried a clipboard and a radio.

I didn't think security guards at nursing homes saw much action, so I was a bit surprised to see so young and beefy a man, wearing a dark blue uniform, a .9mm pistol strapped to his waist. The second guard was inside jotting something down—probably my license plate. He wasn't reading the paper or munching a doughnut; he was watching me. Maybe this was a selling point for Elston Manor—unbreachable security. I supposed I'd want that for my parents, if it came to that.

"Sir?" the guard said crisply, glancing around the inside of the car, taking me in. He behaved like a cop.

"I'm here to see a patient," I said. "His name is Benchley Carrolton." I added, foolishly, "He had a stroke"—as if the guard would feel sorry for me.

He glanced at his clipboard and scribbled something. "Your name, sir? And relationship to the patient?"

"My name is Kit Deleeuw. I'm a friend. A good friend," I said.

The guard leaned down and tipped his cap back so it wouldn't bump against the door frame. "Sir, I'm sorry. Visiting hours are from 10 A.M. to noon and are strictly enforced. We have some people in pretty poor condition in there, so we try to control the environment. You have to call ahead, get on the visitors' list. It's nearly 6 P.M., so visiting hours are long over. And you're not on the visitors' list, so I'm afraid I couldn't let you in, anyway. How's about I give you a phone number. You call first thing in the morning and they'll tell you if Mr. . . . er . . . Carrolton can receive visitors." He wrote a number on a slip of paper and handed it to me, then consulted his clipboard again. "I see from the manifest here that he's in intensive care. Visiting is even more restricted there."

I could tell by this man's face—his nameplate said Handler— that there was no point asking him to bend the rules. He wasn't cold so much as resolutely professional.

"Could I ask a favor? Could I ask you to check on his condition?"

I knew the answer before he gave it, but one of the cardinal rules in my line of work is always to ask.

"I'm afraid not, sir. They don't give out that information except to authorized people or members of the family. Sorry."

I made it to the Garden Center in less than fifteen minutes. The "Closed" sign had been dragged up over the entrance, even though closing time in the spring usually wasn't until 9 P.M. I got out, unhooked the sign, and walked into the office.

The Garden Center office resembled a country living room more than a retail center. There was a cash register on one shelf, but also plump chairs and comfy sofas usually occupied by schmoozing customers squabbling about aphid control. A teapot was always simmering and for the kids there was hot chocolate or lemonade, depending on the season.

Benchley's golden retriever, Melody, lumbered over to stick her nose in my crotch and lick my hand. Rose Klock was sitting with another worker, staring out the window.

I didn't know Rose very well. She was a European refugee, a concentration camp survivor, I suspected, but I doubted I'd ever know. She didn't talk much, and Benchley never discussed the people he collected and offered refuge to.

Rose lived on the second floor above the Garden Center office, just down the hill from Benchley's 150-year-old clapboard
farmhouse. Sometimes when I drove in to see Benchley, I
thought I saw the curtains move in her window. I had the sense
that she was intensely protective of Benchley, always watching
over him, suspicious and sometimes resentful of the many people
for whom he made time. She functioned as a sort of assistant and
housekeeper. Benchley was fanatically self-sufficient, not the
sort to have somebody cook for him, but Rose did tidy his house
and office, and sometimes I'd see her toting plastic containers of
soup and stew into his kitchen, depositing them in the refrigerator.

Benchley sometimes said he felt bad about her. He was glad
she had a safe and comfortable place to be; he needed and valued
her; but he was conscious of the fact that Rose seemed unable to
construct a life to replace the one she'd lost. She had no family,
had made no friends, and other than occasionally bicycling into
town to see a movie or pick up groceries, she rarely left the Garden Center. When she wasn't working, she sat up in her room
reading or gazing out the window, keeping an eye on Benchley's
house.

She was gazing out at it now.

"Rose, I'm so sorry," I said. "Can you tell me what happened?"

She looked down at an untouched cup of tea at her elbow,
then up at me again. Then she seemed to steel herself. "Two
days ago. It was late at night . . ."

"This was Sunday?" I asked. She nodded.

"Mr. Carrolton is very regular. Very orderly. He always goes
to sleep at eleven-thirty. He watches the evening news, then he
does his exercises. Then, lights out at quarter to midnight. Always."

I knew this to be true. Benchley was meticulous and organized. Intensely interested in news of the outside world, he never
missed the local news—particularly the local forecast, because it
affected his garden and everybody else's. These were rituals,

along with breakfast at 6 A.M. (a bran muffin and tea), a salad at one, pasta and steamed vegetables for dinner at seven. Benchley's pacifism extended to beef cattle and chickens. All creatures, he said, were sacred, repositories of God's spirit—except for mosquitoes, which he swatted without hesitation. "Not God's creatures," he'd say. "And even if they were, a mistake."

I handed Rose her cup of tea and she sipped from it, then put it back on an end table. She'd pulled a woolen shawl over her shoulders, even though it was quite warm. I saw that her eyes were bloodshot, her face drawn beneath her steel-gray hair. Benchley was her universe.

"At two in the morning, I looked out and saw his lights were still on."

"You were awake?"

"I don't sleep much," she said. "I rang Mr. Carrolton—Benchley. There was no answer. You see, I knew something was wrong. I am good at that." This last statement was made quietly, with resignation. I bet she was, too.

"I knew something was wrong. All the downstairs lights were on. I thought he had to be sick . . . or . . ." She didn't finish the thought.

"So I put on my robe and ran over," she said, gesturing toward the rambling house with her head. Home to many generations of Carroltons, it had been added onto until it sprawled.

"I have a key," Rose said, which I also knew to be true. She seemed ready to recount the story, as if she had been rehearsing it. "He was lying on the floor, right in front of the TV. His eyes were open . . ." She started to sob. I put my arm on her shoulder, but she recoiled, and I quickly withdrew it.

"I yelled, 'Mr. Carrolton, Mr. Carrolton, what is wrong?' But he couldn't answer me. I saw he had been sick . . . he had . . ." she struggled for this word ". . . vomited. He was breathing but he couldn't move or speak or answer me. I called the police. The ambulance came. The attendant said he had had a stroke."

Rose wasn't allowed to visit Benchley in intensive care. But she'd sat in the hospital waiting room for hours. She hadn't called anybody, she said, because he had no family and the doctors had told her he couldn't see any visitors. Besides, she admitted, she was too frightened to think of it.

"But yesterday . . . I intended to call you yesterday, Mr. Deleeuw, because you are Mr. Carrolton's close friend, and he would have wanted you to know. But he had left a letter . . . this letter. He told me just a few weeks ago that if there were an emergency I should read it and do just as it instructed."

She handed me a crumpled sheet, printed on a computer and addressed to her:

Rose,

In the event of a medical emergency that is disabling, please call my attorney immediately. He has instructions as to what my wishes are. Please follow them carefully. I would prefer that you not contact anyone else without his permission. I hope you will never have to read this letter, but I am past eighty, and it seems prudent to be realistic. Thanks more than I can ever say for your great care of me. My lawyer, Mr. Levin, will also see that you are taken care of. Please ask him about this.

Thanks, Benchley.

She took back the letter and reread it, as if to make sure she had done the right thing. "Yesterday morning I returned to the hospital and they told me Mr. Carrolton was gone! He had been taken to this Elston Manor."

She started shaking. I gave her a minute to calm down.

"Do you know how that happened?"

She shook her head. "I never heard Mr. Carrolton mention the place. I have no idea what it is. I told the nurse I was worried and she gave me this card . . ." She rose from the chair, walked slowly to her purse near the cash register, and returned with a business card. It read "Transitions, Inc. James Goodell, Chairman. Flip Kimball, President. A new kind of assisted care facility."

The back of the card listed residences scattered around the New York area, the last being Elston Manor.

The name Goodell was familiar. James Goodell was the New Jersey Senate majority leader, one of the state's most powerful political figures.

"I called this place, but they said no visitors," Rose went on as I stood holding the card, puzzled, hoping it would explain things. "Mr. Carrolton said if there were ever any trouble, if anything happened to him, I should call his lawyer. But Mr. Levin said I was not to call anyone, that Mr. Carrolton had left very careful instructions. He wanted to be moved immediately to this . . . this . . . Manor."

I asked Rose if she needed anything, but she shook her head. "Why is he there, Mr. Deleeuw? Why did they take him from the hospital?"

"I don't know, Rose," I said truthfully. "But I promise you I will find out and let you know."

I looked at my watch. In an hour and a half I was to meet with a flock of worried parents at the Wyndham Episcopal Church.

"May I use the phone?" I called Eric Levin, my lawyer as well as Benchley's; he came on the phone in seconds. Levin had helped me out in several investigations, most notably when Rochambeau Police Chief Frank Leeming had me locked up for obstructing justice during a dicey murder investigation. Levin mostly handled wills and real estate closings; my brief arrest was high adventure by comparison. But I liked him. He was a straight shooter.

"Kit," he said. "I've been expecting your call."

"Eric. I want to find out what the hell is going on with Benchley and why I can't see him. That nursing home is guarded like the White House."

There was a too long pause. "Don't waste your time, Kit. I can't talk to you about this. It's confidential. All I can tell you is that it's all in accordance with Benchley's written wishes, which I have in a notarized letter delivered a few months ago. He wanted to go to Elston Manor. There was no ambiguity about it. He repeated this in a telephone call. He didn't want anybody called until he was established there. I don't know why, and couldn't say if I did. He had some sort of relationship with James Goodell. I was surprised, as I suspect you are. Goodell is a very big deal in this state and I didn't even know Benchley knew him. But I can't talk to you about the arrangements."

I was astonished. Why all the secrecy? Benchley and I talked about death quite openly, all the time. He had told me repeatedly that, when the time came, he had made arrangements to live in a Quaker-run retirement complex. The Friends ran a string of highly regarded assisted care communities that were famous for the dignity they accorded their residents. Why had he changed his mind? And what on earth did he have to do with a slickie like Goodell?

"Eric," I said. "I respect confidentiality, especially in my line of work. But I've got to see Benchley. Either I get in or I'll get another lawyer and file a lawsuit. Then I'll call the cops and the papers and make an enormous stink. I'll say he was kidnapped from the hospital. I don't know what I'll do, but I want in. Or I'm coming back with the Marines, okay? I love this man. He's my closest friend."

Levin took a deep breath. He knew the futility of talking me out of something when I was in full crank. "I'll call Goodell," he finally said. "I have some concerns about Benchley's affairs I want to discuss anyway. Maybe he can arrange something. Meanwhile, Kit, stay cool, will you? I know you're upset about Benchley, but he hasn't been abducted. This is what he wanted, and you and I both know his mind was crystal clear."

This was true. But I had to see Benchley for myself before I could relax.

I called Jane, who had just gotten home. Evelyn had thoughtfully called her with the news. "Kit, I'm so sorry. Have you seen him?"

I told her why I hadn't.

"I'm on my way to my meeting in Wyndham," I said. "I'll fill you in when I get back. The kids okay?" I wanted to know that everyone was safe.

"Em's here. Ben's got practice; I'm going to pick him up at eight."

Our family had had a tough time the past few years. To help save our home and provide us with a health plan, Jane had been working in a clinic and had gone back to school to become a full-fledged psychologist. Now she was one. I still did a lot of the child care, but I was no longer the sole driver and scheduler. We were all happier and I was a tad less frantic.

But this wasn't going to be a happy week. I understood that. I headed onto the Parkway south, relieved to focus on my report. Most people would think what I had to say was great news, but I had the feeling it would not be well received.

three

SOME PEOPLE might say raising money for college is the toughest thing about having kids. Or fending off drugs and booze, particularly in combination with the family minivan. Surviving your offspring's adolescence would get a substantial chunk of the vote.

But if I were singling out the one hardest task for middle-class parents, I'd say it's the Butt Out Problem. Learning how to withdraw from the micromanagement of children's lives. And how to stay out.

When all is said and done, the most striking thing about my generation of parents is our fearfulness. We're ceaselessly trying to create perfect worlds in which creativity is ever encouraged, education is meaningful, plentiful friends are always available, and life's disappointments are anticipated, avoided, or, if all else fails, navigated hand in hand with Mom or Dad.

Rochambeau parents called teachers incessantly to dither about grades. They dreaded free time for their children as if it were cholera, filling it up with a whirl of music, art, and drama lessons. They hired SAT tutors and pricey college consultants to help ensure their teenagers' acceptance at the handful of colleges deemed worthy of them. It was nuts.

The adults left little room for kids to make decisions, mess up, take responsibility. Our own lives got hopelessly tangled up with theirs. Legions of therapists made comfortable livings pointing this out to suburban parents across America.

"You'd think people would know that if kids don't make mistakes, they can't learn how to avoid them," Jane often mused. "But people don't, do they?"

They don't.

At least once a week, I turned down the chance to make considerable money spying on middle-class children whose parents were worried. I'd bitten the first few times, taking money from clients who feared their kids might be hanging out with a "bad crowd" or loitering on the "tough" side of town (featuring, in Rochambeau, a Grateful Dead memorabilia store that an aging hippie had opened in an abandoned gas station). I didn't take many of these cases anymore, suggesting that the parents go see a shrink first to make sure their fears were founded. If the shrink agreed, I said, call me back. Few did.

Jane and I suffered this problem as severely as anyone. She had spent so much of the past few years working and taking graduate courses at night that she felt guilty about being too remote from the kids. This had led for a while to The Interrogatories, during which Emily and Ben were debriefed nightly, like turncoat spies at Langley, encouraged to regurgitate every detail of their lives.

My own problem was more classic: a nightmare childhood. I'd grown up an isolated geek, pursued by bullies, ignored by teachers, criticized by my parents. My father's position was that any problem I had was my fault. He neither enjoyed my company nor sought it out. Mostly, I felt like a piece of lawn furniture he had acquired by mistake but was trying to live with. He never abused me—I can't claim to be any special sort of victim—but from the time I was ten or so, we just didn't have anything to do with each other. We used to talk once a year, at Christmas, but it was such a chore for both of us that we didn't even do that anymore. I didn't want my kids to suffer that way. I thought for years I could create sunny, pain-free childhoods for them.

But one of the great advantages of being married to a psychologist is that your consciousness gets raised in a hurry. Jane and I sat down one day and acknowledged that we both had a Butt Out Problem. She therefore devised the Butt Out Quiz. I failed it weekly for months before its lessons finally penetrated. The quiz still hangs on our refrigerator between the school lunch menus and the reminder of Percentage's rabies shot appointment. Get more than three items wrong and you've got serious work to do.

BUTT OUT QUIZ

—When people ask your kid a question, do you answer, even if the kid's right there? As in, "Do you want to come over and play today, Emily?" and you say, "No, she's got a violin lesson."
—Do you overprogram your kid with activities that require your participation and involvement? So many sports teams and lessons that you function as a driver more than a parent?
—Is your conversation chronically child-centered? When you encounter another adult, do your inquire about her children, their school experiences, their camp choices, their field hockey prowess—and never ask the parent how she is?
—Do you ask your kids more than you need to know about their lives? Pump their teachers and friends' parents for information? Discover how every single class went, who they ate with at lunch, who they sat with on the bus?

And so forth. It's staggering how much kids can figure out for themselves, given the opportunity.

This was all on my mind this evening because I was reporting on the results of a Butt Out assignment, one of those that seemed legitimate at first but really turned out to involve parents who were looking for ways to stay involved, to not Butt Out. That's why I was driving to Wyndham, fifteen miles west.

Wyndham is a wealthy suburban enclave favored by Wall Street's up-and-coming Masters of the Universe. It's mostly a young-family community, because by age fifty the Masters are largely unemployed. They get downsized or they take their money and run; in either case they tend to pull up stakes and leave Jersey behind.

The Wyndham town zoning code makes Rochambeau look like the South Bronx—no more than one house every five acres. In fact, people usually owned much more land than that. Wyndham residents needed binoculars to see their neighbors. Their sprawling contemporaries, restored Victorians, and magnificant old clapboard colonials sat far back from the main road, their lights and alarm systems peeking and blinking through the woods.

It's fun to make fun of the rich, but in my work, I'd developed some appreciation for them. They were, in my experience, generally nice people, perhaps because they could afford to be. Unburdened by such nasty little cares as mortgage payments, college tuition, and medical bills, they often relied on members of my profession to untangle their sometimes messy affairs. They didn't nickel and dime me over expenses and they paid their bills on time. I had always comforted myself with the idea that money didn't buy happiness, but I was reassessing.

The Episcopal church, a fieldstone beauty circa 1796, sat on a ridge overlooking the post office and tasteful florist's shop that constituted downtown Wyndham. I pulled into its parking lot, next to a row of Mercedes, BMWs, several Land Rovers, and a Lexus or two.

Donna Lake had seen a story about one of my more notorious cases in the Morristown paper. The press had picked up on Shelly Bloomfield, aka "The Last Housewife." An unrepentant homemaker in an era when most women headed off to work, her arrest for the murder of a feminist middle-school principal had rocked Rochambeau to its shrubs.

"I read about you in the paper," Lake had said when she called. "Of course, I wouldn't know how to find a private detective otherwise." Of course. We talked briefly. She explained. I agreed. A certified check for $3,000 arrived, express mail, at the mall next morning.

She had called me because of a strange kind of panic gripping the town. Donna and her husband, Gilly—why do the Mob and old money love nicknames so?—had recently moved to Wyndham from Frankfurt, where he ran European operations for some global bank. The first thing she noticed was that no child in Wyndham, of any age, stood and waited alone for the school bus. A parent, or in some cases, a nanny or a housekeeper, waited with every kid, even the high school students. When Donna wondered about this, her neighbors whispered that several times in recent years, strange men in big cars had attempted to kidnap town children. Donna heard detailed and bone-chilling stories about kids running shrieking through deserted woods toward their distant homes, calling for help but always too far away for anybody to hear. They emerged scratched and bloody from thorns and branches. She was shocked, and not a little ticked, since the real estate agent had sworn that crime was unheard of in Wyndham, and her eight-bedroom house and barn with pool had cost—well, she was too well bred to say, but Willie found out in thirty seconds: $1.4 million.

"You see this stuff on the news," Donna said to me, shocked, "but the biggest thing I expected to worry about out here was deer eating the forsythia." Suspicious, she'd begun asking her new friends—in the Garden Club, at the League of Women Voters—about these stories. Everyone had heard about the kidnappings. Everyone believed them. Of course, they were true. Don't you watch TV? Happens all the time! So why hadn't they made the papers? The town burghers had told everyone to be quiet about it. Kidnappings were not known for improving property values.

"But what about your kids?" I asked Donna.

"Well, I wait with them just like everybody else," she said, exasperated at the question. "What if I weren't there—I have two daughters, ten and thirteen—and something happened to them? How would I feel then? Besides," she added, almost mumbling the words, "it's quality time."

That probably should have tipped me off right there. "Quality time," part of the lexicology of the child-crazed suburban middle class, ostensibly meant time to be close to your kid.

But everyone knew what it really meant: a license for neurotic parents to drive their kids to school daily rather than send them on the bus, to sit in the waiting room so they could listen to every note of their piano lessons. If these kids were any closer to us, they'd fuse.

Maybe what Donna Lake really wanted was for me to confirm something troubling, so she'd have an excuse to continue her quality time at the bus stop.

It wasn't my kind of case, really, but a part of me was fascinated by the degree to which rumors and myths got woven into the subconscious of suburban communities. The case would be even more interesting if the stories were true and the police were, in fact, covering them up.

And there was, of course, the practical to be considered. Our dishwasher had literally blown a gasket, winter storms had left sections of the roof denuded of shingles, in danger of rotting through. If I didn't paint the outside of the house soon, my neighbors would start tossing rocks through the windows. Jane's practice was just getting started, her income was still wobbly and uncertain.

Donna Lake and two of her friends had come up with the $3,000. If I found the reports were true, they'd continue to sit in their cars at the ends of their driveways. If the stories were false or only partly true, they would approach the president of the Junior League and other influential people in the town to call a meeting at which the parents would consider my evidence and learn to relax about their kids.

I could understand why people felt vulnerable: Wyndham was potentially a great place to kidnap a kid. Abductors could cruise the winding country roads unobserved by townspeople or the two cops and one detective who comprised the local PD.

I had heard various phobic myths myself about kidnappings—the small girl snatched in a mall, whisked into a restroom, and hurriedly disguised with a haircut and dye was the most popular—and investigated several.

The reality was, it almost never happened. Kidnapping was an extraordinarily rare crime in America, outside of domestic disputes and custody cases. Law enforcement tended to organize quickly, and punishments were swift and severe. The whole thing sounded a little kablooey.

I put Willie to work on the stats. A lanky, cherub-faced blond who inspired crushes among young women everywhere, who worked (and occasionally lived) in a dark room next to my office in the mall, Willie could get his hands on any recent credit card purchase, bank loan agreement, or checking account withdrawal with startling speed. All he needed was a name, an address, a Social Security number, or even a town name, along with his Power Mac equipped with every known Web browser and search engine. He pulled up deeds, birth certificates, tax payments, autopsy results, verdicts in civil and criminal trials. Crime stats were a snap, available on state, county, and federal Web sites with a few clicks. Through means I didn't understand or want to understand, he could tell me if somebody had bought a major appliance in San Diego last month.

So after I deposited the check and while Willie downloaded FBI stats (he was at the moment sucking out of the ether every shred of information there was about Elston Manor and the people who owned and ran it), I called every police department in the county and then the Chief of the tiny Wyndham PD, Sal DeCiccio. A former Newark detective, he sounded perpetually weary, but pleasant and cooperative. I told him Donna's story, and he guffawed.

"These people," he said. "This is where the kid runs screaming through the woods, right? All bloody? And we're supposedly covering up? The problem in this town is that if you say something happened, people freak. If you say nothing happened, they assume you're lying. Like they're saying, 'Hey, I'm rich and I have this fabulous house and three great cars. How can all these shitheads in New York City and Newark not be ogling me, my house, my kids?' Not that they want anything to happen, mind you, just that they assume everybody wants what they got."

And, I prompted, "everybody" didn't?

"First off, this town is far from the street rats," DeCiccio explained, more patiently than I might have. "People cruising Wyndham from Newark and Brooklyn would be—how can I put this?—conspicuous. Know what I mean?" I knew what he meant.

"And there's only one major road in or out of town. There are plenty of towns with VCRs, bikes, and jewelry that are closer to Newark and the city than this one and much easier to get in and out of. There just isn't a lot of crime here." Willie's stats had borne that out. Police departments can sometimes fudge the way they report robberies or burglaries, but it's hard to play with violent crime stats.

The Chief went on: "Some burglaries in the summer and over the holidays. Some vandalism. That's about it. And this silly shit you're asking me about. All over town, every morning at 8 A.M., every housewife is sitting in her Lexus at the end of her driveway with Junior or Sis watching for the bus. Hell, if the burglars around here were half awake, that's when they'd strike, 'cause nobody's fucking home. It's bullshit. Never been a kidnapping here. Never been an attempt."

I scribbled notes. "Nothing like it?"

"No," said the Chief. "You probably know that all kidnappings are federal and have to be reported to the FBI. Nobody covers up a kidnapping, and why the fuck would I? I'd get to double my budget if somebody tried to grab one of the darlings in this town."

I pressed him to think what might have prompted such fears. "The only thing that might have any bearing is four years ago when some dentist drove by Shaketown Road in his Town Car and called a twelve-year-old girl over to the car. He had his fly unzipped and waved his dong around. She did run screaming through the fucking woods, yelling loud enough to wake the dead, believe me. We got the guy still sitting there, trying to zip up," he added proudly.

He guffawed. "Our local oral surgeon. Offered girls money to pose in the nude while he took some snapshots. It was amazing to arrest Doc Porter, and it was even more amazing 'cause he had twenty-five pictures hidden in his bedroom. Some of the town's leading private school girls had picked up a few extra bucks. Boy, that lit the place up, I can tell you. He did six months for lewdness and moved away. Running a motel in Florida, they tell me. That's our only drama, take my word for it."

I thanked him.

"That's okay. Have a good 'un."

I had called some local townspeople, too, a few at random, a few that Donna Lake said claimed to have information. Most of those I called didn't want to talk to me at all. A couple huffed that they had heard about this firsthand. "I don't know the exact address but it was right here on my street. The poor girl barely escaped with her life. Of course I'm sure of it." But when I got the reverse phone directory and called every house on the road (all four of them), nobody knew anything. It was someplace else that the "incidents" had occurred, I was assured.

It was fascinating if grotesque. Why did these people pass this story around so insistently? These were people with access to all kinds of resources, but no one I talked to had even tried to check these rumors out. Was this an inevitable by-product of the grisly fare on the evening news? The result of being too isolated from the masses of humanity? Just another way to keep the kids tethered?

I didn't have any more stats to locate or leads to track down. I was ready to present my findings, and I was relieved that I was done. I had to clear my schedule for Benchley.

In a small meeting room in the church basement, a couple of dozen people were milling around, murmuring in anticipation. A slim, brown-haired woman in her forties, tastefully dressed in a tweed skirt and silk blouse with a scarf around her throat, came up smiling warmly and introduced herself. Donna Lake looked tanned and fit—a tennis player, I'd bet—and the tiniest bit apprehensive, wondering what she'd wrought.

Ordinarily, I would have enjoyed an encounter like this. A chance to poke people right in their suburban phobias was always a hoot. But tonight I was just anxious to get home so that I could talk to Jane and start working the phones. I was going to get into Elston Manor one way or the other. I had to be as available to Benchley as he wanted me to be. That meant rearranging my calendar, postponing the many overdue insurance reports, declining new cases or referring them to other PIs. And the meeting was not, as it turned out, enjoyable.

Against all reason and experience, I'd hoped that these people would be relieved at my unglamorous but thorough investigating. Who wants there to be a kidnapper in the neighborhood?

Instead, there was an almost visible disappointment in the room as I wound up my brief account. One woman stood up before I could even ask for questions. "You're not saying it isn't dangerous out there, are you?"

That sort of threw me. "I wouldn't suggest that life doesn't have its dangers," I said carefully, not wanting to give offense. "But I feel pretty confident that your kid isn't likely to get kidnapped waiting for the school bus."

A few people were clearly ticked off; others looked embarrassed. They'd heard the story so often they had a hard time believing it wasn't true.

One woman in the back, her hair tied with a big yellow ribbon, seemed particularly flushed and angry-looking. "Look, Mr. Deleeuw, you don't live here. I do. I know a child was nearly kidnapped right on Highland Road. I know another who ran for her life while being chased through the woods near the Nature Preserve. I know the fear those families have lived with. I have no idea where you're getting your information, but it's junk, pure junk. I don't care how many charts you have. I sit with my daughters every single morning and I will until the day they go off to college." If you ever let them go to college, I thought.

She poked her husband in the arm, as if to encourage him to join in the denunciation, but he shook his head, and she sat down.

The outburst seemed to jolt the people in the room, who were, I am sure, unaccustomed to raised voices. "Well, he is a professional detective," I heard one man murmur, from the right side of the room.

"I understand your concern," I said. "But I am very certain about what I'm telling you. It's not up to me how you respond to my report. My job is to make sure it's accurate, and it is. This is a safe community. Your children are not in danger."

After fielding a few halfhearted questions about my sources and statistics, I stepped down, shook hands with Donna Lake, who smiled wanly, and walked out quickly. The irony was almost delicious, I thought as I backed the Volvo out of the church lot. Parents were supposed to be shocked by reports that there were dangers. In contemporary America, parents were distraught when there weren't. Most kids in Wyndham would be sitting with their parents waiting for the school bus for a long time.

Back on the highway, I dialed Elston Manor.

I got a voice recording. "You have reached the Elston Manor Rehabilitation Facility. Our offices are open from 9 A.M. to 5 P.M. If you are inquiring about Elston Manor, please press 3 and leave your name, address, and telephone number and a representative will be in touch with you. If this is an emergency, please press 0 and someone will assist you. Otherwise, please call us during business hours. Thank you."

I had no compunction about hitting zero. This was an emergency as far as I was concerned. And a woman's voice, crisp and businesslike, did materialize right away. "Nursing station. Supervisor Rodberg. How can I help you?"

"I'm sorry to call on the emergency line," I said, "but this is sort of an emergency. I'm calling about a friend . . ."

"Excuse me for interrupting," she said. "Are you a member of the family?"

"No," I said. "I'm a close friend. I just want to know how

Benchley Carrolton is. My name is Kit Deleeuw and you can ask him if you want. I'd appreciate it if you could tell me how he's doing."

"I'm sorry, Mr. Deleeuw," she said. "You'll have to call back in the morning. I'm not permitted to give out information to anyone who's not on my list of preapproved family members. I have no option."

I spent many hours in my work wheedling information out of people, in person or on the phone. Most people were cooperative or wanted to be; they would help if they could. All I needed or wanted was some sense that Benchley was holding his own.

But remembering the security at the Elston Manor gate, I doubted I would get it. "Is he conscious?" I asked, the words catching in my throat.

"Sorry sir. We are very busy right now. Please call in the morning."

The line went dead.

four

WHEN I GOT HOME at nine-thirty, Jane was in
the kitchen in her bathrobe catching up on the mail
and the *Times*. She got up and circled her arms around my neck.
"Hey, hon. How are you? How's Benchley?"

"I don't know," I said, hugging her hard. "I haven't been able
to get into the place . . . it's called Elston Manor. I can't even
figure why he's there, let alone what his condition is." I shook
my head. What *was* he doing there?

These kitchen encounters were a regular part of the family
ritual in recent years. Jane would get home late, talk to the kids,
sit down at the kitchen table with a stack of files until I'd find
her nodding off and shoo her up to bed.

Like a lot of people, we had experienced a 6.8 Richter scale
role reversal in the wake of the '80s, little of it voluntary. We'd
all set about raising our families with one notion of what life
and work were about, and before we were halfway through, the
assumptions we'd brought into adulthood had been upended or
obliterated.

The only thing that was still true was that we needed to make enough money to keep a house going, pay for camp and lessons and orthodonture, take care of aging parents, and desperately stash money away for college. Retirement seemed a moot point for our generation. We'd be manning the grills at The Lightning Burger when we were seventy, if we were lucky, right about the time Social Security was scheduled to collapse of its own poorly funded weight. In addition to which—a disturbing trend I was noticing all over Rochambeau—though we heard plenty of whining from friends about how they dreaded the Empty Nest, the nests all seemed pretty full to me, with young men and women hanging around long after they were supposed to be gone.

Anyway, the 1980s were over and I found myself not only a private investigator, which was weird enough, but also, in the jargon of the times, a Primary Caretaker.

Between work and daily domestic chores, I ferried Ben, Emily, and various pals all over creation, to soccer meets, dentists and pediatricians, friends' houses.

I didn't mind all the driving, because a strange psychological phenomenon takes place in the backseat of a car: Kids who would never give you the time of day blabber on to one another about friends, school, and the dramas and scandals of their lives. Parents become invisible when they're sitting in the front seat of a car. All you have to do is shut up and you can glean everything you need to know. Ask a question about the same subject at home ten minutes later, and you get grunts and shrugs.

I used to work hard when I was on Wall Street, but when I was done for the day, I was done. These days, I was never done; nobody was. What harried people the boomers were, poor bastards. We thought we were going to change the world, but we ended up just trying to survive it. Losing my job was liberating in one big way: I had no career left to lose, no choice but to redesign our lives—in our case, for the better. So the winners became the losers, and the losers the ultimate winners, happy but broke.

I put the teakettle on. It would be a comfort just to tell Jane about my long and troubling day. "I wanted to know about this place he's in," I said. "But it was like Fort Knox. Let me go say good night to the kids; I'll be right back."

Percentage was, as usual, stunned to see me enter the hallway three feet in front of him and rushed to grab one of his chew-bones. His tail began the side-to-side thump that would go on for five minutes or so until he had brought me a large pile of toys and presents and properly expressed his joy at my arrival. I had to make an equally big fuss over him or he'd wiggle around like that all night. Fortunately, after the first couple of years Labradors are innately sedentary beasts; the energy expended in welcoming is good for two hours of solid sleeping.

I tapped at Ben's door; he grunted back. Em was already asleep. I'd always felt a bit of a pang when I couldn't say good night, but I don't think it matters much anymore. I'd probably just end up annoying her.

"Oh, Kit, I forgot to tell you," Jane said, pouring tea as I came back into the kitchen. "Eric Levin called tonight. He said to give you a three-word message."

"Three words?"

"Yeah, just three. 'No can do.'"

five

WHAT, REALLY, can you say about adolescence that's helpful? It's a conundrum, a challenge, not a single dread thing but a series of dread things. Almost no one is ready for it. Almost no one is good at it. Every interesting adult describes it as the worst time of his or her life. Every parent is taken aback, convinced he or she was so loving or sensitive as to be able to avoid it.

It is inherently illogical and unpredictable, and there is no peaceable way to negotiate it because it is a profound conflict with high stakes whose very point is conflict. If you don't go after them, they'll come after you; it's what they need. You're not supposed to like it, but you will survive it, and the kid will too, if you keep your sense of humor and perspective. Or so I've been promised.

Even if she thinks you're stupid. Or will cross a street to avoid being seen with you. Even if much of what you say, do, and are is patently offensive. If your clothes are dull, your taste in music witless, your jokes flat. Even if your most prominent trait is your instinctive and unfailing gift for saying just the wrong thing at the wrong time. Even if your very existence on the earth is profoundly embarrassing.

Why, I asked myself, couldn't we all just agree that separation was inevitable and independence admirable? Have some moving familial ceremony, perhaps, shake hands, and move on? Why did we need to plunge into this protracted and explosive drama? God works in mysterious ways, Jane said. A psychologist, for chrissake, and that was the best she could do.

"Good morning" was my polite greeting as Ben and Em came staggering down the stairs for school the next morning. Little kids bounded. Adolescents dragged sullenly along like prisoners getting off the van to walk into the big house: Since life was nothing but oppressive misery, what was the rush?

"Em," I said, trying to sound subdued—cheerfulness was never welcome in the morning—"I put out a muffin for you." Both of my kids were old enough to make breakfast for themselves, and sometimes did, but mornings were a chance to take advantage of their bleariness by slipping in something healthy, like Total or a bran muffin.

"I know," she muttered, just the smallest hint of disgust in her voice. The import was clear: I can see the damned muffin, dummy. Do you think I'm blind?

Ben was out the door in three minutes, muttering something I barely heard about practice later—he would call and leave a message on my machine. After which Em, inexplicably, came over and gave me a big hug.

Had she forgotten what a dolt I was? How intrusive and uncool? "Love you, Dad," she said. Go figure.

When the kids were off to school—Jane was long gone—Percentage watched me closely to see if I grabbed the leash, which would mean he was coming with me to the mall or on one of my stakeouts. He was an easy office-mate and a great cover for a stakeout. Nobody expected a PI to be walking a big black Lab, especially one with a gimpy leg. On the other hand, you sometimes had to break off a surveillance to let him go pee.

"Not today, pal," I said. He understood, and went to investigate the possibility of muffin crumbs under the table.

I decided to work the phones from home, rather than go into the office. I left Evelyn a voice mail message, then called Luis. The Lightning Burger was on the ground floor of the Amway, directly below my second-story office, one of a row of obscure little businesses—collection agencies, an answering service, a temp placement firm—hidden away above the mall's walkways and shops. Luis answered himself. "Lightning Burger," he said in his courtly Cuban accent. "How may we serve you?"

Luis and the Lightning Burger always seemed mismatched. Once a highly successful and, by all accounts, brilliant criminal lawyer in Havana, Luis had opposed and then fled the Castro regime. For reasons he never talked about, his family didn't make it out with him. He still looked the part of the prosperous attorney—tall, gracious, elegantly dressed, even at the Lightning Burger. He ran the place with great care, courtesy, and efficiency, beloved by his staff for his gentleness and generosity, and by those customers who got to know him for his courtesy. Nobody really held him responsible for the food. Why had he never attempted to practice law in the United States? I didn't really know that, either.

Along with Benchley, he had become one of my closest friends, yet I had never penetrated the reserve and privacy that enveloped him, and I probably never would. I'd never been to Luis's home, and despite several invitations, he'd never been inside mine. Still, his keen and experienced legal mind was one of my greatest resources. Luis could cut through the complexities of a case in a way I never saw anyone else do and surely couldn't do myself. I never took a major case without touching base with him, and he often steered me in fruitful directions.

We'd sit in one of his spotless booths, Luis in his well-tailored suit, me in my wrinkled chinos and mocs, picking at our burgers or sipping bad coffee. I'd lay out the details of a case, and he would nod and smile, interjecting a question here or there, asking me to repeat something. After he had all the information he wanted, he might gently suggest a question, point out an inconsistency, or express puzzlement about something someone had said. I'd get the hint, listening with extra care because Luis always expressed himself in a soft-spoken way. When he heard something that he really didn't like or that didn't make sense, however, he'd sit up straighter, bear in on me, perhaps raise one eyebrow. You could picture him standing in some steamy Havana courtroom, a fan revolving overhead, eviscerating some hapless malefactor.

And all the while, I was asking myself unspoken questions. How had Luis survived in Cuba for years after the revolution? Why did he never mention the family I knew he had (I had seen a faded photo tucked into the visor on the single occasion when I'd been in his car)? What had become of them? How did he pass the time in those few hours he wasn't at the Lightning Burger? Did he have a girlfriend? Hobbies? Did he go to ball games? Sit in a restaurant laughing with friends? I couldn't picture it. What kind of house or apartment did he have in Jersey City? Why didn't he want anyone to go there?

I didn't know the answers, and it would have seemed far too smarmy to sniff around. Whatever his reasons, Luis would stiffen at personal questions, and I had long ago stopped asking them. He was entitled to his privacy.

My sense was that Luis had plunged or been dragged into some political drama and lost. Clearly he had suffered greatly and lost much, and he had chosen to run this small corner of the world with class and courage. But I couldn't help feeling some sadness at how a man with so much charisma and intelligence had ended up presiding over twenty-two orange-and-white Formica booths in an aging mall in northern New Jersey.

"Luis," I said. "I don't know if you've heard. Benchley Carrolton's had a stroke. He's in a nursing home, an arrangement he apparently made some time ago."

I heard a sharp intake of breath. "May God bless him," Luis

said softly. "He's not in a hospital? What nursing home? Did he ever mention this arrangement?"

I could tell from Luis's tone that he was just as puzzled as I was. Benchley had joined us several times for coffee or lunch when he was near the mall. The two men felt warmly toward one another, each recognizing the grace and spirit of the other.

"A place called Elston Manor. And no, he never said anything about it. In fact, Benchley always made it clear that he didn't want to be kept alive by extraordinary means. He talked often of the way he wanted to die. He said Quakers celebrated a person's life, and didn't mourn their death. He even said he wanted to die right in the Garden Center. Is that my imagination—"

"No," Luis said. "I heard him say the same things, several times. Among the elderly, talk of death is common and sometimes morbid. But Benchley was never afraid of it. He said it was his last great journey. This Quaker notion—celebrating life, not mourning death—it was very real for him. I never heard him mention this place either, and I can see you feel something is not right." I smiled. Only Luis could "see" my disturbance over the phone. But it was valuable to learn that his anxiety mirrored mine.

But that didn't mean there wasn't an easy explanation. Maybe Benchley had recovered sufficiently quickly to no longer require a hospital, but still needed too much care to be sent home. Maybe he didn't want to bother any of his friends. Maybe he thought he was making provisions to keep from being a burden. I could see all of that. Benchley had the right to make his own decisions. But why be so secretive?

It was time to find out. I told Luis I'd fill him in when I knew more, then dialed Trenton information and called State Senator James Goodell's office. Rochambeau was in his district, something of which I guess I was vaguely aware.

Goodell was one of those militantly moderate politicians who characterize New Jersey. New Jersey doesn't get into flaps about gay rights or make lots of ruckus about abortion. New Jersey is a place people go to raise families and commute to their jobs.

The government is merely supposed to keep the infrastructure running—get the Turnpike repaved, prevent the beaches from eroding, issue driver's licenses—and otherwise leave its citizens alone, which is what generally happens.

Goodell was one of the best-known and most powerful politicians in the state. He ran the State Senate so handily that no governor could pass legislation without his approval. A political moderate who understood the inner workings of government, he always got endorsements from the big papers. I had never heard his name in connection with nursing homes, though. It was a surprise to find out he was the nominal head of Transitions, Inc., which ran Elston Manor and was headquartered, according to Willie, in Ridgewood.

A secretary said Goodell wasn't available, but wouldn't say where I could reach him. So I called Transitions, Inc.

"Is Senator Goodell there?" I asked. "It's urgent."

"May I tell him what the call is in reference to?" asked the young woman on the phone. So he was there.

"My name is Kit Deleeuw. It's urgent that I talk to the senator. It's about a friend of mine who's in one of his nursing homes. I need to get in to see him."

"And the name of your friend?"

"Benchley Carrolton. He's in Elston Manor in Clifton."

"Just a minute, please."

But it was several minutes before Goodell came on. "Mr. Deleeuw? I am deeply sorry to have kept you waiting. I was in a meeting and I just had to wait for it to break up. I apologize. I hate being on hold and try never to do it to other people. I'm pleased to hear from you." The voice was smooth, gracious, confident, the voice I imagined a skilled politician should have. "You're the one they call the Suburban Detective, right?"

"Right," I said. "I'm flattered you've heard of me."

"Oh, I keep tabs on my constituents," he said. "Besides, how many famous detectives are there in New Jersey?"

Wow, he really *was* smooth. My last three cases had generated considerable publicity in New Jersey and, more important, in

New York. I'd been flooded with calls about my battles with the Russian mob in the last case, but I'd declined all of the TV and interview requests; they would be good for business, probably, but I valued my family's privacy. And I thought a good investigator ought to be able to move around without being recognized. I had become somewhat well known, but that was a far cry from being famous. Actually, I doubted Goodell had been in a meeting at all. I suspected he'd used those minutes to run a computer check on me. The newspaper stories about my cases would pop up in a second on Nexis.

So Goodell was blowing smoke, but why? He had no reason to kiss my ass, though I knew enough about politicians to understand that the good ones did it instinctively.

"That's very kind of you," I said. "I don't know how famous I am, but I need a favor, as a constituent and a friend, not as a detective." I thought that might put him at ease.

"Shoot," he said.

"One of my closest friends, Benchley Carrolton, is in Elston Manor, Senator, recovering from a stroke. I'm a bit surprised he's there, frankly. Apparently your company has a contract of some sort with him, one he never mentioned to anybody. But the real problem is that your people won't let me in to see him. I'm not related. There's a lot of security there . . ."

"Jeannie will be on the phone the second you hang up to see that you get access. I hear some concern in your voice, Mr. Deleeuw. Let me try to alleviate it. I asked her to call up Mr. Carrolton's file, which I now have in front of me. First, you will have visiting privileges. I don't know if you called the Manor or not, but the policy is that guards let no one in without administrative approval. We've had some robberies and a few months ago one of our patients was assaulted on the grounds. People who contract with assisted care facilities become rightly angry when they hear about such incidents, and we mean to see nothing like that ever happens again. Did you call Elston Manor and ask to see Mr. Carrolton?"

I had to admit, a bit awkwardly, that I hadn't. The guards were so emphatic I'd thought it would get me nowhere. But it was true, I'd jumped to conclusions.

"No problem," Goodell chuckled understandingly. "People get rattled when their closest friends get sick. As to the arrangements, I'm sure you, of all people, understand they are confidential. But I can tell you we have a letter on file from Mr. Carrolton's attorney . . ."

"That would be Eric Levin, right?"

"That's right. The contract was negotiated with Flip Kimball; she's the president of Transitions. The only thing surprising about that is that she usually delegates these negotiations to other people. But Mr. Carrolton is someone special. The arrangements were made six months ago."

I asked exactly what kind of facility Elston Manor was.

"Mr. Deleeuw," he said, "politicians don't have the finest image these days. When my father died recently, I had the opportunity to invest some money. I chose to invest in assisted care facilities. They're profitable, to be sure, but I could have bought a couple of McDonald's just as easily. I think this is important work. People at this time of life need help and support. Too many people die alone, suffering without help or attention. I hope to see Transitions grow to the point where that isn't necessary. We charge patients who can afford it, but we are the only licensed private health care provider in the state to reserve fifteen per cent of our beds for people who can't afford to pay our fees. Mr. Carrolton was involved in helping the elderly. He worked in the hospice movement and he often lobbied and demonstrated in Trenton on behalf of the elderly and the poor, as you probably know. That's where I met him."

I did know. Benchley was off to Trenton every other week, it seemed, demonstrating against the death penalty, or in favor of better prison conditions or housing aid for the elderly. Benchley was probably a familiar face in the halls of the state capitol. It was perfectly logical he would have met Goodell there.

"I told him more than once about my plans for building a dozen assisted care facilities that weren't just warehouses, that provided good medical care, but also made sure the people inside led active and productive lives. He even helped us design the basic model for these centers—residences, community service programs, recreation and exercise facilities. He's a friend of mine, too, Mr. Deleeuw. He was pleased to have a chance to do something positive for old people."

That was definitely true. Benchley often visited nursing homes in Rochambeau. One of the reasons he often talked about death, it occurred to me, was that he was seeing so much of it. How could I have overlooked that? It made sense now that Benchley would have made some arrangement to spare himself the fate he was witnessing in others. But why not tell anybody, including his housekeeper and closest friends? I wondered if anyone in his Quaker Meeting knew. I made a note to call.

"Six months ago, after a dizzy spell, Benchley came in to meet with me and Ms. Kimball," Goodell was saying. "I don't run the centers day to day, so I left the two of them to work it out, and they did. I'm afraid I do have to run now, but I hope this answers your questions. By the time you get to Elston Manor, you'll be on the approved list. Please call me back, or Ms. Kimball, if you have any questions at all. We'll be here. And please give my best to Benchley. Tell him we're praying for him."

I thanked the senator and hung up. Everything he said made sense.

Next, I called the Friends Meeting House in Rochambeau. Between the day care center in the basement and the many counseling programs offered in the evening, someone was always around.

"Friends Meeting. Jessica Welsh here. Can I help you?"

I had met Welsh several times. She was an elder in the Meeting and Benchley's close friend as well as an avid gardener, so she was often at his house or the Garden Center.

She had heard about Benchley, but like him and the other Quakers I'd met, she had a different response to adversity.

"I hope he's well," she said. "Benchley has had a wonderful life, truly full and satisfying and rewarding. I hope he'll be able to return to it." No lament or grief—in Quaker practice, death and trauma were a part of life.

"Jessica, can I ask if you knew that Benchley was going to a nursing home called Elston Manor?"

"I didn't, Kit. I was very surprised, we all were. If he were well enough, why didn't he come home? A hundred people were ready to care for him here. Or if he needed an assisted living facility, Benchley has long had arrangements to go to Oakvale, the Friends' residence outside of Philadelphia. I know because I've made the same arrangements and we've often discussed it. We look forward to the time when we can be with other Friends and prepare for the final journey, as Benchley calls it. No one in the Meeting quite understands why Benchley would make plans like this and not share them with us. Although," she added, "he surely has the right to do so without any judgment from anyone."

I thanked her, took Percentage out for a brief walk, then disappointed him bitterly by not inviting him along for the ride. But I was headed for Elston Manor.

For Benchley, Quakerism wasn't something you practiced an hour a week. It was woven into every part of his life. He never made more profit than he absolutely had to, and he did countless good deeds every day of his life. I'd been the beneficiary of any number of them.

I was fanatically loyal to my clients. I took them on believing in their causes, but whatever happened, once they signed that contract I worked for them. I never stopped, no matter what. And Benchley didn't need a contract to become a client of mine.

six

JAMES GOODELL was one politician who was as good as his word: The guard at Elston Manor, another brawny, thick-necked guy with a gun strapped to his hip, waved me through the minute I mentioned my name. What was even more impressive, he pronounced my name correctly, something as rare as leftover money at the end of the month.

"Yes, sir," he said. "Morning, Mr. Duh LOO. You're on Mr. Carrolton's visitor list. You're welcome to visit him anytime between the hours of ten and noon, seven days a week. No food, please. Or flowers. And no friends who aren't on the list. No more than two visitors at a time, no longer than fifteen minutes at a time—that's doctors' orders. Can't extend past that for medical reasons. The nurse will go over this with you. Okay, sir? Please sign in." I nodded and signed the clipboard, the first visitor of the day.

Goodell wasn't kidding about making sure there were no more mishaps, but perhaps the security wasn't so strange. Elston Manor wasn't far from one of the rougher stretches of Paterson, where Jane used to work in a mental health clinic. She still went there once a week to see some of her clients. A bunch of sick and elderly people would be easy prey for robbers or crackheads.

Though I worried plenty about Benchley's health, I was more at ease about his being at Elston Manor after my talk with Goodell. I had no idea what the man was really like, how sincere he was or wasn't, but at least he appeared to be open and accessible. And what would there be to hide, anyway? Rose's hurt feelings aside, just what did I think had happened—that Benchley had been kidnapped by psychotic predators and spirited away into one of the state's most expensive and nicest-looking assisted care facilities? As Jane had reminded me, people waited years to get into such places.

Maybe the problem was that, like Rose, I just didn't want to accept the idea that Benchley was too ill to care for himself or, worse, that he'd made arrangements to be taken care of that didn't include me. Butt Out, I reminded myself.

Easier said than done. I wanted Benchley back at the Rochambeau Garden Center, sitting in a grove of young oak and maple saplings when it was warm, inside one of his fragrant greenhouses when it was cold, sipping his legendary cider and talking over the mysteries of life. It was in one of Benchley's greenhouses that I'd decided to become a PI. And I had spent countless evenings in one fertile corner or another of the Garden Center, yakking about my cases, my kids, my problems. I wanted Benchley back there where he belonged.

But he probably wasn't coming back.

I remember first moving to the suburbs with two small kids, our lives revolving almost completely around them and other little children, around schools and play groups and lessons. But as we rounded forty, our children old enough to fend for themselves much of the time, the concept of mortality seemed less distant. It had become a constant buzz in the background. I knew that one reason Benchley's stroke was hitting me so hard was this frightening new reality.

I drove slowly down the driveway. The same Latino gardener

was riding a mower along the already perfect lawn. It seemed clear enough now what had happened.

During one of his myriad good deeds on behalf of the infirm and the elderly, or during one of his many protests and demonstrations, Benchley had gotten to know Goodell in Trenton. Benchley had decided that this kind of assisted living facility was worthwhile and, in exchange for assurances that the poor would get some slots in Goodell's homes, Benchley had agreed to help plan them. Maybe he'd arranged to get some of his friends involved, too. Then, typically, he'd decided to put his money where his mouth was and sign up.

He would have said nothing about this. Benchley had never done great or spectacular deeds that cried out for recognition. Just the opposite: He did countless small ones, quietly paying a deserving kid's camp costs or plucking lonely people out of rest homes for the day and taking them to the giant movieplex down the highway. It never occurred to him to broadcast his activities.

The sprawling brick and glass complex curved around to my left, much of it hidden behind trees and shrubs. I saw some cinder walking trails and benches farther down the gently sloping hill. There was nothing institutional about the place, nothing ugly or depressing.

The visitors' parking lot was behind the building. Another security guard with a walkie-talkie stood waiting by the back door. My name was on his list, too, presumably because the guard at the front booth had radioed him. I expected him to give me directions, but instead he escorted me into the lobby and, veering to the right, into an airy waiting area with enormous floor-to-ceiling windows and ficus trees in big brass planters. The effort to make Elston Manor bright and cheerful was obvious and clearly expensive.

At a giant walnut desk, beeping monitors flashed digital readings from the still invisible patients. It was the only suggestion of what purpose the facility served. Except for a few stainless steel carts here and there, there was not a piece of medical equipment in sight.

The lawns, shrubs, and flowers outside the vast windows were well spaced, weed-free, and flourishing, something that would please Benchley no end. It was all too common for him to pull over when he was driving through Rochambeau and spotted weeds choking off some newly planted ash tree. "I'm sure these folks won't mind a little help," he'd say. They never seemed to.

"Visitors' Center: Please Check In Here," read a discreet sign at the front desk. I looked around and noticed a few patients being pushed through the garden in wheelchairs. Far down the hall—maybe fifty yards away—two women with walkers had taken seats before a large-screen color monitor. Behind the women watching TV, I could make out two others playing cards at a small table.

The staff, most in civilian clothes and sneakers, wearing small nameplates, passed quietly along the corridor. A lot of Hispanics, it appeared.

I kept waiting for the guard to point me somewhere and leave, but he stood right alongside me until a big, cheerful-looking woman with unnaturally red hair looked up from her paperwork and offered me her hand. She was wearing a functional navy pantsuit and a nameplate that announced she was Mary O'Brien, Head Nurse. I introduced myself. She was big-boned, tall, and wide, with a fearsome grip, and a tough, appraising gaze. I suspected she didn't take any stuff from anybody, and I wasn't planning to give her any.

"I'm here to see Benchley Carrolton," I said. "I gather I'm on your list." There was no way I was leaving Elston Manor this morning without seeing Benchley.

"Yes, we're expecting you," she said. "Can I ask you to come with me first?" She led me toward a small conference room; the guard, seeing I was in good hands, wished me a pleasant visit and left.

I took one of the chairs around an oak table; O'Brien took another. She carried a folder containing what I assumed was Benchley's chart.

"I've been told to treat you like family, though I gather you're actually a close friend," she said. "May I ask how long you've known Mr. Carrolton?"

"About six years. And yes, he's a very close friend." She nodded. I am always careful to stay on the good side of people like Mary O'Brien. If I was rude or demanding, Benchley could pay for it, not me. "That means giving you the whole story then, which, I'm sorry to say, is not pleasant. We've been getting lots of calls from other friends and members of his Quaker Meeting. Are you ready for this?"

She was asking if I was prepared for bad news. My throat tightened, but sure, I was ready. My job was to get at the truth and help him out as best I could; my own feelings and struggles could come later.

"Shoot," I said. I liked Mary O'Brien, who clearly wasn't into bullshit. "I can handle it, Ms. O'Brien. How's Benchley?"

"Medical or lay terms?" she asked. "And please call me Mary."

"Plain English, please."

"Mr. Carrolton has had a massive and disabling stroke. He nearly died at Rochambeau Memorial, but his vital signs have stabilized. However, he cannot speak and he has very little movement in his arms and legs. He can't move his fingers. He can't control his bodily functions. We don't know if he's retained much mental function; he doesn't seem to respond when we talk to him or ask questions."

That was about as disheartening a report as I could have imagined. I looked at the floor and blinked hard. I couldn't picture this most active of men paralyzed and silent.

"What's the prognosis?" I asked.

"You'll have to talk to the doctor, though I don't believe he's here right now. Stroke patients may improve through rehabilitation and therapy, but I don't want to kid you, either, Mr. Deleeuw. Your friend is badly damaged, and, of course, he's not a young man. Sometimes his eyes respond to light and visual stimulation. It's possible that he can see, hear, and think but that he can't organize his thoughts yet or vocalize them. But more likely, he's not aware of anything that's happening to him. Medically, that's about all I can tell you. We don't really know what's working and what isn't. He has round-the-clock supervision, because if anything should happen we want to be there. Okay?"

I nodded numbly. It was hitting me now. I told Mary I just wanted to see Benchley, and I would get more information later.

"Room 120, then," she said. "Around the corner, on the left. We can't let you stay longer than a few minutes."

He had the room to himself—almost. A middle-aged nurse sat across from the door, reading a magazine. The room was spotless, the windows clean, the floor polished. Outside the window, a mass of azaleas was about to bloom. All the sheets on the bed were crisp and neatly arranged. A digital monitor sat above Benchley's bed, flashing numbers and readings.

I saw a catheter tube attached to a plastic bag, tubes going into his nose, an IV in his neck and in one arm. He looked aged and spent. Until a few days ago, I'd have said that Benchley was in much better shape at eighty-one than I was. He walked for twenty minutes on the treadmill each evening, took a vigorous hike over the hill behind his house each morning. Now, he seemed to be staring vacantly at the ceiling. His right hand trembled. A thin line of spittle issued from the side of his mouth. The room was eerily still, except for the beeps and clicks from the monitors.

I walked to the side of the bed. The nurse—Alma Olivera, her name tag said—nodded, but didn't say anything. She didn't take her eyes off me, either, except to glance once in a while at the monitors flashing up above Benchley's bed.

Heartbroken is the only word I can think of for my reaction to what I was seeing. Who was this aged, dying man? Where was my friend?

I stook at the side of his bed. Nurse Olivera held up a warning hand to keep me from getting closer.

"Benchley?" I said softly. "Benchley? It's Kit. I'm here. I'm sorry . . . I'm so sorry this happened to you."

The nurse looked away; perhaps even professionals hesitate to trespass on such intimate moments. Benchley blinked. His head turned and his eyes focused on mine. His gaze was steady and clear. That was his look. I smiled. I had no doubt he was seeing me.

"He probably cannot recognize you, sir," said the nurse, in accented English, as if she were reading my mind. "He is not responsive to stimuli."

Benchley blinked again.

I knelt down by the bed. "Could you give us a minute?" I asked the nurse.

She shook her head slowly. "No, sir. I am not permitted. I could be dismissed for leaving the room. Mr. Carrolton must be under constant observation. I'm sorry."

"Then could you step back? Just give us a bit of privacy? You can see the monitors from the doorway, can't you?"

She seemed confused by the request, uncertain, as if she'd been given clear instructions about leaving, but not about moving.

"Please? I'll only be a second. He's my closest friend."

She hesitated, then rose and walked toward the door. But she didn't take her eyes off us, and if she listened carefully, she might have heard us as well.

Benchley's eyes were still fixed on my face. He blinked again. I couldn't believe he didn't know me.

"Benchley," I whispered, drawing closer. "Hey there. Hey there. Blink twice if you know this is Kit."

One blink. Then another.

The IV pump whirred, then clicked. I saw drops filtering down from one of the bags into the plastic line going into his arm. The spittle continued to trickle down the side of his jaw. But his face, if anything, grew more intense. Olivera stepped back toward us, apologizing halfheartedly and fiddling with one of the IV pumps. She stepped back.

"Benchley. Blink once if you know where you are." He blinked, and as I leaned forward, supporting myself on the bed frame, I felt a tap on my left hand. It was his thumb. He could move it. But O'Brien had said he couldn't. Had my arrival inspired him? Or had he hidden this? I was bewildered, unprepared. I should have called for the nurse to tell her Benchley could move one finger, but some instinct held me back. Why was it so hard to get in here? Why were they watching him so closely? I'd been in intensive care units where nurses weren't sitting and staring by the bedside. Why had O'Brien said he was so unaware when his expression was so unmistakably alert? Or was I misreading him, seeing only what I wanted to?

"Wiggle your thumb if you can, Benchley." He wiggled his thumb. He could definitely hear me and understand. And react. That urgent look in his eyes—was it the effect of the stroke? Or of something else? I'd been a PI for only five years, but had taken to it. I was surprised to learn that I did have an instinct for when people were lying and when they were telling the truth, when something was wrong and when it wasn't. Suffering a stroke is reason enough for an elderly man to look alarmed; why did there have to be a more sinister explanation? But in my work, instincts were ultimately all you really had, along with good help and good luck.

"Did you make a deal to come here, Benchley? Is that right? I'm just making sure." He seemed to hesitate, his eyes tearing. "Blink twice if you did." He blinked twice.

"Is everything okay here? Blink twice if it is." He didn't blink at all. I realized it was a tough question to answer. It forced him to hold his eyes open and it was too general.

"Never mind, Benchley." The nurse moved toward us again.

"I'm just telling him I love him, in case I don't get a chance later . . ." I tried to look grief-stricken—it wasn't hard—and supplicatory, as if I knew she'd understand and help. She nodded sympathetically, stepped back a bit. But Benchley's IV began beeping.

"I must change this," Olivera said. "I will bring another bag. When I return, you must leave him." I nodded, relieved, as she left the room.

"Benchley, is something wrong? If something is wrong, wiggle your thumb." His thumb moved.

"Are you in danger? Wiggle your thumb if you are." There was a small response, as if he didn't know or wasn't sure or was growing too tired to continue. I had very little time, and I wasn't sure I'd get this chance again.

"Have you seen something you don't like? Something that bothers you? Wiggle your thumb." This time he did.

"Doesn't that put you in some danger, then?" He moved his thumb harder, pressing it against my hand. The nurse came in with Mary O'Brien, even as Benchley's eyes closed and he seemed to fade out. Of course, I thought. The nurse had fiddled with his IV to put him to sleep. I looked up at the bag but couldn't read the markings.

"Sorry, Mr. Deleeuw," said O'Brien. "But that's it for today. You've exceeded the time limit. I have to insist. Come back tomorrow, okay?" She gently but firmly took my arm and urged me out the door. I turned back to Benchley, but he seemed to be asleep.

Nurse Olivera stayed behind.

"I'm sure that was difficult," O'Brien said, as we headed back down the hall.

I put a hand on her shoulder and guided her back into the conference room. I locked the door.

"Look, I might seem paranoid and strange. If so, I apologize," I said quietly. "But on the off chance that I'm right, I would never forgive myself if I didn't speak up."

She didn't say anything, which was odd. I might have expected confusion, or even outrage. But she was anything but outraged and not the least bit confused. She stayed as cool as a winter breeze, her eyes locked onto mine almost as firmly as Benchley's had.

"Ms. O'Brien, I am nervous and upset. I don't know why or how Benchley got here. I wasn't prepared for him to have a stroke, to be totally paralyzed, to be in a place like this. He can't move a finger."

At this, I sensed she relaxed a bit. Just another overwrought visitor horrified by what illness and age could do.

"I simply want you to know how much I care about him. If anything should happen to him, I will insist on involving the criminal justice system to the full extent possible. Police, autopsy, lab work-ups, the whole thing, okay? Do you follow me?"

She didn't look relaxed any longer.

I was winging it here, treating Benchley as a client, assuming he was in distress on the skimpiest of evidence. If I was wrong, they'd just figure I was a nut. If I was right, I was playing with his safety by alerting the staff to my suspicions. But he was helpless and powerless. They needed to know, the dedicated staff and administration of elegant Elston Manor, that somebody was paying attention, somebody would be back. At the moment, it seemed the only way I could protect Benchley.

O'Brien kept her voice as level as her gaze. This was a woman who didn't rattle easily. "I don't follow you, Mr. Deleeuw. We take very good care of our patients, and Mr. Carrolton will be no exception. I can't even imagine . . ."

I opened the door onto the hallway and turned halfway back. "I just wanted to be clear, Mary. I feel better now. I'll be back. Tomorrow and every day." A hollow threat, but the only one I could think of. This was as tough a guy as I could play. Since I look as menacing as a high school history teacher, Jane says, I had to let them know that if anything untoward happened to Benchley, I'd be back and I'd be bringing the cavalry with me.

Why did I think I'd need the cavalry? Just because the whole thing felt wrong. Because Benchley was, of all the humans I knew, sensitive to others. He didn't have to tell the people who cared about him all the decisions he'd made, but he would have tried to avoid surprising, excluding, or alarming his friends. Because this decision seemed precipitous and uncharacteristic. Because this place was too high-powered, too sealed off, too much like some beautifully designed containment facility.

Odds were, I was being a jerk. If I was, I'd be embarrassed. If

I wasn't, something horrible could happen to Benchley and I didn't have much time to stop it.

I felt frantic, almost panicky, but I didn't want O'Brien to see that. They could kill Benchley in a second if they had reason to. Did they have reason? Was he really conscious of being in peril? Was he really communicating with me? I couldn't be sure.

The guard at the back door made me sign out, as did the guard at the gatehouse. But then the gate didn't rise to let the Volvo through. Instead, the guard stepped out of his booth and leaned over the door of the wagon. I rolled my window down.

He leaned down. "Mr. Deleeuw, I've been asked to tell you that your name has been taken off the visitors' list. It's being restricted to family only. You can't come here anymore."

His face was impassive. He was unapologetic, just businesslike. He clearly wasn't going to say one word more than he had to.

"What? Why? Benchley doesn't have any family."

But he was already back in the booth and on the phone while I was still sputtering. Despite the flowers and sunshine, I felt suddenly cold.

seven

I DROVE to the American Way as quickly as I could. The Volvo was straining on even the smallest hill. And I was pushing it, wondering again if it was time to get a speedier, flashier car.

My sense of urgency was real. I had to move very quickly, be cleverer than I had been. This wasn't an ordinary case. I might have only a few hours or days to help protect one of the people I most loved, a person who might be in horrible danger.

Or might not.

I needed a reality check. I worried that I was too freaked to think clearly, something no PI can afford. There were the multiple shocks of the stroke, Benchley's vanishing into Elston Manor, my bizarre efforts to communicate in that creepy, over-guarded place.

I couldn't call the police, because I had no concrete evidence that anything was wrong. Chief Leeming would laugh me right out of town if I went to him with reports of Benchley's thumb-jiggling.

And I had no legal standing to try to get Benchley wrested

from the place. In fact, the reverse was true: He had left explicit instructions that in the event of a decline or medical crisis he'd move into Elston Manor, one of the new assisted care facilities set up by one of the state's most powerful political figures.

I called Jane at work and asked her to drive to the Amway. It was not a place she frequented: She hated malls, crowds, fast food, and kids in hordes. Besides, I think she was still a bit uncertain about this whole private-eye thing. "You didn't have to reinvent yourself that much," she'd say at odd intervals, such as when I'd been shot, beaten up, threatened by Russian mobsters, or thrown in jail by the local police. Wasn't there some intermediate step between the life of a Wall Street trader making pots of money and the life of a PI called out at all hours of the day and night on bizarre, sometimes murderous cases?

Still, I needed her. So she'd be there. Whatever messes I had made of my life, marrying Jane was a stellar move. Not only did she provide a health plan and some revenue when I desperately needed both, she provided strength, support, understanding, love, and friendship. Sex, too, when we managed to sandwich it in.

I called Luis at the Lightning Burger and asked if he could join us. Standard Operating Procedure: I never made a serious move, if I could help it, without running it by Luis.

Evelyn would be there, too. Probably the least likely person in Rochambeau to work in a PI's office, she'd saved my work life, organizing my office, screening out bad clients, forcing me to meet deadlines, file insurance reports, and keep actual tax records.

We'd need Willie, too. He had easily made the transition from genial hacker to genial investigator. When he wasn't scarfing up information from the Net, he could blend effortlessly into just about any suburban environment. Young, blond, tall, and good-looking, you could drop him into a mall, a park, a high school parking lot, and he would melt in, chatting up total strangers, drawing girls like flies.

I parked by the American Way's back entrance and half-jogged, half-ran inside. Late morning was one of the quiet times in Mallville, after the elderly had finished their daily exercise and before the housewives gathered to lunch and shop.

I passed the wholesome family of mannequins in their usual window at Cicchelli's Furniture Store, sporting their new spring sneakers and Mets windbreakers.

I waved to Plain James, who was lining up the R&B tapes and CDs on his vendor's cart, the "Soul Shack," and sipping the first of what would be a half-dozen or so espressos through the day. He was resplendent this morning in a sequined red dress, platinum wig, and ropes of rhinestones. He'd fled Manhattan and an agonizingly complex love life for what he called the "saner, tamer," life of a pushcart tycoon in the American Way. When the mall management discovered he was a transvestite, the company had flirted with the idea of tossing James out. But Luis and I and Murray Grobstein, the powerful owner of Shoe World, had threatened a lawsuit if anyone bothered him. Management backed down, and James turned out to be a fine mall citizen—meticulous, profitable, great legs.

James waved back but didn't speak. He still trekked into the city many nights and sometimes didn't return to New Jersey until it was time to open for business. "Morning is not my best time, honey. Come on around when the sun goes down," he'd coo.

The first few times Luis and James had met, I thought Luis was going to pass out in shock. The culture clash between the machismo world of Havana and the seedier reaches of the East Village was staggering. But the two men got used to each other and we all came to look forward to coffee, such as it was, at the Lightning Burger. Plain James and Luis were both, after all, outsiders and refugees, pilgrims in suburbia, making their way in a new world under radically changed circumstances. So was I, the former Wall Street bond trader trying desperately to keep from defaulting on his mortgage. Welcome to the '90s.

As for Murray Grobstein, he was my favorite mall entrepreneur. Downsized in the late '80s, like me, but twice as smart, he'd noticed that well-off kids were spending fortunes trying to look like poor black kids from the city. So he drove around Brooklyn and Harlem on weekends and then, on Monday, ordered large quantities of whatever he saw kids wearing on their feet. Murray had caught this boom at the precise moment when black athletic superstars were becoming gazillion-dollar cultural icons. He sold shoes that lit up, hissed, inflated, weighed ten pounds, and leaped right into the arms of eager New Jersey teenagers. As a result, Murray smoked imported cigars, drove a Jag with the license plate "SNKR KING," spent January in Aruba and much of the rest of the year working his butt off to keep up with suburbia's successive footwear fads.

"It's a great country, isn't it?" he often chirped. "I love eight-foot-tall black guys who play basketball."

Why were white kids into black culture so deeply, from the NBA to hip-hop music? I always suspected it was because the suburbs don't offer a distinct culture of their own. So many types got tossed into the blender of middle-class suburban life—Jews, Catholics, Muslims, gays, lesbians, Japanese, Irish, Iranians. Rochambeau's most popular soccer coach was a refugee from the Ayatollah, a mathematician turned science teacher; his assistant was a lesbian who'd adopted four kids of varying ethnic backgrounds. Black street culture, distinct from them all, seemed by comparison rich and alluring.

I hadn't quite got past the mall's multicolored fountain when two lean, crew-cutted men in suits—they might as well have had C-O-P-S stenciled across their foreheads—stepped in front of me.

"Kit Deleeuw," said the one on the left. I nodded. He flashed a State Police Detective Sergeant's badge. "I'm Detective Sergeant Rosetto. This is Detective Weir." Rosetto wore a black suit, Weir a dark blue one, both suits cheap and well rumpled. In fact, the two of them looked as if they'd been cruising the Garden State Parkway for the last couple of hours.

"How can I help you gentlemen?" I asked. "I'm in a bit of an emergency."

That seemed to pass right over them. Rosetto, it seemed, was going to do the talking. "We're here on behalf of the state Private Investigations Licensing Office," he said. "Can I see your shield, please?"

The NJPILO gave us our badges and licenses. It also took them away. PIs were intensely regulated in New Jersey. To get a license, you had to pass a six-month training course, submit to a meticulous background investigation, and agree to follow a million persnickety rules and regulations.

Since my former career was destroyed as the result of a federal investigation into insider trading, my license took an extra few months to arrive. The FBI, still ticked because I wouldn't testify against my friends and former colleagues, didn't make things easier. I finally got my ID and certificate, however.

But the Licensing Office could yank our shields for any reason and take its sweet time investigating whatever complaints had arisen about our work. There wasn't much we could do about it but starve. Rochambeau PD Chief Frank Leeming loved threatening to call the LO whenever he caught me overstepping my bounds, withholding information, or making him look bad on a case—things that had happened with some frequency in my brief but intense career.

"Please . . ." I said.

Detective Rosetto held up his hand and scanned his notebook. "We understand you threatened a nurse at the Elston Manor assisted care residence this morning. Is that right?"

I blinked. Perhaps I'd been distracted, but was I so damned dumb that I had forgotten I was diddling with the most powerful politician in the state? That despite his genial demeanor, I now represented trouble to him and his major investment in assisted living? That an unmistakably clear message was required to shut this problem down? The only thing I didn't know yet was how strong a message—would they pull my shield then and there? Or give me another chance?

Of course, they gave me a chance. That would be the politician's way. Yanking my license would enrage me, back me into a corner, leave me with nothing to lose. Threatening to yank, on the other hand, would give me an incentive to behave, if I wanted to keep food on the table and pay my bills. I had already had one traumatic career change; I didn't have any more to pull out of the hat.

I denied that I had threatened, abused, or mishandled anyone at Elston Manor or anywhere else. I explained I was just inquiring about a friend whom I was deeply concerned about. I sputtered about my excellent record. Both men took copious notes. Weir asked me a few questions. What was my relationship with Mr. Carrolton? What was my recollection of my encounters with the Elston Manor staff?

But all three of us understood what was happening.

"Mr. Deleeuw," said Rosetto, "we have to investigate this matter. This is still a preliminary inquiry. The complaint could be withdrawn, or we could find the charges unfounded. But if we find there's a basis for them, we'll file a report with the LO and they will be in touch with you about any possible disciplinary action. If not, then you will, of course, be free to go about your business."

That was clear enough. If I dropped my questions about Benchley, Goodell and his pals wouldn't bother me. If I didn't, the LO would yank my license while investigating me for, oh, about the next three or four years. And what, exactly, would I do about it? I had no evidence that anything was wrong.

I watched the cheap suits recede. Murray Grobstein, repositioning some $160 sneakers in his window, was watching. So was Plain James, who could spot a cop miles away. And so, I noticed, was Luis, standing in the front window of the Lightning Burger. I waved to him and pointed upstairs. He held up a finger as if to say, "I'll be there in a minute."

I walked over to a nearly invisible blue door and climbed the stairs to Deleeuw Investigations. It might not be in operation by this time next week, but for now, there was work to do.

eight

THE DELEEUW IRREGULARS were already gathering in my two-room office. Since it was nearly lunchtime, Luis had graciously agreed to cater. And here he came, with one of his earnestly monosyllabic young employees toting the grub. There were two trays of burgers and cheeseburgers (Willie could chug three or four all by himself), chicken sandwiches, fries, and soft drinks. Luis never wanted to take my money, something he found deeply embarrassing, but I knew the Lightning Burger didn't have a community service budget, so we each put five dollars in a bucket and sent it down to his cashier. Sometimes, the irony of all our lives swept over Luis and he would turn mischievous, arriving with wine, candles, and a linen tablecloth.

But not this day. "Is everything okay, Kit?" Luis asked politely. He was obviously curious about my encounter with the two detectives, but wouldn't ask outright.

Jane charged in right after he did, lugging her usual fifteen pounds of books, files, laptop, and vast handbag. I was very happy to see her. "Thanks for coming, sweetheart. I appreciate it. It's real good to see your face."

"Hey, sport," she said, giving me a big hug, something neither of us often did in public. "How's Benchley?" I shrugged and shook my head. She squeezed my hand, then went over to yak with Evelyn, ever the stereotypical librarian in wire-rimmed spectacles and prim bun.

The librarians I knew were distinctly modern techies, as likely to be surfing the Web as reshelving in the stacks. Evelyn, though, came from another age, a superior one as far as she was concerned. She had done some surveillance on a case, and was eager for more adventurous work, but it made me nervous.

In fact, Evelyn looked drawn and a bit edgy this morning. Maybe it was the news about Benchley, which might have struck close to home. I didn't know how old Evelyn was, and I wouldn't dare ask her, but she had to be advancing past seventy. I knew she spent many afternoons visiting friends in hospitals and nursing homes and attended plenty of funerals.

Deleeuw Investigations was not, fortunately, a business that depended on foot traffic. In our hidden corner of the American Way, we rarely saw anybody from the credit agencies or telemarketing firms that lined the hallway. We rarely saw anyone at all. I'd started in a single office with a view of the highway—it was mesmerizing to stare out at rush hour traffic, which began at 4:07 each weekday afternoon—and the parking lot. As befitted my PI status, the office was spare, filled with used store-display furniture, most of it damaged, bought from Cicchelli's down below. There was a safe where I had put my .38 five years ago and from which I'd never taken it, plus a small anteroom where Evelyn worked part-time.

The office had grown with my practice, though. We were computerized now, and on the World Wide Web. We had broken through the wall of the office next door and made a space for Willie, though I thought of it more as a lair. He'd hooked up a network on which we e-mailed each other all day, which was fine by me, since I didn't have to go into Willie's cave.

I wasn't even certain when he was there, since he came and went at odd hours, sometimes hanging around bars and high school parking lots looking for runaways or gathering information on drug dealers, sometimes trailing Deadbeat Dads and collecting information on their hidden financial dealings, often listening to CDs by candlelight and prowling the farthest corners of the Internet for information.

But he was here now, the smell of cheeseburgers and fries having lured him from his den. He was somewhere in his twenties, though with a tousled mop of dirty blond hair always hanging over his forehead, bright blue eyes that seemed lit from within, and a "Sex and Lies" tattoo on his right forearm, he looked even younger. Depending on how he dressed, Willie could do choirboy or druggie, the boy you dreamed your daughter would date or your worst nightmare.

Willie was an instinctive trailer, a suburban hunter tracking people on bike, motorcycle, and roller blades. He could follow you all day through a mall and you'd never see him. Or glide past you a dozen times on his skateboard and look like one more goofy middle-class kid in the neighborhood.

Just last week he'd arranged a racquetball game with a computer store owner who had filed a $3 million lawsuit against the Rochambeau PD, claiming that a drunk-driving arrest had somehow left him with crippling back injuries. And the dummy had let Willie videotape the encounter so that they could both improve their game! Not only would this disclosure earn us a nice fee from the town's insurance company, but we'd gain several loyal police sources as well.

I worried about Willie sometimes. He lived alone in one of those bland garden apartments and didn't seem to be making much progress at constructing a real life, though he never wanted for girlfriends. Like Luis, he kept his personal life very personal. All I knew was that he'd been a reverse refugee, starting out in San Francisco, then moving to New Jersey. Some problem must have sent him East instead of going with the flow, especially given his computer-whiz background.

But I wasn't his dad. Like me, he seemed to have grown up without one. Problem was, I was a dad, with all those paternal instincts, and I didn't want Willie living like Sam Spade in fifteen years. It was easy enough to do in this line of work, where you could work all day and all night if you wanted.

A retiring PI had passed him along to me as a source of information. Willie worked for a giant credit firm, and with his keyboard wizardry could find out in seconds if somebody had bought dinner in St. Louis with a credit card the preceding week. He would leave his reports out by a designated Dumpster at night; I'd leave two hundred dollars under his apartment door. The arrangement eventually came to bother me. I was encouraging Willie to break the law, and I was doing it myself. I decided to make him legit, to make him officially my associate, and he jumped at the chance. No more hacking, I said. Right, he twinkled.

He was always in touch, flashing me reports of the latest surveillance, responding at odd hours to emergency research requests. As long as I'd known him, he'd traveled with wireless modem-equipped laptops, cell phones as thin as sliced prosciutto, pagers, and beepers. We were close, yet we weren't. If he vanished or moved, as I suspected he would one day, I wouldn't have the slightest idea where to look for him or how to contact him, except through e-mail.

"Luis, my man!" was his greeting as he fell upon a burger. It took him a while to notice the rest of us, but somewhere between the first and second cheeseburger he greeted Jane.

So we were all here: Jane, Evelyn, Luis, Willie, and me, the Brain Trust, my own little operations team. An odd mix, but no investigator ever had better or smarter backup.

"Hey, folks," I said. "Thanks for being here." I sat on Evelyn's desk, the others in a semicircle on the floor, the sofa, odd chairs. I went over my talk with Goodell yesterday, the visit with Benchley that morning, the taps and blinks I was positive were efforts to communicate. I left out, till I could brief Jane privately, the intimidation tactics by the State Police.

"You understand, Kit, that there's a strong possibility your imagination is taking flight here, don't you?" Jane was getting down to business as usual. "That Benchley, who suffered a massive stroke, might be responding to stimuli in ways you take as messages when they aren't . . ."

Luis couched it more delicately. "Or even," he added, "that Benchley is confused. That he may think he faces danger when he does not. After all, he has been through an extraordinary trauma."

I had considered the possibility that I was overreacting, but not that Benchley himself might be unclear about what was happening. Still, didn't stroke victims sometimes lose clarity about what they were experiencing?

I reviewed what I'd seen and heard, step by step. Jane made a few notes, looking every bit the working professional in a dark brown pantsuit with a white shirt open at the collar. As a psychologist, she'd studied the effects of strokes.

"Kit, I'm not minimizing your instincts, which I trust. I'm pointing out that strokes vary wildly. Sometimes people are fine in hours; sometimes they literally have to learn to think all over again, to remember how to connect the dots. Sometimes they think in disjointed ways and sequences, hear words differently than they are spoken, understand them in idiosyncratic ways. It's possible that a series of events that would be perfectly comprehensible to Benchley before the stroke might be interpreted completely differently afterward. Just a caution."

Luis asked me to go through Benchley's responses to my questions again. I did. "It wasn't just the blinks and wiggles of his thumb," I added. "Mostly, it was the look in his eyes. He was frightened. Maybe frightened of the stroke, I have no trouble buying that. But I just had a sense he was in danger. It didn't come just from him, it was the place, too. There were too many security people there, watching too closely. What were they afraid of? They didn't want to leave me alone with Benchley for a second. Why not? Wouldn't they want him to have company?"

Willie, who'd been sorting through some pictures, cleared his throat. "Chief, I've been on-line and on the phone gathering material about Goodell. He's got four of these centers up and running already, Elston Manor plus two in Connecticut and one in Westchester. Eight more are under construction, all of them in New Jersey. According to the bank records, they are rated very highly as excellent investment risks for limited partnerships. Assisted care is growing, and these centers aim at wealthy elderly people. They have very high staff-to-patient ratios and make a big deal out of security; they are all certified by the states involved and get the highest rating from nonprofit monitoring groups. The word in Trenton is, Goodell plans to go national with Transitions, Inc. He's tired of state politics and wants to make some real money."

"Anything off about him? Anything I should know?" I asked.

"Maybe. I don't really know yet," Willie said. "On-line I found something about a lawsuit filed in Southampton, Connecticut, against his facility there, Puritan Homes. It's right along I-95, a big one-hundred-and-ten-bed unit that's been operating for eighteen months. The lawsuit was filed by the son of a man who died there." Willie glanced up from his papers, having noticed something he hadn't before. "Of a stroke," he added.

"What was the suit about?" Evelyn asked, looking a bit pale.

"That he was given too many injections of a drug called Hemavero, a blood thinner, and that it killed him. From the papers filed, it sounds like a nasty suit, suggesting the drug was administered even though the doctors knew the dose was dangerous. The patient—eighty-nine-year-old man named Wilford Hamilton—went into a vegetative state." Willie read from his printouts. "The suit was settled six months later, with a nondisclosure agreement on both sides. Sounds like they bought off the son, Bill Hamilton, just before it went to trial. I've got his address and phone number if you want to talk to him. He's a lawyer, semiretired."

"Thanks, Willie. Hard to know if it's relevant or not. I can't imagine you could run a facility like that these days without picking up a few lawsuits."

Luis stood up. He nodded toward Jane, then to Evelyn. Luis still nodded to women whenever he spoke, and he always would, even though in America that probably puzzled more women than it charmed.

"Kit, you could easily have misinterpreted or overreacted," he began. "But perhaps not. It is strange that Benchley made these arrangements without telling anyone. He is a deeply religious man; I can't imagine that he wouldn't have wanted to be among the Quakers. Why go into this new facility, which is both expensive and unfamiliar? And you know Benchley quite well. If you believe he was frightened, he may very well have been. I agree with you about this matter of security, as well. Nursing homes for the elderly are not usually the targets of robbers. There are always people around. And what is there to steal? I know all too well that security is used as often to keep people in as it is to keep them out."

I was surprised by this obvious allusion to Cuba, which he ordinarily never mentioned. But Benchley's plight might have struck a deep chord with Luis.

Before he could say more, the phone warbled. Evelyn took the call. Meanwhile, Jane's pager began to beep insistently. Willie shrugged and ambled back into his lair to commune with the Internet. Modern communication. All news travels fast, including, it seemed, bad news.

Evelyn was gesturing in alarm. "What is it?" I asked. She waved me into my inner office with what looked like a phone message in her hand. Evelyn was tough as hardwood, befitting a veteran civil servant with decades of service and a keen instinct for taking on bureaucracy, but she looked distinctly rattled.

"Kit, the strangest call. It was from a man named Jim Weitzman in the Essex County Prosecutor's Office. He didn't even ask if he could speak with you. He just said to give you a message. He said the call was a courtesy, that he wanted to let us

know that his office might be instituting a witness-tampering
and perjury inquiry against you . . ."

My jaw must have dropped several inches. "Perjury? This is a
joke, right?"

"No, Kit," she said. "Mr. Weitzman said a witness in an insurance fraud case—he wouldn't say which one—had come forth to
say you paid him to give false testimony. That your own testimony was also false. This Weitzman said the prosecutors were
looking into the allegations. I took down every word he said,
Kit, but I didn't know how to respond. Do we need a lawyer?"

That threw me. My lawyer was Eric Levin, but I could hardly
call him after he'd arranged for Benchley to go into Elston
Manor and hadn't arranged for me to see him.

What a bizarre phone call. Prosecutors didn't call you up as
"a courtesy" to alert you to the fact that you might be a target
of a criminal investigation. They would assign the case to investigators and see whether there was anything to it. If they had
real reason to suspect me of either perjury or witness-tampering,
they'd simply barrel into my office with half a dozen cops, seize
every file I had, and haul me before a magistrate.

A "courtesy" call was translatable enough: it was another
warning. Stay away from Elston Manor or get your ass indicted
and your license yanked. I did need a good lawyer, and I had
one right in the anteroom, waiting—Luis. He might have to be
unofficial, but there was nobody better. I murmured a few sen-
tences and suggested we adjourn to the Lightning Burger to talk.

Downstairs, supplied with so-called coffee, I relayed the few
facts Evelyn had told me along with the particulars of the State
Police visit. Did Goodell have any other unpleasant surprises in
store? I badly needed Luis's reassurance, but I was in no sense
prepared for what came out of his mouth.

"Kit," he said. "I have given more thought to this case. It
troubles me. I have thought of that poor gentleman lying helpless in a hospital bed. Don't worry about these threats, my
friend." He dismissed them airily. "If the authorities were prepared to move against you, you would be in handcuffs on your

way to the arraignment. These warnings simply mean that the senator wants you to go away. You must pretend to do that. You may visit Benchley if you can, chat with him, that is all. Otherwise, you must make no overt moves in this case. Tell Willie to stop his searches. Make no further phone calls. There's only one way we can help Benchley."

I was glad he had an idea, because I was running out. I waited.

"This Elston Manor is near Paterson, am I right?"

I nodded.

"A number of Cubanos work there, I believe?"

I couldn't identify their nationalities, but there were Hispanic workers—gardeners, orderlies, Nurse Olivera—all around Elston Manor. I had noticed that. "What are you getting at?" I asked him. He wore an odd expression, both amused and determined.

"I too have asked some questions," Luis said. "I've heard some things about Elston Manor. The administrators aren't kind to their employees. They pay very poorly. People say it's not a happy place. It's tense. Heavily guarded, lots of secrecy, places where even the help can't go, rooms janitors can't clean and orderlies have no keys for."

I was having a hard time grasping this. "Off-limits rooms? Are the patients there very ill?"

Luis shrugged. "I cannot say. Down the block, my neighbor Hector Juarez is janitor there, part-time. There seem to be many part-time jobs there. Hector complains there's no friendship, no socializing, no place for employees to sit and talk. You do your work, then you get out. It's a grim business."

Was that so unusual? "But Luis, facilities for the aged and infirm aren't usually happy places."

He shrugged. "Perhaps. But even at hospitals, the workers can make a few jokes, have coffee in a lounge, or talk in the cafeteria. This place is extremely—what do the kids say?—uptight." He paused, sipping at his coffee again. "So I've been thinking—I might be able to help," he said.

"Hold on, Luis," I said. "I'm the detective. This is my case."

"Not precisely," he said calmly. "Benchley didn't hire you, Kit. Nobody did. You have involved yourself because you wish to help a fine man. I propose to involve myself for the same reason. None of us can walk away from somebody in trouble. I am sure you understand."

His voice remained affable, but his eyes were blazing. I had the sense it would not be healthy or feasible to tell him I disagreed. I could only imagine the agonies Luis must have suffered—the loss of family and friends, the ruin of his proud career, perhaps imprisonment or even torture, exile, poverty, the indignity of grinding out burgers in a graying mall. What I suspect sustained him through all of it was an old-world sense of honor. Life in one way seemed simple for Luis: You determined what the right thing was, and you did it.

"I'm putting my assistant manager in charge here, then I'm going home to change," he continued. "Then I'm going to apply for work as an orderly at Elston Manor and learn what on earth is going on. Hector says it is not difficult to be hired there because so many workers leave. He will speak for me. He owes me a debt. I helped get him into the United States."

And how had he done that? I wondered. Had Luis smuggled refugees or political prisoners out of Cuba and through some pipeline to the mainland? I would probably never know, just as I had never understood why he hadn't passed the bar and taken up the practice of law here. Maybe he'd lost heart, or run out of money. Maybe he'd committed some felony that would come back to haunt him. Maybe I'd put Willie on it one day and find out for sure. Maybe I wouldn't dare.

My mouth opened but nothing intelligible came out. Luis going undercover? My first response was to refuse to drag Luis into such a situation. But it was, I had to admit, a terrific idea. What better way to have a look around the place, and who less likely to draw attention than a courtly, middle-aged, Spanish-speaking man? Normally, I would never have let Luis stick his neck out. But Benchley's life might be hanging in the balance.

Before I could answer, Jane appeared at my side, looking

shaken, as Evelyn had. As everybody in the state seemed to be today.

"Kit, I got a call from the psychologists' licensing board. There's been a complaint against me by a former patient. It's outrageous and insane. I've been accused of violating confidentiality and of overcharging." She laughed briefly. Overcharging! "The man from the licensing board said he wasn't sure they'd formally investigate the charges, but they were putting me on notice that it was a possibility. My God, I can't imagine what this is about . . ."

She sat down in the booth next to me. Luis and I exchanged heavy glances but said nothing. Jane put her head on my shoulder. She had worked like a demon to get trained and certified, and she loved her work. A scandal, whatever its eventual outcome, would devastate her, and almost certainly ruin her practice.

I slipped my arm around her shoulder. The phone call had scared the hell out of her, and I didn't blame her. It was hard to damage a private detective's reputation: The worse people thought about you, the more effective they thought you were. Harming a psychologist's reputation, on the other hand, was all too simple. Rumors alone would suffice. Nobody would go near a psychologist whose license had been suspended or who was under investigation. A single ugly newspaper story—even if it were later corrected—could prove lethal.

I was beginning to grasp what pressure really meant. I'd thought the heat I'd taken from the FBI a few years back was intense, but this was a whole new level of harassment. I'd been emboldened in my conflict with the feds by the belief that they had some rules they had to play by. Goodell didn't seem to have any.

But he was also demonstrating that he wasn't particularly bright. There was no way I would turn my back on Benchley, no way Jane would want me to, and, despite the threats, no way Luis would let me. Goodell had flexed some impressive muscle but hadn't bothered to do his homework. I never walked away from clients, even when they sometimes wanted me to. And I never walked away from friends.

I offered Luis my hand. "You're in, podnah," I said. When you feel like a squashed beetle, it sometimes helps to sound like John Wayne.

nine

JANE AND I decided the only possible response to Benchley's stroke, and to these sudden and frightening threats to our livelihoods, was pizza. We'd spent a couple of desultory hours in my office, trying and failing to concentrate on our respective paperwork, before we gave up. It wasn't working. We were too unnerved. So I called home, told Ben and Em to heat up the leftover spaghetti in the fridge—and don't forget to cut up some veggies, Jane had chimed in—and we headed out.

We sought refuge at Pizzeria Uno, where we usually dined, to use a too elegant word, before movies at the Sony Gigaplex. This ritual was the closest thing there was to a sacred rite in our happy if complicated marriage. It never varied. I always had a sausage Plizzetta. Jane always ordered a plain deep-dish pizza. We always split a Caesar salad.

Normally, such meals were followed by pot-luck movies, so called because sometimes we knew what we wanted to see and sometimes we went in blind. We turned off our pagers and cell phones. I got some pretzel bites. She bought a box of Goobers. We holed up in the dark theater, leaned back in our reclining seats, put our drinks in their nifty plastic cup-holders, and guessed the movie trivia quiz questions, which, by now, we knew by heart. It just didn't get much mellower than that.

Jane and I had had our ups and downs over the years. Ironically, our marriage was in the most trouble when I was the most financially secure. The truth was, Jane had hated being a housewife. She valued child care as important work, but it wasn't for her. She felt her life shrinking, the boundaries of her world defined by play dates and gripes about teachers. She was secretly thrilled when I lost my Wall Street job and she launched her career as a psychologist. Meanwhile, it turned out that I had a gift for domesticity that had never been called into play, and that I was better at shopping, scheduling car pools, and attending to the details of child care than she was. It wasn't because I was a better parent, more that I had never previously had the chance to be much of a parent at all.

Jane knew she was a loving mom, but she didn't revel in the details of child care; she found them tiresome and suffocating. I found them riveting and miraculous. It was a kick to learn the ins and outs of the supermarket, to figure out the political intricacies of a young girl's social life, to sense when to move in on children's lives and when to Butt Out. Most men didn't get to do that, and it felt like a privilege to be able to learn how, as my reenergized wife pursued her training and even acquired a health plan. We both ended up twice as happy, our marriage twice as strong. Losing all that—I didn't want to think about it.

We sat in the not yet crowded pizzeria—we had timed our arrival to be just ahead of the hordes—doing what parents do when they're finally alone, talking about the kids. There was always plenty to talk about. Ben had morphed from a sullen adolescent who struggled with grades and smoked pot at every opportunity to a sullen adolescent who drank beer at every opportunity but was somehow on the honor roll.

"At least it's trending the right way," I said.

Emily was in motion, too, as kids always are. Though she found me stupid and repulsive, except when I was driving, she still confided in Jane occasionally. "This boy she says is hot pulled her hair a few days ago, and by suppertime everyone in the school was buzzing about it," Jane informed me. "Then, the next day, he pulled this other girl's hair, and Em was practically in tears." Some things never change.

We nibbled at our food, trying to combat fear with mozzarella. I checked out the parade of Jerseyites out on the town— stonewashed denims, big new sneakers, lots of gold chains, Devils jackets. One of the many things I love about New Jersey is that you almost never feel unhip here.

"Look," I said, as the waiter cleared our plates. "I know today was scary, but Luis was right. We can't freak out. Goodell wouldn't have warned us first if he had really decided to pursue these investigations. We would have been served with papers or hauled off to court. I know how much your career means to you and how hard you've worked to get it, and Lord knows I've been through enough to get established. But this stuff is just meant as a warning."

Jane held up her hand. "Kit, I know. I'm on edge and I know you are too. But we have to help Benchley. There's no other option. If they try to mess with us, we'll just have to fight. Meanwhile—" She stopped and looked at me quizzically. "What?"

Close couples develop a sort of intuitive sonar. Jane was picking up a blip on the screen.

"I'm going to Connecticut tomorrow."

"Connecticut? But you told me Luis said to stop investigating, to pretend to be scared off."

"Yup. Luis said we should lie low, but I need to check out this rest home that Transitions owns in Southampton."

"The one Willie mentioned, where there was a lawsuit?"

"Right. Filed by this Hamilton guy. I called him this afternoon; he agreed to see me, said that under the terms of the settlement he couldn't say much. But the fact that he was willing to see me at all is interesting."

Jane gave me the fish eye. "But Kit, didn't Luis caution you? Aren't you taking a pointless risk?" And then, aware that she was having no effect at all, she smiled thinly, wanting to look calmer than she felt. "Okay, okay, sorry. Just be careful."

When we got home, there were three messages blinking on our answering machine. One was from a female admirer of Ben's, pretending to be calling about homework, one from a client of Jane's wanting a referral.

The third was from my cousin Harriet, telling me my Uncle Dan was in a hospital in Evanston, scheduled for emergency bypass surgery. She'd keep my mother informed on his progress, she said.

My uncle had been a healthy guy, playing tennis almost daily on the courts his condo association maintained, bragging about his victories to me via e-mail, which he'd mastered in his late sixties and regarded as a wonderful new toy. He also kept tabs, from a distance, on my father. "Kit, I think you're going to have to come out here and get the old prick into a nursing home," he had messaged me recently. "I know this is a particular burden for you, but there really isn't anyone else. He sure won't listen to me. He won't even stay on the phone. He just hangs up." He wouldn't listen to me either, I thought; Jack Deleeuw never listened to anybody. Now Dan was suddenly in trouble himself.

So here it was again, this unwelcome sensation of becoming increasingly aware of something I never used to think about. It seemed to me there were two kinds of people in the world, those who thought they and their loved ones would never die, and those who no longer had any doubt.

I had just rounded forty and had two kids. I had plenty of time ahead of me. I had years of serious parenting to do, and I intended to be the world's most enthusiastic granddaddy. Jane and I had all sorts of exotic retirement fantasies, from buying a Cape Cod cottage to heading for Santa Fe. It wasn't as if I needed to start making my funeral arrangements. But mortality was suddenly a factor in my life, popping up on my answering machine.

I took Percentage out for a walk. He dragged his bum leg behind him. Rounding the block, I wondered about Dan's surgery. Maybe he'd be good as new, back on the courts in a month or two. Didn't that happen a lot after bypass surgery these days? Or maybe he'd never recover his full vitality. Maybe it would soon be his time.

But Benchley's time, I thought, had not come. His life wasn't finished, he didn't seem ready to go. I realized these really weren't my decisions to make, but I had a strong sense that what was happening to Benchley wasn't a natural progression. The man I'd seen in Elston Manor wasn't at peace, ready to embark on his final journey. He was afraid, and his fierce eyes were signaling "Help me."

ten

PEOPLE WITH REAL MONEY are preoccupied not only with slamming the door shut behind them, but with using the full power of the law to keep anybody else from prying it open.

That had obviously happened in elegant Southampton. There wasn't a fast-food franchise or garish gas station to be seen. The discreet little Main Street, just four blocks long, was a quaint Disney version of a small-town center, with striped green awnings over the storefronts and tulips in wooden planters.

Following the street signs—tasteful and color-coordinated—according to Hamilton's directions, I drove past a pillared and corniced brick municipal building that looked as if it had been designed by Thomas Jefferson. I practically expected a sign that said Ye Olde Town Hall.

I made a small detour when I happened on a sign for Puritan Homes. Like Elston Manor, it resembled a high-end garden apartment complex more than a residence for the impaired elderly.

It was almost certainly designed by the same architect, with the same gatehouse in front, and the same meticulously land-scaped lawns and gardens, another institution that didn't look like an institution but was, Lord knows, safe and secure.

Goodell seemed to have assembled a large, well-oiled com-pany. Was Bill Hamilton's settlement on behalf of his father a chink in the armor that I could use to keep Goodell's wolves from my door? Or to shed some light on how Benchley had gotten to Elston Manor and what might be happening to him there?

My expectations weren't high, but this was the only lead I had. In the meantime, Willie was going to hang out in a burger joint down the road from Elston Manor and see if he could get some conversations going. Luis might already be chatting with other workers as they swabbed toilets or washed dishes. And Jane was on the phone with some of her therapist and health care pals to see if anybody had heard, observed, or surmised anything un-usual about the place. Evelyn, now a competent Web trawler thanks to Willie's instruction, was checking on-line for other lawsuits, deeds, or public transactions that might help us.

In a day or two, maybe I'd know if anything unusual or liti-gious was going on at Elston Manor or Transitions, Inc. But Goodell, if he was as savvy as he appeared, would also know that I hadn't been frightened off. It's almost impossible to make so many inquiries without tipping off your target. An employee currying favor, a computer tech noticing a query, a state health care worker passing along some questions—somebody would let Goodell or his people know that someone was asking questions.

That could mean an ugly confrontation for Jane and me. I felt an icy stab somewhere in my midsection, the same kind I felt whenever I thought of Benchley.

My mind was racing. Goodell and his heavy-handed threats. These absurd state probes. Benchley in Elston Manor. Luis im-personating a janitor. And all of this had somehow triggered feelings about my father that I'd successfully pushed away for years. Thanks to so many reminders of the aging and illness, he was back, dogging my thoughts.

I wondered for a moment if my father could survive in a residence like this one. Truth was, I had no idea. I knew more about Em and Ben's teachers than I knew about Jack Deleeuw, other than the universal description: He was reclusive, mean-spirited, and stubborn.

He must have had a pleasant side, once. He had managed an insurance company office, and I've never met an insurance salesman who couldn't turn on some charm. I couldn't locate any memory of charm, though. All I could reconstruct was the proverbial man of few words. It was rare for him to initiate a conversation, or even to pay attention to one.

He and my mother fought bitterly, loudly, and continually, but it wasn't until he added infidelity to a rotten disposition that she got fed up and left. If that bothered him, he never showed it. In any case, I hadn't talked to him since.

Maybe he had some code, principles he hung on to for dear life, and that's why everybody found him so difficult. Or maybe he was just a rotten bastard.

I'd grown up rarely thinking about him—until now, when I seemed to think about him every day. If Dan died, I'd be the only person left who'd care a whit about Jack Deleeuw, and I didn't care all that much. The prospect of taking Ben's and Emily's small college savings accounts—all we'd managed to salvage during the collapse of my career on Wall Street—was ghastly. But so was the prospect of a phone call telling me that my father had been found wandering the neighborhood in his pajamas, or starving in his unkempt apartment, or drowned in the bathtub. When all this was over, I'd have to go see him. Even if I couldn't figure out how to help.

But for now, I might be able to help someone who did pay attention to me, who'd been a confidant and friend, who was ailing and in need of my peculiar services. Maybe I could be useful to Benchley.

I called Willie on my cell phone and asked him to ride out to the Rochambeau Garden Center and check on Rose Klock. I'd nearly forgotten about her since my visit; she must be devastated and alone. She might even have remembered something helpful.

"Make sure she's okay, that she has food and everything she needs. I'm worried about her emotional state too," I told him.

He passed along a message: Jessica Welsh had called to say that the Quakers had heard from Eric Levin. Benchley's will provided a substantial bequest to the Meeting, and the lawyer was suggesting they get together to discuss it. "Ms. Welsh sounded real upset," Willie reported. "She said Levin seemed to assume that Benchley was going to die. She said they agreed to sit down with the lawyer, but they were plenty confused, y'know?"

I knew.

Bill Hamilton lived at 23 Wheeler Avenue, a well-tended brick Georgian. Compared to the palaces I'd just passed, it was imposing but not spectacular, which around here meant an $850,000 house rather than a $1.3 million one. The grounds were spotless and lush; the dogwood was in bloom.

I hadn't told Hamilton why I wanted to see him, other than my interest in the lawsuit against Puritan Homes. But few people have the willpower to refuse to see a private investigator; we still have a bit of mystique. Though your contemporary PI is much more likely to be sitting in front of a computer screen than slugging it out with some gunsel, people are curious about us. Sometimes they dread some skeleton dug up from the past; other times they think I'm tracking *them* down on behalf of lawyers for a wealthy deceased relative, with a fat check in my jacket pocket.

Bill Hamilton made me wait a bit in the stone archway before his front door. I heard the chimes pealing and echoing throughout the house. When the door opened, I was looking at a man a decade or so older than me, minus some hair and plus a substantial girth. He was somewhat formally dressed: gray slacks, a blue oxford-cloth shirt, and a sweater vest. I caught the whiff of cologne, heard opera playing somewhere inside. There was no sign of anybody else around.

Hamilton offered a perfunctory handshake and waved me into a spotless sitting room with facing sofas, clubby chairs, and silver-framed photographs on most surfaces, pictures of a couple progressing from their wedding into old age. I took the man to be Hamilton's recently departed father, Wilford. His mother's name, Willie told me, had been Delia; she'd died several years earlier of a sudden heart attack, according to the death certificate Willie had pulled up from the state's computerized records. She'd still been living in this house when she died.

"Smoke?" Hamilton asked me, lighting up. He looked impatient and uncomfortable, ready to dispense with this unpleasant task as quickly as possible.

I shook my head.

We both sat down. He was being courteous but not making me too comfortable, as in offering me anything to eat or drink. He looked at his watch. Clearly, he found a visit from a PI a bit nose-wrinkling.

"I have an appointment in a few minutes, so forgive me if I'm abrupt, Mr. Deleeuw." I doubted this was true, but Hamilton seemed to read my thoughts. "Squash. Twice a week."

I nodded. I wouldn't have used the term "appointment" to describe a weekly recreational activity, but I could see that he would; he was formal, a bit old-fashioned, suspicious, but too well bred to say so.

"I believe I told you that I'm a private investigator," I began.

He interrupted before I could launch my appeal. "Mr. Deleeuw, forgive me, but I really should ask for more identification, shouldn't I?" He should, actually. I would have. He seemed to relax a bit at my plastic folder and shield; I hoped I'd still have them in a week, once Goodell got through with me.

"Sorry," Hamilton said, "but you know . . ."

"I know," I said, trying to put him at ease. "You can't be too careful." Deciding that a businesslike approach was the best tack—this guy was not the chatty type—I got down to it. "I'd

like to ask you a few questions about the circumstances surrounding your father's death."

He pursed his lips and frowned.

"No," he said.

The mantel clock ticked. Sunlight streamed through the window. It was a pretty house, beautifully maintained—perhaps because it didn't look as if kids had ever lived in it, at least not for
a long time. Hamilton appeared to be a bachelor, the type that
used to be called "confirmed." Why had he agreed to see me if
he was going to respond in monosyllables?

"I can't talk about it," he said. "Under the terms of the settlement with the insurance company, I am enjoined from discuss-
ing the settlement, or the circumstances of my father's death,
with anybody. I don't know you, Mr. Deleeuw, but as a private
investigator I'm sure you're savvy enough to know there's no
reason on earth why I would risk a substantial financial settlement to discuss my father's death with a total stranger for no
reason . . . unless I'm mistaken and there is some reason."

He looked at me curiously. Discussions like this one were
chess battles, with strategic gambits and feints. He'd said no flat
out, yet he hadn't stood up and tossed me out. Always a good
sign.

"There might be a terrific reason," I said. "But I can't know
that without getting a little more information. And as an attorney, Mr. Hamilton, you know quite well that you'd have to do
something shocking and egregious—write a book or hold a press
conference—to have Puritan Homes haul you into court and
take its money back."

"You'd have to think I was naive to buy that argument," he
countered smoothly. "How do you know, for example, they
don't pay me in installments, precisely to forestall discussions
like this?"

He had me there. Of course, they paid in chunks. Otherwise,
they'd have no recourse if he misbehaved.

Now it was my turn to look at him. If I left, he'd spend a few
sleepless nights wondering why I wanted to know what I wanted

to know. But how often did curiosity triumph over money? The next few minutes would decide if there was a middle ground.

"Mr. Deleeuw, let me be frank," he said after a tense moment. "I'm a corporate lawyer and accountant, very respectable, not used to game-playing. Transitions, Inc. was quite generous in its settlement. I am wondering what brought you here, as you have undoubtedly surmised, and would be pleased if both of us ended this meeting getting what we want—you, a bit of information that isn't really very spectacular, and me, the reason for your visit. But that would necessitate my trusting you, and as I've never laid eyes on you before, I can't see why I should."

As it happens, I was not unprepared.

"Do you know David Sandwell?"

"The head of the New York State Bar Association?" He was stunned.

"Yes, that's the one."

"I've met him one or two times, and I surely know *of* him. He's one of the most respected lawyers in the country. Do *you* know him?" This was said a bit too incredulously.

I reached into my wallet, copied down a number, and handed it to him on a slip of paper. "This is his private number. If he's in, he'll pick up the phone. Ask Sandwell if you can trust me, and whether or not I am discreet even unto torture. Here's my card so you don't forget the name. I'll wait outside the door."

I walked out before he could ask any more questions. Hamilton would never know that Sandwell had hired me eighteen months ago to wrest his son from a crack den in Jersey City without harming the kid, attracting the police, or making any messes that would impede the lad's trajectory toward Harvard.

Willie and I had located the abandoned brownstone, lured the dazed boy out on a slick pretense, and—pretty dramatically, for me—jumped him from behind, wrestled him into the back of a rented minivan, and delivered him to Papa in Westchester, unhurt and free of any legal or other complications.

To be honest, the kid was so dopey he barely grasped what

was happening to him, which was a good thing. He was bundled off to a treatment facility the next day.

When I told Sandwell three days later that the den had been raided by the New Jersey State Police (without spelling out that I was the one who'd tipped off Lieutenant William Tagg—the twelfth solid lead I'd handed the guy in three years—so that he would owe me even more than he already did), he was profusely grateful. Sandwell offered me tons of money above my fee, which I declined. But I did ask him to vouch for me on occasion if the need arose. And the need had arisen.

A couple of minutes later, I was back in Hamilton's sitting room.

"This is all strictly confidential?" he asked, looking at me even more strangely now, wondering what a PI from New Jersey could possibly have in common with one of the country's most prestigious litigators.

"Glad it's all settled," I said. "Yes, this is absolutely confidential on both sides. This conversation never happened unless both of us decide that it did happen, for some reason I can't fathom now. Okay?"

Pretty slick for a guy who was a bond trader just five years ago, I complimented myself. I decided to use another old PI bluff, pretending to know more than I did.

"I'm here, Mr. Hamilton—"

"Call me Bill, please." We were suddenly on a first-name basis.

"Bill, I gather that you sued because there was evidence that Hemavero, the anticoagulant drug given your father, was administered, ah, inappropriately? Perhaps too liberally?"

"You're guessing," he said, shortly. "The truth is, I sued because of both reasons you mentioned. The drug probably shouldn't have been administered at all, although there's some debate about that. It's a powerful drug. Taken in the wrong doses, it can cause heart failure. The lawyers argued that under the circumstances—my father had had a severe, sudden stroke—it was a risk worth taking in order to save his life. Several doctors told my lawyers that Hemavero is very dangerous and shouldn't be prescribed for people with heart conditions. My father had had heart trouble for years. Of course, their experts disagreed—you know how medicine is these days—and called the stuff a miracle medicine of last resort."

Here was a man determined to be evenhanded about his own lawsuit. "You're dealing with institutions where people—forgive my frankness—go to die," Hamilton went on. "They may spend months or years in apartments there, living more or less independently, going on field trips to antique shows. But once they've moved into the nursing home wing, that's a one-way trip and everyone in the place knows it, so people aren't surprised, or in many cases even upset, when someone dies. I will be candid: I couldn't bear seeing my father degenerate further; I was somewhat relieved myself. But I'd wanted him to die naturally, not as the result of a careless overdose."

"Is that what it was?"

Hamilton looked at his watch, then out the window. He might have been relieved, as he said, but the pain in his face suggested a more complicated set of responses.

He went on: "The most solid grounds for a lawsuit—heck, I could have probably pressed for criminal prosecution—were that the dosage was literally four times the recommended maximum. Four times! It's hard to believe. And the really shocking thing is that Puritan Homes is one of the best assisted care facilities in the Northeast. Passes all of its accreditation examinations with flying colors. Costs a fortune. The care seemed splendid, really. Otherwise, I would never have agreed to place Wilford there.

"The reasons for the secrecy clause are, of course, so that word of the staff's dreadful incompetence won't get around," he said. "I understand that things can happen anywhere, in any institution. But part of me wanted to see justice done for my father."

And another part wanted to live in a gracious house in Southampton, with imported carpets and oil paintings, I thought. And to play squash at the club. But maybe that was unfair. I was slipping into cynicism.

Hamilton wasn't being evasive; he didn't seem to have anything to hide or be ashamed of. I can't say his reasons left me overflowing with respect, but I didn't find his motives complex or hard to understand. I had little feeling for my own father. Perhaps I wouldn't want hush money if he was killed by incompetence, but I couldn't say for sure. If my father had a medical accident and a settlement could send Ben or Emily to a first-rate college or open up a spanking new office for Jane, could I swear I wouldn't go for it?

"Mr. Hamilton . . . Bill . . . I assume from what you've told me that there was no reason to suspect any foul play? You're convinced this overdose was just incompetence?"

He sat up sharply. "Why would you ask that? And please, don't dissemble. If you want the truth, offer some."

Hamilton's businesslike nature was working to my advantage. He would tell me what I wanted to know if I would tell him something in exchange. "Well, I have a client in one of Transitions, Inc.'s facilities in New Jersey. I'm trying to make sure he's safe there. I have no reason to suspect the company of any wrongdoing, but the place does seem unusually secretive and security-conscious. And giving a patient four times the maximum dosage of a drug doesn't strike me as a casual mistake."

He took that in. "I know it sounds hard to believe," he said, "but here's what happened. The pumps Puritan Homes was using to administer intravenous doses of medicine are set by staff physicians every morning. A nurse comes in to check on them. A Spanish-speaking nurse—from Nicaragua, I believe—was on duty the morning my father died. It was her second day at work, only her third week in America. She was turning Wilford over. He was completely immobilized by the stroke; he couldn't speak or move, though he seemed to be mentally alert. Anyway, she knocked the IV pumps over onto the floor, hard, and that threw the dosage settings completely out of whack. She pulled the pump upright, but didn't notice that the dosage had been affected. And, of course, she didn't want to tell anybody about knocking them over, thinking she could lose her job. And I'm sure she was also thinking, who would care about this old man who'd had a stroke and was about to die, anyway? My father was in a coma by the time a doctor came in and checked on him in the early afternoon. I have to say the doctors were impressive, seemed top-notch. I had no complaints of any sort about them. Up to that point, Puritan Homes had delivered on every promise it made."

For the first time, a look of sadness crept across his smooth face. I think he missed having a family, squash club or no. "Dad died four days later. He didn't ever regain consciousness. The doctors there said he probably would have died from the stroke anyway, unless I kept him on life support, which he had explicitly asked that I not do, and which I wouldn't have done in any case." Here, I thought, was an example of somebody being candid and forthcoming. What a witness Hamilton would make at a trial.

In fact, he anticipated my next question. "Eventually, the pump did send an alarm to the nursing station. With the setting out of kilter, the IV solution emptied more quickly than it was supposed to. But by then it was much too late, given my father's weakened condition. This was a potential weakness in going to court, Mr. Deleeuw—there is little doubt my father would not have lived long anyway, and there were no earnings issues or anything like that. Still, the company is growing and expanding and a trial wouldn't have done them any good. But there was no possible motive for anyone to harm my father deliberately. Quite the opposite—the nurse had no idea what she'd done. She got fired anyway, of course. She came by here in tears a week or two after the funeral, and apologized profusely. She was moving back to Nicaragua, she said. I felt badly for her."

But, I thought, the bottom line is that you wouldn't have gotten so sweet a settlement if her horrible mistake had become public.

"I did agonize about moving Wilford there, Mr. Deleeuw, more than you probably suspect. My father was a formal man, just as I am; we weren't intimates, but we were quite cordial. Before the stroke, I called him every day. I visited every week, usually twice. I brought him books, took him for walks. He seemed comfortable there. Had I had any reason to believe this was more than a dreadful mistake, believe me, I would have involved the police. But I saw no purpose to be served in this poor woman's going to jail, either. Puritan has purchased new pumps, the kind that sound alarms instantly if the settings are changed without punching in the proper code. So my decision was either to seek more money and a public scandal or to accept the fact that my father wasn't going to live much longer anyway—I don't think he knew me after the stroke—and at least enjoy this lovely house and a comfortable life. Puritan Homes cost over three thousand dollars a month, Mr. Deleeuw. I had to borrow on my previous home after my father went through his savings. I'd given him first-rate care for five years, so much so that financing for my own retirement had become a major question mark. That's the dilemma of our generation, isn't it? Just when we need to care for ourselves, we have to care for our parents. And I don't even have children to worry about.

"So I made my decision and am mostly at peace with it. There was no evidence of anything more than a dreadful mishap. Perhaps the hospital shouldn't have hired a foreign nurse, I don't know; maybe her training was inadequate. But the consulting firm my attorneys hired said confidentially that Puritan Homes is an exceptionally well-run facility and that this aberration could—and probably does—happen anywhere. My attorneys, Nick Britton and Peter Mackley, advised settling."

But, I wondered, wouldn't publicizing the overdose at least alert other families and nursing home administrators that this problem might be occurring? Don't go there, I told myself. I wasn't the Ralph Nader of health care. I was here to see if there was any connection between Benchley's plight, Goodell's strong-arm tactics, and this man's father's death. There didn't seem to be. Meanwhile, the clock was ticking on poor Benchley, who might be at the mercy of some new hire at Elston Manor.

Surprisingly, I liked Bill Hamilton. I appreciated his directness, and even his choices, as different as the two of us were. Would I have made the same ones? Forced to choose between my father's and my own family's life, what would I do? I was about to find out.

Jane and I were still heavily in debt. The abrupt collapse of my career and the cost of Jane's education had drained us. But there was no one else to pay for my father's nursing home care, should he really be as sick as my uncle had told me. And he probably was. I guess I identified with Bill Hamilton because I didn't like the way I felt, but I felt it nonetheless.

Back in the Volvo, I turned my cell phone back on. It rang almost instantly. As I veered onto the Interstate heading south, I flipped the phone open. It was Willie, sounding distinctly rattled.

"What's up, Will?"

"Chief," he said, "it's Rose Klock. I don't know how close you were to her . . ."

"Not close at all. Why?"

I heard noises and sirens in the background. How close you *were*, he'd said. The hair on the back of my neck was rising.

"She's dead, Kit. I got to the Center, and one of the employees said they hadn't seen her for a day or so. I went around back, to her apartment, and rang. Nobody answered. The door was unlocked, so I opened it, and there she was, sitting in a chair. It was awful, man."

Awful, yes. Rose had suffered plenty in her life, and the loss of her beloved Benchley was grievous, more than she could bear, maybe.

"I called the police, then waited outside."

"Will," I said, hoping against hope. "Did you look around before you called the police?"

"Sure, Kit."

Whew, I thought. The kid *is* good. "What? Can you talk?"

"Yeah. But Chief Leeming wants to talk to you."

I bet. "What did you find, Will?"

He sounded shaken, disoriented. His first corpse. And he wasn't even thirty.

"Nothing, Kit. There was no blood, no sign of any struggle. She was sitting in a big soft green chair with her head back and her eyes closed, as if she'd died taking a nap. No note, nothing disheveled or broken, no pills or anything."

I sighed. "That's terrible. Is it possible that there's a bullet or stab wound so small or hidden that you didn't see it?"

"It's possible, Kit. But I doubt it. There are no homicide people here either," he said. "The paramedics seem pretty mellow. No county sheriff or State Police or anything." Willie knew what to look for by now. The Rochambeau PD wasn't very experienced in dealing with homicide, so they usually called in outside help when they encountered one. But from Willie's description, it sounded as if Rose had just passed away quietly.

"I called Evelyn at home and asked her to come into the office, Kit, in case there was anything you needed. She just called and said she wanted you to call her right away. It's urgent."

That didn't sound good. Willie had done a great job, and I told him so, and that I was sorry I had sent him walking into that sad scene. I asked him to hang around to see what he could pick up, and he said the Rochambeau PD had ordered him to stay, so he wasn't going anywhere.

At which point, Frank Leeming came on the phone, busy and gruff. "Deleeuw," he snapped. "You involved in this one, too? Sorry to hear from your kid here that your pal Benchley's sick. The kid says he was here because you told him to come. That so?" There was never any beating around the bush with Chief Leeming, no chitchat or pleasantries. He wanted to know if I was involved, and he also wanted confirmation that Willie had business there.

"Chief, I don't know a single thing about this. I sent Willie over because Rose seemed depressed about Benchley's being taken to a nursing home. I just wanted him to check on her."

"Seems he was too late," said Leeming, with his usual sensitivity. "Anything going on here that I should know?"

"Chief, you know I've learned the hard way not to withhold things from you."

"Yeah, but your gift for bullshit seems intact."

"C'mon, this is a sad thing. Rose Klock suffered a lot in her life. I think she was depressed, but it doesn't sound like there's anything to suggest she harmed herself."

"Oh?" Leeming asked, all innocence. "Did your boy check the place out here? 'Cause if he did, he could be looking at tampering with evidence."

I assured the Chief that Will wouldn't tamper with a thing, and told him about my conversation with Rose earlier in the week. Leeming was invariably tight-lipped, but this case didn't suggest any complications for him, so he graciously told me there was no note or sign of suicide or murder. "The paramedics think she had a coronary right in her sleep."

Leeming seemed satisfied. I got Willie back on the phone, and asked him to try to find out one or two more things if he could get back into Rose Klock's apartment. He said he would.

Poor woman. Benchley had tried many times to persuade Rose to travel a bit; he'd even offered to send her to Florida for a vacation. She'd have none of it. She liked to sit up in her room, stare out the window, listen to Brahms. I wondered if she'd died of too much grief.

I called Evelyn, who answered instantly. "Kit, I heard the terrible news about Benchley's housekeeper," she said. "She must've had enough trouble for five lifetimes. I came into the office after Willie called me, and, Kit, the first thing I saw in the stack of mail was a letter. The return address, handwritten, said 'R. Klock, Rochambeau Garden Center.' Should I open it?" she asked. I said yes.

Rose's letter had been postmarked two days earlier. She must have written it just after I'd left her.

"Dear Mr. Deleeuw," Evelyn read aloud, in a slightly shaky voice. "I hope you are well. It is lonely here. I am so upset about Mr. Carrolton. Without him here, I have little to do. I only hope Mr. Carrolton is well. I tried to call the Elston Manor, but was told I could not visit him, as I am not family. I don't know what else to do. I have tried to take good care of him. Maybe I did too good a job. I have lost everybody. Sincerely, Rose Klock."

I didn't know what to make of the bleak note, and neither did Evelyn. Rose had never written to me before, but since I was Benchley's friend and we had just talked about his illness, perhaps it seemed logical to her to contact me. I couldn't know if her tone was unusually depressed or typical. The only person who might know was Benchley.

Was it a suicide note? That wasn't clear. Mostly, she seemed to want to see Benchley; without him, she must have felt adrift, purposeless.

Though theirs was obviously a platonic relationship, it was impossible to be around the two of them without seeing that she adored him. She fussed over his every sniffle and ache, brought him his vitamins, scolded him to get more rest and come inside when it was cold. He was the only outlet available for her boundless nurturing, someone who could fill a bit of the void left by whatever tragedies had brought her here, rootless and alone.

Benchley never got more rest or came inside, but he never bristled or showed annoyance at Rose's fussing. He just smiled and did what he wanted. She didn't seem to mind.

I told Evelyn to call Chief Leeming's office and have the cops come get the note. I could imagine the explosion if Leeming found out about it and I hadn't reported it. I doubted it would make him think any differently about Rose's death.

Benchley had told me Rose had her own health problems, a mild stroke whose effects went undetected for weeks, and some heart troubles. She had seemed alert and healthy when I'd talked to her, but maybe I'd underestimated the devastating effect of Benchley's sudden illness. She'd found him on the floor, after all. Why hadn't I called or visited her yesterday?

This drama only seemed to get fuzzier and more complicated, and I didn't think I was one step closer to getting Benchley out of that place. Plus, there was an additional problem now, to be cold-blooded about it: When we did get Benchley out, there would no longer be anyone at home to care for him. I made a note on one of my handy Post-Its to call a nursing service and pasted it on the visor above my seat.

Driving down I-95, I thought of feeble, lonely, possibly confused Rose Klock, who seemed to have lost everything once and now, decades later, had lost everything again. It wasn't hard to picture her deciding to end her pain. But why wouldn't she simply say so? There would surely be an autopsy; maybe that would tell us something.

eleven

'D CROSSED the Tappan Zee and was headed down the Parkway when the cell phone warbled. Evelyn said Luis wanted me to meet him at the Tick-Tock.

The Tick-Tock was a proud silvery Jersey diner, sitting alongside Route 3 like a brightly lit ocean liner, its defiant motto, "Eat Heavy," displayed in neon for all the commuters to see. It was a put-on-your-polyester-clothes-and-bring-Grandma-for-brunch kind of place. The food came in about ninety seconds; the quantities, like the choices, were prodigious; fat and cholesterol were not major concerns.

An intensely private man, Luis had declined my many invitations to visit us in Rochambeau and had never invited me to his apartment in Jersey City, where a bunch of Cuban immigrants had moved in. Luis wasn't antisocial—he was a charming, gracious man. Perhaps his reticence had to do with a struggle to come to terms with his trajectory from legendary Havana lawyer to fast-food franchise manager. For all his grace, there was something wounded and fatalistic about Luis, as if he'd experienced such a loss that none of life's lesser annoyances bothered him.

So Luis and I had lunch or coffee at the American Way several times a week, and I told him just about everything that went on in my life, while he told me nothing about his. And it was a good deal. The closest he'd ever come to acknowledging our curious relationship was a remark he'd made at lunch one day, after declining the hundredth invitation to have dinner at our house. "You're a good friend to me, Kit," he said. "All you have to be to be a good friend is simply to exist."

This adventure was a first all around. Luis had never before actually joined an investigation himself. I hoped he could handle himself. Goodell obviously knew how to play hardball. What if he got Luis deported to Havana? Forced out of the mall? It was one thing for me to take risks, quite another to put my friends and family in peril.

I told Evelyn to put me through to Willie's voice mail. "Will, it's Kit. Can you make a couple of calls, find out where our friend Senator Goodell is this afternoon? ASAP." Might take two minutes if Willie was sleepy.

I veered east and was at the Tick-Tock in fifteen minutes. Luis was at a booth in the back of the diner, looking like a regal maintenance man, but very much transformed. I'd never seen him without a suit, tie, and white shirt. Now, the most sophisticated fast-food franchise manager on the planet had trashed himself up pretty good. He hadn't shaved, he'd pushed his hair forward over his forehead, his fingernails were dirty. He actually looked rumpled in a dark blue jumpsuit with "Transitions, Inc." embroidered over the left pocket, and his name printed in black marker.

I shook hands and laughed. "Wow. Is this the Luis that's been waiting to come out?"

"This is the Luis who almost couldn't get seated here when they took a look at me." He chuckled. We ordered coffee and breakfast, even though it was past noon. Jersey diners serve breakfast all day long, every day of the year.

I told him about my encounter with Bill Hamilton. He took it all in as usual. I could see why Luis had been a brilliant criminal attorney: He could feel his way through illogic and instinctively point me toward the truth.

But today, he had news of his own to deliver. "No problem getting in," he said. "My neighbor Hector told me they were looking for a janitor. He said the cleaning staff rotates all over almost every day. I hope that later this afternoon I may be able to see Benchley. I start in two hours."

I asked if he'd learned anything so far.

Luis frowned. "I cannot be sure, Kit. There are five wings, A through E. E wing is not accessible to most employees. There are a fair number of deaths, Hector tells me, but that is not unusual in such a facility. That is why people go there, no? Because in this country their families do not want them to die at home." He shook his head at what must have struck him as an especially barbarous American trait.

"But this Elston Manor seems very well run. It's clean. The kitchen has plenty of good food, well prepared. People are not left alone or unsupervised. The staff seems well trained and dedicated. There are many supervisors, and doctors come in and out frequently. I would rate it highly, if I were evaluating it."

Though it seemed suspiciously easy to get hired. Luis said his friend had called the personnel office, and they had asked that he come in right away.

"There is apparently a large turnover," Luis said. "They had openings in the kitchen and on the maintenance and grounds staffs. Staffing is a big problem, I know this from the Lightning Burger. There are constant vacancies in the low-level jobs because everybody wants to climb the ladder quickly."

Luis said he'd gone in, filled out an application, and been hired on the spot. "They said they would check my references later, but that Hector's reference was good enough. I filled out a short questionnaire, using my real name and address so they cannot claim I falsified my employment application, which is a crime. Then they took me down the hall to a uniform closet.

With a stencil card, they wrote *Luis* here on the jumpsuit pocket. When I report to work, the instructions are to sweep each room in the C wing, then to mop all the floors with detergent and disinfectant. There will be a supervisor's inspection each night, and if I fail two nights in a row, I will be relieved of this job."

I thought about the Nicaraguan nurse who'd tended the elder Hamilton at Puritan Homes, hoping the hiring practices for the health care professionals and medical staff were more rigorous. Ted Bundy could have strolled into Elston Manor and landed a job as a janitor.

But Luis said that was typical in America. "In Cuba, a janitor's job is a good one, with security. You might have it for life. Here everybody understands that humble jobs—like those at my restaurant—are temporary. You hire whoever walks in the door. I do this myself. Probably it is different for doctors and nurses, but even the best-run institutions in America have little choice but to hire minimum-wage workers in this way."

Most minimum-wage workers, however, aren't in a position to knock over an IV pump and send somebody into a coma. You send parents or other people you love off to institutions run by strangers, taking a real leap of faith that the people there will care for them and treat them with dignity and respect. But how can you ever know? It's a question of trust, and when it came to Transitions, Inc., I didn't have much.

"What is the E wing?" I asked.

"Apparently the home works in this way, Kit," said Luis, sipping his black coffee. "On A wing are the healthiest people, quite self-sufficient patients. E is where patients are taken to die. So the patients on A wing require little help, but those patients in the other wings are progressively more ill and in greater need of attention. The E wing staff is hired specially, and doesn't move around. Probably they require special training. People do not often wander in and out of there. And there is a great deal of security. Maybe a bit too much."

"Benchley?"

"Is on D wing," he said. "Which is not good, because that is where patients who are critical go before they are sent to E. People don't often return from there, I am told."

Luis seemed to be hesitating.

"What?" I prompted.

"They call E wing 'Death Row,'" he said.

Jesus, I thought. Death Row. Perfect.

"Couldn't you find out anything about Benchley?"

"Just a bit," said Luis. "I was given a brief tour and I didn't have reason to linger on Benchley's ward. But afterward I walked through again, planning to tell anyone who asked that I was lost. But no one stopped me. It's true what they say: If you are an immigrant maintenance person, people will see right through you sometimes.

"There was a doctor in his room. And a nurse. Benchley's head was hidden by a curtain. I kept walking. But later today or tonight, perhaps, I will find a way to get assigned to that ward, even to clean that room."

"Are you sure you want to be doing this, Luis? I don't know the details of your immigration, but . . ."

He held up his hand. The subject was closed. "I can stand to give up selling hamburgers for a few days," he said, smiling suddenly. "And this job pays above the minimum wage—seven dollars an hour. I want to do this. Benchley is a wonderful man. He . . ." Luis looked down at his coffee, hesitating. "Last year I had a problem. A person in Cuba . . . my daughter, in fact . . . was having a very serious time."

The diner, full of lunchtime customers, seemed eerily quiet to me now. I said nothing, just listened.

"I called Benchley because I know there is a Quaker Mission in Havana. They have remained in Fidel's good graces, partly as a channel to the United States and other countries. The Quakers . . . have been very helpful to people who have been imprisoned." It was obvious he wasn't talking about other people. It was also obvious that I should keep my mouth shut.

"Benchley invited me to the Garden Center. I met with him several times; it took many hours of his time to resolve this matter. He helped me. A great deal. Now I have a chance, perhaps, to help him."

I guess I felt a bit wounded. Why hadn't Luis come to me? Why hadn't he or Benchley mentioned this? But that was a selfish response. Luis had done what he had to, and Benchley was extremely discreet. I often didn't know about the people he helped. I wondered if I'd ever know what had happened to Luis's daughter. Not likely. Even revealing this much was a big step for Luis, and another mere hint of what he'd been through.

He asked me a few more questions about Hamilton. We also agreed it would be helpful if Luis could grab Benchley's chart and make a copy of it. He said there were copying machines on each wing. "But I have to be careful here, Kit. It makes sense that I might get lost as a new employee, but there is no possible reason a janitor would legitimately copy a patient's chart." We both decided that keeping his job, maintaining access to the place, might have to take precedence over active sleuthing.

"It was both reassuring and disappointing, Kit. It seems a very well-run place," Luis said, "yet it still feels as if something is wrong."

I paused as a waitress—the personalized enamel frying pan on her aqua uniform read "Justine"—provided one of the Tick-Tock's eternal refills.

"Are you sure, Luis? Is it possible that we—I—just don't want to accept the truth that's right in front of my nose: that Benchley decided for whatever reason that he wanted to be treated at Elston Manor, and I can't accept it because he never confided in me?"

Luis shook his head. "No," he said. "You cannot accept it because it does not make any sense, not for Benchley. He would have told *someone*—you, his housekeeper, someone at his Quaker Meeting. You checked there, didn't you?"

"I did. They are very surprised. There is a wonderful Quaker retirement home in Bucks County, Pennsylvania; he'd long ago made arrangements to live there along with some others." I told him about the upcoming meeting with Eric Levin. Luis took that in as I paid the check.

"Perhaps this will become clearer to us very soon" was all he said. He shook my hand and walked off to find his car. I hoped he'd learn something helpful before Benchley progressed to Death Row.

twelve

WHEN I WAS WORKING a case like this, my family knew the drill. Jane assumed shopping, cooking, and kid supervision. Ben walked Percentage, two bucks for each outing. We paid a retired nanny to take over the middle-school car pool and drive Emily to lessons and friends' houses, as she complained bitterly about being too old for a sitter. I vanished. Benchley couldn't wait while I struck a meaningful and satisfying balance between work and personal life.

After a case was over, it always took a couple of weeks to get back into the rhythms of life: to remember the car pool schedule, to get to the market and buy everybody's favorite cereal, to catch up on stockpiled laundry.

In the meantime, parenting was a haphazard activity at best. I checked in via cell phone. Em, just home from school, answered. "Hey, Dad," she said, forgetting for a moment that she hated my guts. "How's Benchley?" I told her he was holding his own, and I was going to try and get him home soon. "How are you, sweetie?" I asked. By now, she had remembered. "Maggie's coming over," she said, sounding bored. "Everything's okay.

Maggie'll be here any minute." This meant everything was fine so would I get off the phone already? So I did.

I was speeding west on an impulsive mission. I'd decided to drop in on State Senator James Goodell. Willie, supplying directions, assured me I'd find him at home now that the legislature was out of session. It was better not to know how he knew.

I hadn't told Luis, who would not have approved. A lawyer through and through, he always counseled caution, discretion, careful timing. As he would no doubt point out, popping up unannounced at Goodell's house was dangerous on several levels. It escalated our little conflict. It was in itself grounds for action by the Licensing Office, since Goodell might claim I was intimidating or harassing him. It could provoke him into action. So far, we'd just been warned. If somebody showed up tomorrow and yanked my shield, what good would I be to Benchley, or to anyone?

But there are moments, I've learned in this new career, when you just have to work on instinct. And my instinct said I needed to have a face-to-face with this guy. Make personal contact. Talking to him on the phone, I'd gotten the sense of a practical, accommodating foe, not a menacing psycho.

Besides, we live in an era when it isn't possible to control institutions like media or the law as easily as it once might have been. He could yank my license or Jane's, but I could also sue his ass for a hundred million bucks and scream to the press that he was trying to scare me away from a potentially threatening investigation. I didn't want this hanging over us. If Goodell and I were going to war, so be it. But I wanted at least to make sure we were reading one another correctly.

I turned south. New Jersey is a bedroom state, and one of its priciest bedrooms is Short Hills, favored nesting place for CEOs, Wall Street moguls, and state senators building nursing home empires. Goodell's house was comparatively modest, appropriate for a state politician. A rambling three-story white clapboard affair, it was less grand than most of those I was passing. A Honda hatchback and a Volvo station wagon sat in the driveway. You'd never catch a politico with any brain cells driving a Beamer or a Benz.

New Jersey politicians seem to have learned that they can survive and prosper simply by not annoying anybody unduly and running the government quietly. Half the time, because the TV stations focus on New York or Philadelphia news, you never even know what they look like. So I'm not positive I would have placed the guy in jeans and a flannel shirt, digging in the garden at the side of the house, had I not known he lived there.

Goodell looked up with a friendly smile. "How do you do!" he explained, offering his hand as if he'd been waiting all day for me to appear.

"Just fine," I said. "Sorry to bother you unannounced like this, Senator. I'm Kit Deleeuw. We talked on the telephone a bit the other day, about Elston Manor."

There was nothing in Goodell's face to suggest that he was the least bit bothered by my showing up like this. Not even a flicker of wariness at the appearance of a man he had recently threatened.

The only indication of any tension was that he stood there holding his shovel, not inviting me to sit down on one of the nearby redwood benches or ushering me inside.

"I remember. You were asking about Benchley Carrolton." He shook his head. "That's rough, a major stroke. He's a fine man. I'm proud to have him in Elston Manor, I can tell you that." He leaned his shovel against a tree and got down to business. "I believe you wanted to get in to see him."

"I'll just be frank," I interrupted. "You're wondering what I'm doing here. There's no point in wasting time by tap-dancing around, is there?"

He looked puzzled, but waited for me to go on.

"First off, I'm gravely worried about Benchley. As I'm sure you know, I am no longer permitted to visit him. I'm worried that he's in some sort of danger."

Now Goodell looked genuinely incredulous. "Danger? Jesus, Deleeuw."

Moving closer, he jabbed a finger in my chest. He was a large man, in good shape, square-shouldered. And he was not pleased. "Look, Deleeuw, I resent this. I've killed myself the past ten years to build a chain of facilities that have earned the highest possible rating five year in a row from the American Association of Assisted Care Residences. And from the United States Nursing Home Association. And from the New Jersey Board of Licensing. Elston Manor has had at least twenty major inspections in the past three years. Aside from one report suggesting two more wheelchair ramps and one more night duty nurse—all of which are now in place—there wasn't any criticism. None. I'm proud of these places. Nursing homes can be frightening and depressing. Mine are well run, cheerful, and beautiful. What are you insinuating? That I'm some sort of scum who bleeds old people dry?"

I blinked a couple of times, but stood my ground. His finger hurt, actually. And his anger seemed quite genuine.

"I'm just looking out for my friend," I said quietly. "Nobody who knows him can figure out why Benchley would sign papers committing himself to your home—"

"That's easy," Goodell interrupted. "I told Benchley I would keep this confidential, but I don't want trouble here. And I see you're not going to go away. I have nothing to hide. Quite the opposite. But it's part of our agreement. What I tell you has to be confidential; will you honor that?"

"Sure, if it doesn't endanger—"

"Oh, bullshit, Deleeuw. Benchley Carrolton's in no danger from me. What kind of monster am I supposed to be, anyway?" He'd grown flushed, but stepped back and collected himself. I'd noticed the curtains parting in the front window as his voice rose. He looked over his shoulder and waved to whoever was there.

"Benchley is a well-known figure in northern New Jersey. He's active in Quaker activities; he's involved in historic preservation. He's very much known and admired among the elderly.

Elston Manor should be the crown jewel in my company, but it's also the facility struggling the hardest. Too much competition."

"Some of it from the Quaker home?" I guessed.

"Some, yeah. But the problem with the Quaker place is that it can't take the most seriously ill residents; it has to transfer them to medical facilities. So it ships people out. It's tough."

Goodell ran his hand through his hair—gunmetal gray, mediagenic, perfect for a pol. "But I do get competition from lots of places around here. Especially this one chain—Greystone, Inc., British company. Opened up five or six facilities that have really undercut me pricewise. We just couldn't keep our occupancy rate up. I want to sell out to a huge insurance company that's moving into the business. Its due-diligence people are going to inspect me in six months and there's a lot of money riding on higher occupancy, at least more full than forty-five per cent.

"I think the problem is that everybody moves away from New Jersey when they get near retirement," he added, more conversationally now, as though we were two fellow entrepreneurs. "Besides, a lot of people are afraid of places like this. And I'll be honest about it: Few kids spend top dollar on a first-class facility, especially if they can spend half of what we charge and figure their parents will hardly know the difference. Who really knows? I only know we need to fill that place up.

"Every place we went to talk about Elston Manor, to drum up interest, we ran into Benchley Carrolton. I loved the guy, and I think he liked what I was trying to do. So I made him a deal."

A deal. With politicians, it was always a deal.

"I offered a hundred thousand dollars to a nonprofit organization of his choosing, which turned out to be his Quaker Meeting. And another fifty thousand for the soup kitchen he works with in Paterson. He couldn't believe it. You know, the Meeting is in danger of having to sell its building, because many of the members are old and they can't afford to maintain it. With this money, his friends could fix up the Meeting House and stay there forever. Plus the soup kitchen, which lives off donations week to week, could stay in operation for years. Plus I offered to admit to Elston Manor, for reduced fees, the people from the Quacker residence who were too ill to remain there. So they could get good care and still stay together."

"Very generous, Goodell. And in return?"

"In return, he'd agree to move to Elston Manor—no charge, of course—when he needed care. That was the main thing. Because if Benchley Carrolton came to Elston, he'd bring countless people with him. I would be a signal to people in this area, since he is so well known, especially . . ."

Especially among older people contemplating death and decline, I thought. Goodell had been candid about his motives for helping Benchley. Even $150,000 wasn't a huge investment—three or four new residents lured by Benchley's presence would spend that much in a year or two. Accustomed to wheeling and dealing, Goodell had his eye on the bottom line. That wasn't always a character flaw, though. If what he'd said was true, everybody seemed to benefit.

"Why, we've had half a dozen people call for brochures just since Benchley got sick," Goodell added. "Why on earth do you think I'd hurt him?"

I didn't really know what to think. "It was a shock, Senator," I said lamely. "He never even mentioned . . ."

"That was his doing, Deleeuw, not mine. He wanted these gifts to be anonymous; that was the nature of the man. You know that as well as I do, probably better." He was right about that. Benchley thought anonymous charity was the finest sort. "Confidentiality was a condition—*his* condition."

Goodell glanced back toward the house, then reached into his pocket and pulled out a pack of matches and a thin black cigar. He lit it carefully, cupping his hands to protect the flame. "Benchley agreed that if he was incapacitated he would go to Elston Manor. That was what I got out of it. He was uniquely visible in the community. It would signal people that this was the place to go—and it has."

I mulled how much to tell him. I had to balance getting at the truth with a concern for Benchley's safety. Neither Luis nor anybody else—not even Jane, Willie, or Evelyn—knew I'd come, I guess because they all would have warned me not to. So Goodell could easily add harassment to the other charges against me. He might even decide that Benchley wasn't worth all this trouble and harm him.

But having come, there was no point in leaving without a shot at getting some answers.

"Senator Goodell, you're being blunt, so I'll be blunt. When I visited Benchley the other day—under the extremely watchful eyes of your nursing staff—I was able to communicate with him, to send signals." I decided not to be any more specific. "I felt he was clearly warning me that something was wrong. And I felt the nurses were crowding me, monitoring my visit with unusual vigilance. Why couldn't I be alone with him?"

Goodell took another puff on his skinny cigar. "This off the record?"

I nodded, adding, "Unless there's some reason it affects Benchley's health."

"We've had some legal problems."

"You mean the case in Connecticut? Bill Hamilton's?"

"Shit," said Goodell, quietly and ominously. "It's the first rule of politics, never underestimate anybody. I see I underestimated you. Right, the Connecticut case. And Burlington County, too."

"Burlington County?"

He shrugged. "You found out about one, you'll find out about the other. An eager man visiting his very sick father—the kid was a former paramedic—adjusted the IV pump to hasten matters along a bit. The father died, we prosecuted his son—the case is still pending—and now the widow is suing us. I've got to tell you, Deleeuw, this assisted care stuff gets intense. People are driven nuts by the cost of caring for their parents. It's a nightmare. You have to choose between your mom or dad or getting your kid through college and being able to retire yourself. If it weren't a conflict of interest—and if it wouldn't get me run right out of office—I'd propose that government step in here. But that's a liberal idea, right, Deleeuw? Hopelessly liberal. Mean-

while, I've got people in these homes, and their kids are waiting—praying—for them to die. It sounds awful, but I see the
pressure they're under.

"So we instituted some tough new rules. No leaving visitors,
especially first-time visitors, alone with life support equipment
and IV pumps unless they are spouses or we know them very
well. Our lawyers say that will keep us from being found 'egre-
giously negligent' as we might have been in both Burlington
County and Connecticut."

"So you're telling me all this hypersecurity is just a legal pre-
caution?"

"That's right."

"But what about the signals Benchley was sending?"

"Look, Deleeuw, I'd advise you to talk to some gerontologists.
Benchley Carrolton had a massive stroke. I'm sure he's frightened and confused. Wouldn't you be? We don't know if he understands what happened to him. Or remembers where he is or
why he's there. My God, what do you think a stroke is, anyway?
It's not a minor headache; it affects the brain. I'm sure he's
scared out of his mind, poor guy. But we can't have nonfamily
visitors hanging around unsupervised."

He tapped his cigar ash into a bed of pachysandra. Listening
to this guy long enough could actually convince you he was a
caring but prudent businessman.

I don't exactly know what made me ask, but the question
popped out. "Do you know Rose Klock?"

That seemed to befuddle him. "Give me a clue."

"She worked for Benchley."

"Ah, the housekeeper? I don't know her, but now I remember
the name."

"How come?"

"Because that was part of his deal. His housekeeper—
Holocaust survivor, I believe he said?—would be admitted to
Elston Manor, no charge, for as long as she needed. He wanted
that in writing, part of the agreement we signed with his
lawyer."

"Would you let me see that agreement?"

"No. Benchley wanted it confidential and we agreed. The whole arrangement would be violated, legally and morally, if we started passing around the agreement." He didn't seem to want to negotiate, even though he seemed willing to tell me what was in it.

"Anything else I should know before I turn it up myself?"

Goodell looked tired, as if this had become more than he intended to take on. He was contemplating a wealthy political after-life with his millions from that big insurance company. He wasn't really going anywhere in state politics—he'd been defeated in a bid for governor two years earlier—and had probably worked like a demon to set up these model assisted care facilities. Now there was all this trouble, including me.

"You'll probably hear about Bennett," he said.

"Bennett?"

"Dr. Stillwell Bennett. Silly Bennett. He was the medical director for all our facilities, including Elston Manor. I fired him two months ago. He's lucky he's not in jail."

Here was a new wrinkle. I waited.

"We caught him taking kickbacks from a drug company. Monthly payments from a pharmaceutical manufacturer for stocking, recommending, and prescribing—some might say over-prescribing—some powerful medication."

This sent my eyebrows up. "Wouldn't be Hemavero, would it?"

He sighed. "You're pretty good, Deleeuw. Let me know if you want another client. Hemavero, yeah. The same drug that killed the guy in Connecticut, Mr. Hamilton."

"How did this scam work, exactly?"

"Hemavero is a perfectly good drug, but very potent. Administered in doses that are too large, it can be fatal, sometimes triggering heart attacks. Bennett used it liberally. We only know of that one case where it actually harmed anybody—the accident caused by the nurse. But . . ."

Two seconds. Five seconds. "But what?"

"Who knows what the son of a bitch might have done?" Goodell said angrily. "I got rid of him, fired him on the spot, once a surprise audit turned up an unusually large quantity of the drug in Elston Manor and our other facilities." He shook his head. "This is a complicated business, and there are some not very nice people in it who make politicians look like choirboys."

"Why isn't this guy facing charges?"

Goodell gave me a don't-push-your-luck-stare, a reminder that he was a tougher and more powerful person than I was. "He's under investigation. At the moment, it wouldn't be very helpful for Transitions, Inc., to have its medical director on trial for taking kickbacks from a drug company, given that said drug was responsible for the accidental death of a patient."

Shut up about this, I told myself. You can deal with it later. The trick is to help Benchley.

"Can I see Benchley?"

"No."

"I want him out of there."

"Can't do that either. He's in good hands."

Next question.

"Did you sic the Licensing Office on me?"

Goodell said nothing, which was a pretty clear answer.

"On my wife?"

He winced. "Deleeuw, I've been in politics twenty-five years. When somebody comes at you where you're vulnerable, you try to back them off. I had a nightmare that on top of my other problems, you'd start making noises about mistreating Benchley, our prize patient. So there might be some connection between that and the attention you got from the Licensing Office. But I don't know anything about your wife. That would be over the line. And premature, too."

Nice shot, I thought. Letting me know it could happen, even as he was denying it.

"Because tangling with me that way is bad enough, threatening my livelihood. But going after my wife . . ."

"It would make me nuts," he said, relighting his cigar.

We looked at each other for a moment, waiting for the next feint.

"I understand the rules of the game, Senator," I finally said. "But if you bring me down in some cheap way, like yanking my license before I'm satisfied that Benchley's okay, I will scream to the media. Even if you convince everybody I'm a crank and a crook, which given my Wall Street troubles you could possibly do, I can still make a lot of noise. It will bring you and your company and those inspectors a lot of publicity you don't want, as a politician and a nursing home operator. Now if, on top of that, you're lying to me and going after my wife, then there's a strong possibility of my going nuclear."

Goodell took a long drag on his ministogie. After a minute or so he offered his hand. I took it.

"We understand each other, Deleeuw. I'm not looking to hurt Benchley or you. Certainly not your wife."

"And I'm not looking to hurt you," I said. "I'm sure your facilities are beautifully run. I'm just in this for Benchley. Once I'm convinced he's there because he wants to be, and in safe hands, you won't ever have to hear my name again."

"That would be nice," said Goodell. "*Are* you satisfied?"

"This conversation has helped," I said. "I have to think about it. Nobody would be happier for it to be true, okay?"

When I pulled out of the driveway, Goodell was back to shoveling. What he said made sense. I even believed a lot of it. But he was formidable. He knew how government worked, and had his fingers on the levers that made it move. Who knew what was really going on with this silver-haired squire of Short Hills?

thirteen

WILLIE TRACKED DOWN Stillwell Bennett in
two seconds; he didn't even need to go on-line.

I was always pleased when Willie managed to find out something without resorting to the Internet. I was increasingly worried that computers were killing all our detecting instincts. That
there were no more gumshoes, only killer typists with Web
browsers. Why bother to learn how to do interrogations when
you could pull a will out of the county clerk's office via the
World Wide Web?

But Bennett, it turned out, was in the phone book. (Willie had
every phone book in America on a CD-ROM). A call determined that he was now the president of the Pleasant Hollow
Retirement Center, a half hour down the Parkway in Burlington
County.

"I'm on my way, I guess," I said, feeling tired. I was starting
to feel welded to the Volvo, with the cellular phone attached to
my ear.

"Kit," said Willie, "we need to talk about Rose Klock. I'm
sort of bugged by her note. It reads like a farewell, like a suicide

note. Do you think she mailed it and then just, like, suddenly died in her chair? I mean, the coroner ruled the death a heart attack, given her age and health and all. She had a history of heart trouble, it turned out. They're not planning an autopsy. But it sort of haunts me; I can't get it out of my head."

Willie had sharp instincts; if something was bugging him, it was probably worth pursuing. But at his age, he was also sometimes prone to enthusiastic obsessions.

"Then, like, sort of investigate it," I said. Keanu Reeves joins the Hardy Boys.

I thought he was headed for a dead end. Rose was old and frail and lived a dozen lifetimes already. I had no trouble imagining Benchley's stroke as the last straw that deprived her of one more person she loved, the last one. You didn't have to swallow pills to kill yourself; you could die of a busted heart.

I told Willie what Goodell had said about Rose and the deal Benchley had made for her care. "Then why didn't she tell you about it when you saw her?" Willie wondered. "Why didn't she refer to it? Did she even know about this arrangement? It just seems, like, weird."

It was hard for somebody like Willie to imagine the fatigue and despair Rose Klock might have felt. "Maybe she just had enough, Will. She was a concentration camp survivor, apparently. Seems to have lost her whole family. God knows how much more of life she wanted to face, especially if she was depressed and lonely. I should have gone over to see her."

But I told him to follow his instincts. As with my own kids, he couldn't learn from his mistakes if he didn't get to make any.

Pleasant Hollow. The names of all these homes gave me the creeps. I braced myself for another visit to a "facility," the kind my father might end up in or even, one day, Jane and I. Little as I looked forward to it, making this tour was probably a healthy thing to do.

It was amazing how Americans cushioned the unpleasant aspects of life with marketing terms. "Assisted living" was one of those terms. "Manor," too. "Nursing home" was probably more accurate. And sometimes, Death Row.

Benchley had faced aging pretty directly. Past eighty and quite vital except for what he called constant "patching," he often talked of the time when he wouldn't be able to care for himself, when even the diligent Rose couldn't manage.

"These homes are places to die," he'd say calmly. "I think we all need to understand that. Nobody wants to go to such a place, and nobody wants to send his parents to one, but these are one-way trips, aren't they? You don't move out again. I think honesty requires that we be open about that. But that doesn't mean life ends when we go there."

For Benchley, the toughest part of aging wasn't death, which he often said was an integral part of life, but the impossible traps our culture sets for old people and those responsible for them.

"I don't know an old person who wants to be a burden to his kids or anyone else," Benchley said. "And I barely know one who won't be. I don't know a single young person who isn't struggling with work and the cost of living. And who won't have some rugged choices to make when it comes time to care for some older person he loves."

Now that I thought of it, when we sat out in back of the Garden Center in the summer—surrounded by trees, shrubs, and flowers and the rich smell of damp potting soil—the topic of death came up quite a bit. It had rattled me at first. Like most people my age, I wouldn't have made it number one on my list of dinner-party topics.

"When I'm dead," Benchley would say, "I hope somebody will take over and keep this a garden center. I hope that people like us will always be chatting under the young trees." He and I both knew it was much more likely, given the state's sordid record of controlling growth, that whole bunches of people would be standing in line waiting to check out their purchases at some Discount-O-Rama. Such was the fate of open land in New Jersey.

But Benchley was determined to confront such possibilities

head-on, without euphemisms or denial, which made it all the more peculiar that he hadn't confided his new assisted care plans to anyone. Perhaps, as Goodell suggested, he was just being modest.

Goodell was somebody who set out to build a lucrative new life for himself by catering to affluent boomers worried about and burdened by their elderly grandparents, aunts, uncles, and parents. The whole idea of a place like Elston Manor was that you wouldn't feel bad about leaving somebody you loved there. You barely saw a wheelchair; you could eat off the floor; residents could stroll through lush gardens; there were nurses and health aides all over the place. No stench. No guilt. Goodell figured to trade in the wear and tear of politics for the more rewarding pressures of a millionaire businessperson. He might make it yet.

But things had turned out to be more complicated than he'd planned. If he wasn't careful, he could lose both careers—the political job *and* the nursing home network.

He was learning that aging was complicated, expensive, and difficult to turn a profit on. Boomers didn't have the money to give their parents topnotch care, and many didn't want to spend it that way even if they did have it, not in an era when a year at a good private college started off at $20,000. Old people clung to their homes; doctors took kickbacks from drug companies; nurses banged into IV pumps. The society was litigious about health care, the industry intensely regulated. A scandal was something no one could afford.

On the other hand, as I pulled off the Parkway and onto the four-lane highway just beyond the exit ramp, I saw at once that I was about to develop a new appreciation for the man, and for Transitions, Inc.

If Elston Manor was a model kind of new facility for the ill and infirm, Pleasant Hollow was the Nursing Home from Hell. It sat a scant few feet off Route 206, a clogged highway. A Ford dealership sat twenty feet from its northern wall; a McDonald's bordered it on the south. There was no lawn or yard to speak of, only a concrete terrace, with a dozen webbed lawn chairs and nobody sitting in any of them, fronting the highway.

Pleasant Hollow had apparently started life as a clapboard house, three stories high, with gables and eaves sprouting on the upper floors. A couple of additions now stretched out the back, to an asphalt parking lot. The grounds were barren—no trees, no shrubs, nothing green. "Pleasant Hollow Retirement Center: Dr. Stillwell Bennett, Director," said the sign nailed to the front entrance.

The place was about as different from Elston Manor as it was possible to be. There was no guard or receptionist waiting to question me as I walked inside—only a lobby with a blaring TV and three people in wheelchairs staring at the screen. One of them was yelling "Jeannie!" "Jeannie!" "Jeannie!"—but no Jeannie responded. The room smelled musty, with bare walls and an easy-to-mop linoleum floor.

Two halls led off to the left and the right. Down the corridors, I could see the residents in various states of dishevelment and undress. Some wore nightshirts, others bathrobes; none were dressed in normal clothing. The dark living room off the main lobby door was lined with overstuffed sofas. Playing cards, games, and puzzles were stacked up on a table, but nobody was playing.

A place willing to make so poor an impression from the second you walk in didn't inspire confidence in what might lie deeper inside.

I followed a sign that read "Administration/Visitors" with arrows down the right-handed corridor. I passed a dozen or so private bedrooms, where people were lying in bed or sitting in wheelchairs, staring out the windows at the parking lot. I saw an attendant gently trying to coax one of the residents. "C'mon, Mrs. B. C'mon, now. Take a little soup. Take it for Jimmy. C'mon now, Mrs. B., you got to eat."

The noise from the highway was clearly audible inside; the smell of truck fumes had filtered in, too. I felt claustrophobic.

And determined not to end up in a place like this. James Goodell was suddenly looking pretty good to me.

Outside the administrative office, I picked up a pamphlet from a wall rack. "Pleasant Hollow is a compassionate, efficient, low-cost assisted care facility for your elderly loved one who is unable to care for himself. Let our conscientious, trained, and certified staff help you and yours."

Before I could take in much more, a jowly, balding man in a white jacket came out of the office, bearing down on me. "Good afternoon, good afternoon," he said, beaming. "I'm Dr. Stillwell Bennett, the medical director of Pleasant Hollow. Can I help you? Are you interested in seeing our facilities? I drop in every day for an hour or so; it's lucky you caught me."

It was a lucky day all around. I introduced myself and explained that I was a PI. Four seconds later, the smile was gone and I was sitting across from a far less ebullient Dr. Stillwell. He was an overweight, sunny man it was easy to take an instant dislike to. Maybe it was the six strands of hair plastered all the way across his skull. He looked very prosperous: a sea island cotton shirt beneath the jacket, $250 British oxfords, sharply creased gray wool slacks, and a massive Rolex. His would be the Mercedes I'd noticed parked out back.

His office, by contrast, was so stark that I suspected he barely used it an hour a day: a single plastic chair, in which I was sitting, a wooden swivel chair, which he was using, and a plain metal desk with a phone. A Merck calendar was tacked up on the wall. That was about it.

Bennett didn't seem to harbor any illusions that I was there for any positive reason, so we both dispensed with the formalities. I figured I had only a few minutes before I got thrown out anyway.

"What's this about?" he asked.

"It's about James Goodell and Transitions, Inc. And Hemavero."

He looked startled, but kept his cool. "I can't comment on my relationship with Senator Goodell. I won't discuss that at all."

"I don't blame you," I said brightly. "It wouldn't make for a good pitch when you're trying to get people to drop Mom and Dad off at Pleasant Hollow, would it? Taking kickbacks from a drug company?"

Bennett flushed. "That's one side of the story," he said. "There's another, but I'm not inclined to share it, certainly not with you. Now tell me what you want and get the hell out of here, before I call my lawyer."

"Look, Dr. Bennett," I said. "I'm really not here to cause you any trouble. In fact, if you want to make some mischief for your former boss, Senator Goodell, it might be in your interest to talk with me. Nothing I'm investigating has much bearing on you, one way or the other."

Bennett looked skeptical, but he buzzed for two cups of black coffee. Maybe he needed it to mask the smell of booze wafting across the desk. A silent, beefy woman in a white nurse's uniform brought the coffee in. When the door closed again, he seemed a bit more expansive.

"I've got to go soon," Bennett said, checking his gleaming watch. "I own four of these places and I have to stop in at all of them each day. I know what you think, that they're hellholes. They are; they're death mills. I conform to the minimum state requirements. I can't spend a penny more. It's not a question of what I'd like, it's a question of what I can afford.

"Now Goodell, he's lined up some big investors—some *very* big and demanding investors. He's aiming for a more upscale audience. But these are the parents and grandparents of work-ing-class people. Most of them go deep into hock just to get in here." Something about his bitter ramblings led me to file a mental note: Find out who Goodell's big investors are.

"These people are actually lucky to be here. There's a waiting list," he went on.

"But rooms probably open up pretty often," I needled, "judg-ing from the warm greeting you gave me before you knew who I was."

He shook his head in sorrow at the ignorance and naiveté that existed in the world. "This is a tough business, Mr. Deleeuw."

Ignoring groans from the hallway and unpleasant smells permeating the office, I pushed on. "What makes it so tough?"

"It's brutally expensive. Even this dump costs two thousand a month. Medicare pays a piece of that, usually. And we have a small staff and, admittedly, few amenities—just bed, food, and nursing care. It still drives people mad, caring for their parents this way. We've had people drop old folks here and then take off, just disappear. So now we require collateral."

"Sort of a deposit on Mom's head," I said.

Bennett glared at me. "Mr. Deleeuw, I don't have time for your pious moralizing. You have no idea what this is like, or what I do or don't do for these people. I do care about them."

I raised both my hands. "Sorry, Doctor. I apologize. Look, we don't have to like each other, we just have to talk to each other."

"You've got two more minutes," Bennett said.

"Tell me about the money. The people that take off."

He sighed, took a sip of coffee, and ran his fingers through what remained of his hair. "When people default on their payments, we have to get the state to pay or else send the old folks to public facilities, which have year-long waiting lists. People can die without anybody coming to get their bodies. As I said, we have a poorer clientele than Transitions. By the time some of our residents pass on, their families are so worn out that they don't even have money for a casket. I come by here once a day, make some rounds. But nobody has money to pay for more than minimal medical care—"

"Do you use Hemavero?"

He ignored me. "We've had to hire a collection agency. Lots of the relatives haven't visited in years. It's rough, rough."

"So why are you in it?"

He glowered at me. "I'm in it for the money. Top hospitals aren't begging me to join their staffs. And this is a booming business, if you hold costs down. We have close to one hundred per cent occupancy."

This man and his place were turning my stomach. "You're

pointing out that you're greedy and opportunistic. I get it. I'd like to know, does Goodell run a clean, safe business?"

His eyes flickered a bit. He was probably wondering about continuing this conversation: What might be in it for him? But he probably was also considering the consequences for his state-run and -licensed business if he ticked Goodell off.

"Hypocrites like you make me sick," he said softly. "What do you know about aging and institutions? Have you voted to raise your taxes so these people could have better care? How many nursing homes have you visited in the past year? How many places like this have you driven by without giving them or the people who live in them one single thought? People come here because hospitals won't keep them anymore and their families don't want them at home. Many are in their eighties and nineties and have only the vaguest idea where they are. We don't give them luxury, but we keep them clean and safe."

There was silence in the room. I didn't come out well on any of the questions. I didn't make a practice of visiting nursing homes, or even thinking much about them, though there were a dozen or so in Rochambeau. I hadn't sent any letters to the governor demanding better services for the elderly.

"I'm sorry," I said, after a moment. "Let's help each other out."

He looked up at the ceiling. "There are fine nursing homes and bad ones. I know this place doesn't look like much, but there are plenty worse. Goodell runs one of the better chains. The medical care is excellent. They actually work at keeping people busy and active, which some nursing homes can't afford to do. I'd send my mother there. But I'll be frank with you, Mr. Deleeuw—and I'm not speaking about Goodell here, particularly—you can pass all the laws and regulations you want, but in Pleasant Hollow or in Elston Manor, there's only one attendant between life and death. When a client has trouble breathing, or heart trouble, or a stroke in the middle of the night . . ."

"The attendant can just walk on by?"

"Or be dozing at the desk. Or doing one of a dozen jobs left for the night shift. Nobody will ever know or, in a lot of cases, care. The families are usually relieved. People in some of these places are in a twilight zone, hovering between life and death."

This philosophical riff threw me a bit. "Where do you stand in this? Do *you* fight to keep them alive?"

"Sure, when I can," he said. "No matter what you think of me, I'm a physician. I take my responsibilities seriously. I—" He suddenly looked so distressed that I thought he was about to cry. His voice caught. Then he pulled himself together. "But I'm not here most of the time. Last week, we had a ninety-eight-year-old lady go into heart failure. Her son had brought her here, then moved away six months later. I've been getting some state and Medicare money for her, but she was still costing me eight hundred dollars a week. She hadn't spoken in two years; she was incontinent. An attendant had to turn her frequently to avoid bedsores, which state inspectors don't like to see.

"She passed on a few nights ago. Did the attendant on duty check? Notice? She says no. By the time we called 911, she was beyond help. Should she have been resuscitated? Put on machines? Brought back to nonlife? It's for the Almighty to decide, but in Pleasant Hollow, He has delegated that decision to a twenty-one-year-old health care aide named Frannie Dougherty, because God didn't provide enough government or other funds for a doctor to be here round the clock. And the one RN on duty was helping Mr. Lewis, who had a debilitating stroke three months ago, go to the toilet."

More silence.

"Do you prescribe Hemavero?"

"Sure," he said. "It's a powerful but risky drug. I'm not commenting on Goodell's charges against me, but I'll tell you this, Hemavero is a very important drug. Given in the right dose at the right time, it can save a stroke victim's life. It can limit neurological damage. But it can pose a real risk to the heart. Given too much or too often, it can cause seizures or heart failure. When we use it, which is not often, I administer it myself, or the nurse can if I'm not here. Nobody else is allowed to touch it."

"How is it administered?"

"Usually by injection. It can be administered via IV pump, too. If you're asking me, have I ever overprescribed this drug to help a patient die, the answer is no. There are a lot of easier, more efficient, and legal ways to do that. If you're asking me, can a patient be killed by improper use of this drug, absolutely. Especially since county medical examiners don't spend a lot of time on ninety-eight-year-old stroke victims, Mr. Deleeuw. Nor does anybody else."

"When would Hemavero be indicated?"

"Immediately after a stroke. In the two or three days subsequent, it can significantly lessen the damage. It's also very expensive. We can't afford to use it routinely. Elston Manor can afford it. I maintain that I ordered it in the proper amounts—"

What would a normal dose be, I asked.

"Hard to say; you have to look at each case individually. But the highest I've ever prescribed is fifty milligrams a day, even for the most severe strokes, and then for only two days."

I didn't think there was much more to get out of this man. "So you have nothing bad to say about Senator Goodell?"

"I have lots bad to say about him, but I'll save it for court. None of it bears on Elston Manor. It's a fine facility. As I said, I'd send my mother there in a minute."

I bet, I thought. Better there than here. "So what was the story, Doctor? That you just took some 'gifts' from the pharmaceutical company?"

Bennett stood up. "That's it, Mr. Deleeuw. There's no point in taking this conversation any further." He walked to the door, held it open. No problem; I couldn't wait to get out.

When I looked back from the hallway, Bennett was already reaching for a drawer, where I suspected he'd stashed something that would crank up his coffee a bit. I wondered if he was a drunk who'd become a nursing home operator or vice versa.

"One more thing," I said from the doorway. "Have you ever done any work for Puritan Homes, the Transitions facility in Connecticut?"

He shook his head. "I might have visited there from time to time on my way to New England. But I don't have any official duties there, no." He spat out his answer, not bothering to turn around.

I hadn't been trying to antagonize him. He had scored a point or two by exposing my belated sensitivity to the plight of the elderly and infirm. Still, I was thrilled to get out of Pleasant Hollow. I thought Silly Bennett was pretty sick of the place himself.

I turned on the cell phone in the car as I headed for the Parkway. As was becoming more common, it rang almost immediately. It was Evelyn.

"Luis has been desperate to talk to you," she reported tersely. "He's got a pager. I'm going to page him and give him your number. He'll get to a private place."

It wasn't two minutes before he called. "Kit," he whispered, "I'm calling from a janitor's closet on the ground floor. I must be brief. I have Benchley's chart with me. But I cannot make a copy; the nurse on duty is watching me too closely."

"Is Hemavero on the chart, Luis?"

"Hema . . . Yes, here it is. Sixty milligrams in the morning; sixty in the evening."

I felt a chill along my spine. That was more than twice as much as Bennett said he had ever prescribed. But was it enough to hurt Benchley? How long had he been getting this stuff?

"But Kit," Luis whispered, interrupting my thoughts. "I talked with Benchley. I had ten minutes because the shift nurse had to help with a cardiac arrest and I volunteered to watch her three rooms. Benchley recognized me. He can even speak a little, though we communicated mostly through the finger-tapping method you described. He told me he is frightened, that something is wrong. He told me he overheard two attendants talking after a patient died. He believes they said the patient had an overdose, and that this served her right because she was a witch. Benchley thought this wasn't an accident, but he couldn't be sure."

In the early evening, the lights of the oncoming cars flashed through the median divider. I tried to shake off the weariness of my hours on the road, and of too many dispiriting conversations.

Luis kept his voice low. "Something is terribly wrong, Kit, I have no doubt of it. But Benchley indicated he didn't want us to bring him out. He insisted we shouldn't. He won't leave the others here. One of the patients is a Quaker from his Meeting, just admitted. He won't abandon her."

"I'm not sure Benchley's in any position to be calling the shots, Luis. Where can we talk?"

We agreed to meet at a coffee shop a few blocks from the nursing home when his shift ended. I called Willie and asked him to join us there. I had a plan of my own, half-baked as it was.

Benchley was living on borrowed time, I was sure of it. I had no evidence that would justify calling in the police, but more than enough to convince me we needed to get him the hell out of there.

fourteen

BEBE'S LUNCHEONETTE was three blocks west of Elston Manor. Luis arrived the same time I did, popping out of a car parked a few doors down.

Sitting across from me in a booth, he looked pale and a bit shaken, without his customary regal bearing or calm. Luis was used to working hard; he'd done his share of cleaning grills and flipping burgers. But becoming a faceless peon, maybe that was difficult for him. Or perhaps it was what he'd been seeing as he swept and swabbed.

I'd never seen him so rattled. "We have some serious problems," he said.

He recounted how he'd been mopping outside Benchley's room, his good luck when the attendant was called away, and his shock at how clearheaded Benchley was. "I could see from his eyes that he knew me and understood everything I was saying. And I almost shouted when he spoke to me. He said, 'Luis, I'm so glad you're here.' He spoke slowly, weakly, but quite intelligibly."

But he seemed exhausted, Luis said, so they began communicating mostly through the code I'd explained, using eye blinks and finger taps and few spoken words.

"He was alert, Kit. And even though speaking exhausted him, he was quite clear in his communication. He said he hadn't let the doctors or nurses know that he could talk. His biggest problem, he indicated, is this medication he's being given. He believes it sets him back."

"What else did he tell you?"

Luis looked up at the clock. "Kit, the next dosage is due at 8 P.M. That gives us very little time. I'm concerned—"

"That they will harm him?"

"Yes, or at least medicate him to the point where he can no longer speak or respond. Benchley overheard things that greatly worried him. He was not completely certain of what he was hearing; he said he couldn't swear to it. But the staff people were talking about a patient who died, this 'witch' who'd been 'medicated along.'

"And there's a friend, a member of his Meeting. Her name, he whispered to me, is Elizabeth Keyes. She'd had seizures, and Benchley apparently arranged for her admission to Elston Manor . . ."

The deal with Goodell, I thought.

"The talk he heard was that her bed would be free in the morning. That there would be one less person to worry about. That Nurse O'Brien would be administering the medications herself. And Kit, what really—"

Luis paused as a beefy man in a Navy sweatshirt strode into the coffee shop and took a seat a few booths away.

"You know him?" I asked.

"No," said Luis. "But I know the type."

My mind was spinning. "So you're saying that Benchley thinks he overheard some attendants admitting that some patient was overmedicated to death. And that they're going to do the same to a member of his Meeting, somebody he got into the home? But he's not positive?"

Luis nodded. "Also, Kit, he more than once mentioned 'the

will.' His will. He said it was a mistake to have signed it. I asked what he meant, but I think the subject was too complex for blinking and tapping. I told him to rest."

"And you're sure you saw Hemavero written on his chart?"

"Positive, Kit."

I told Luis what Bennett had said about Hemavero, how powerful it was. And how disturbing it was to me that Bennett—who hardly struck me as a scrupulous rule-follower—had never prescribed more than fifty milligrams. Still, how could you call the police with that? I could just imagine what the cops would make of testimony from an elderly, medicated stroke victim in a nursing home run by a powerful state senator.

"Kit, I think Benchley is in real danger. He is clearly terrified, for himself or for others, or both." The coffee we'd ordered sat untouched before us as we tried to come to terms with this. Suddenly I saw Luis glance out the window, get up, and head toward the back door. "Forgive me," he said abruptly, over his shoulder. "I must leave. I will contact you."

"Luis," I hissed. "I'm going to get him out." I wasn't sure he heard me. And I wasn't sure how I was going to pull this off.

Seconds later, Head Nurse Mary O'Brien came through the door with two other nurses, all resplendent in starched white uniforms. Luis had vanished.

Nurse O'Brien didn't look happy to see me, but as she didn't rule Bebe's, I had as much right to a cup of coffee as she did. She hesitated, then joined her staff at a table.

My mind was racing. Had Luis gone back to Elston Manor? How could I link up with him? Was Benchley in grave danger? Should I call the police, or would that just end up exposing Benchley to greater peril? I had a nightmare vision of spending the rest of my life regretting that I hadn't taken action when it was still possible.

But I could place a sick man in grave physical jeopardy, destroying my own hard-won practice to boot. Not to mention that there might be a few technical problems, such as the small but fanatic army that secured Elston Manor.

I dialed Willie from my cell phone; he was a few blocks away. I told him not to come into Bebe's—I didn't want Nurse Ratchet to see him—but to meet me outside. And I told him to get on-line as soon as he could—operating a laptop from a car posed no great challenge to Mr. Modem—and see if any insurance policies had been taken out on Benchley or on his behalf. Via the Net, you could get such data anytime, especially if you had the Social Security number of the person involved. I did. When I pushed the "end" button, I looked up into the formidable face of Mary O'Brien.

"Mr. Deleeuw, isn't it?" As if she weren't sure.

"Yes, Ms. O'Brien. It's—interesting—to see you again." I wanted to be calm and collected. I thought I saw some anxiety in those eyes.

"Here to visit Elston Manor?" she asked, with about as fake and brittle a smile as anyone could manage. She knew I wouldn't have any other reason to be in the neighborhood.

"I like it around here, Ms. O'Brien. I might just buy in the neighborhood. I'm sure you know that I'm off the VIP visitors' list at Elston Manor. I'm sure that's thanks to you. What I'm not sure about is why my business in this coffee shop is any business of yours." I smiled just as sweetly and falsely.

She was unamused. "If I see you anywhere around Elston Manor, I'll have you arrested for trespassing. We'll see how the state Licensing office likes that." Hmmmm, maybe it was O'Brien who'd called.

In any case, she'd be on the phone to the Manor's security goons before I paid my check. I took a flyer. "I know how to use the phone too. The same Licensing office might be fascinated by the medication levels being administered to various patients at Elston Manor."

The phony smile vanished. "That's a disgusting lie," she said. "It's also libelous."

"It's no more outrageous or false than claiming I threatened you," I shot back.

She turned abruptly and joined her friends, looking upset. My satisfaction lasted about three seconds. Elston Manor seemed like a foreign country to me, an alien, guarded place over which the outside world had little control; it was tempting to poke at one of its potentates. But it didn't help that we'd had this encounter. She'd only be more on her guard. And she looked pretty alert as it was: She'd glanced at the two coffee cups on the table when there was only one person sitting in the booth. But I couldn't imagine she'd have any way of connecting Luis with me.

I paid my bill under her watchful gaze, climbed into the Volvo, and almost drove into Willie cruising down the street in his ancient VW Bug. I flashed my lights and waved for him to follow. We drove three blocks and circled around to the rear of Elston Manor.

Willie pulled in behind me and I filled him in. "We've got to get him out of there, Chief," he said simply. But how? Luis was presumably inside somewhere, but I had no way to reach him. Was Nurse O'Brien smart enough to check the staff log to see which employees had signed out in the past half hour or so? I'd bet she was.

If anybody linked Luis to the coffee shop or to me, we had to get him out of there too. He had, after all, had a long time alone with Benchley, something O'Brien might easily find out once she started checking.

A six-foot chain-link fence topped by barbed wire ran all along the back and sides of the property, bordering maybe three acres of walking trails, lawns, and trees. I hadn't seen residents using the grounds much, but they would appeal to visitors, especially those whose previous stop had been a place like Pleasant Hollow.

I saw some black knobs protruding from the ground about every five feet on the other side of the fence. If they were electronic sensors, there was no way I could risk climbing over: An intrusion would bring not only Manor security but also the Clifton cops. As much as Chief Leeming often wanted to throttle me, he considered me a responsibility as well as a pain in the ass.

I was a Rochambeau local, after all. He'd even given me a break from time to time. Who knew what the Clifton PD might do?

So I would have to go in through the front.

"Okay, instant plan," I said. I tossed Willie my keys. "Willie, leave this shitcan car here. They don't know you, so it won't hurt if they run a registration check and come up with your name."

"But is it safe here?"

I snorted. "God willing, some local thieves'll come after that lawn mower. Then you could get a real car." Willie had 140,000 miles on the Bug and I knew he adored every rusted inch of it. But I didn't see auto theft as our major risk here.

I told Willie to circle the area slowly in my Volvo. To pass the entrance often enough to be near, but not so often as to attract the attention of the guy in the guardhouse. I told him to leave his cell phone on. Then I left him and loped around toward the front door.

The security here was as well designed as the rest of Elston Manor. The rear of the property was fenced in, but the front was open, with clear—and very well-lit—sight lines from the guardhouse, a small box glassed in on all four sides. To get into Elston Manor, you had to drive or walk by the glass house toward the main entrance.

On foot, I'd have to slip past without attracting the guard's attention, which would be hard enough, then proceed down the driveway and somehow get through the main door, which undoubtedly was locked or alarmed at night. Probably surveillance cameras were mounted at key points along the way to back up the guards. The system was designed to preclude precisely what I was trying to do.

The only hiding place was a concrete planter filled with geraniums, just to the left of the guardhouse. I circled around behind it and flattened myself out on the velvety lawn, keeping the planter between me and the guardhouse. Somebody driving by on the street might be able to spot me if he looked carefully. But there hardly *was* anybody on the street, and no reason to scrutinize the lawn. I was wearing a dark blue jacket, which I hoped would blend into the dark shrubs along the front of the building.

When my Wall Street career fell apart, the first thing I thought of was my criminal investigations training in the Army, where I learned all sorts of skills I joked I'd never have reason to use again. I was surprised how many had come in handy.

I pulled my jacket over my head, as I'd been taught, so that my pale face wasn't conspicuous against the dark lawn, and began wriggling forward on my stomach. The trick was to be patient, to move slowly, then stop.

Grass and pebbles scraped against the side of my face; my belt buckle kept gouging up dirt. Every time a car loomed, I stopped and waited for it to pass.

In this fashion, it took fifteen minutes to pull even with the guardhouse. I saw Willie cruise by every now and then in the Volvo. I assumed Luis was inside, mopping floors, and hoped he was near Benchley. I smeared some of the dirt over my face for additional camouflage. By the time I remembered that camouflage might help get me into the Manor, but would freak out everybody once I got inside, I was a mess. As I tried to get to Benchley, which would require me to look presentable, people would run screaming at the sight of me.

If I ever got inside. It was nearing 8 P.M. I needed some car traffic into the compound, to distract the guard, if I was going to pull this off. But there wasn't any. I lay fifteen yards from the guardhouse for ten minutes while my joints stiffened in the cool dampness. Then I waited ten more minutes. Benchley didn't have this kind of time.

The guard inside looked very young but very alert. I would've preferred that he sit with his feet up, reading some cheap mystery; instead he was sitting ramrod straight in the booth, peering alternately out at the grounds and at the monitors in front of him, each showing a different entrance to the building.

Plan A was going nowhere. I had to come up with something better. I rolled away from the guardhouse and, beneath my jacket, dialed Willie on the cell phone and told him about Plan B. He was incredulous, but game.

I wiggled backward slowly, so that the concrete planter was between me and the guardhouse again. Standing up, I brushed myself off, circled back around the side of the building, walked down the street in front of Elston Manor, and waited until Willie circled again.

I suddenly walked right in front of the Volvo. Willie hit the horn, slammed on the brakes. We hadn't practiced this, and under the circumstances I could hardly complain, but I wished he'd stopped just a foot or two shorter. The car bumped me slightly, and I flopped onto the hood, then onto the ground, with pain stabbing my ribs, elbows, and right leg. I wondered if I'd broken anything.

Willie jumped out of the car, looking genuinely frantic, and yelled to the guard that we needed help.

The guard was out of his booth in a flash. "You need an ambulance?" he shouted.

"No," I gasped, sitting up. "Just some bad bruises. Just some scratches." I whispered to Willie, "Tell him I need some water and to use the phone. That's all."

I was banking on this guy's not being a stickler. I don't care how good a security outfit is, nighttime help is mostly kids earning money for college or trade school. They're not Marines.

"He just wants a drank of water and to make a call to his wife," Willie called back. "Can we go inside for just a second?"

The guard, running over, never hesitated. He and Willie helped me to my feet. His name tag said "J. Blank." He was about Willie's age, though far more clean-cut. He kept calling me sir. "You all right, sir?"

It was after they'd steadied me and brushed me off a bit that J. Blank noticed Willie's HotWired T-shirt. "You on the Web?" he asked.

Major break. Even as the two of them were helping me into the front seat, they were yakking about Web browsers. By the time the door closed, Willie was offering to trade e-mail addresses and leading "Jimmy" to various free software sites.

Blank pointed up toward a parking space near the entrance, met us there, politely opened the door. Willie and I walked in. There was no one around, thank God. Blank said he couldn't leave the guardhouse unoccupied for long. We said we'd be out in a flash. He pointed us toward the phones and washrooms.

Willie stayed behind to chat about computers. I needed J. Blank to be occupied for at least ten minutes; fortunately, he and Willie were going at it like two old ladies bragging about their grandchildren.

"Just a few minutes now," Blank said as I limped off. "I'm not supposed to be doing this."

"No problem," I said, feeling a bit of a twinge. He could easily end up losing his job because of his good nature.

I ducked into the men's room, washed off my face. The major challenge would be avoiding my friend Nurse O'Brien, assuming she was on duty. But Benchley's ward was down a hallway, away from the main nursing office.

Still, anyone I encountered would be suspicious of my presence; visiting hours were long over. I took off my jacket, stashed it in a stall, and rolled up my sleeves. People were forever saying I looked like a teacher or an accountant. If anybody asked me, that's just what I was, a part-time accountant in to audit the books. The trick was to look as though I had every right in the world to be there.

Naturally, two technicians walked right into me as I left the bathroom.

"Can we help you?" asked a woman in white pants and a white jacket. I couldn't tell if she was suspicious or trying to be helpful.

"None needed, thanks," I said. "I'm just doing some auditing and needed a bathroom."

She was glancing down curiously at my pant leg, where the right knee, I suddenly noticed, was torn open. Great. Some accountant. I joked about having fallen down getting out of the car. And I kept walking. So dumb. Why didn't I just say I'd been hit by a car and was cleaning up? Why did I mention auditing? I'd been too clever by half: If she'd called the guardhouse, he would have told her it was okay. Now, if she told him about some auditor, they'd both get suspicious.

I kept moving, heading toward Benchley's room. At the end of his hall sat three wheelchairs; I grabbed one and pushed it ahead of me, rushing past three or four rooms.

What if they'd moved him since Luis's visit? But he was in the same room as before, a technician or assistant standing by his bedside adjusting the bag on the IV pump. The guy looked young, a nursing student, perhaps. He wore a diamond stud in his left ear.

"What are you doing?" I barked, sounding official.

"I'm changing the bag," he said. "Why? Who are you?" I pushed the wheelchair toward him, and he stepped back from the bed. Benchley was asleep; I called his name, but he didn't respond.

"Take that IV outta his arm," I ordered. Uncertain, but unnerved, the kid slid the needle out. I pushed the chair to the bed, swept the curtain back, and making sure nothing else was connected to Benchley, leaned forward and scooped him into my arms. He weighed alarmingly little.

"Hey, you can't . . . He's really sick! This is dangerous."

"What's the matter," I yelled, "want to give him some more Hemavero?" I only vaguely remember the next few minutes. I had gone wild.

I put Benchley in the wheelchair, yanked the blanket off the bed to cover him, and pulled out my PI shield. "Police business," I said. "Interfere and you'll be arrested."

The guy hesitated. "But you can't . . . I haven't checked his pulse or heart. He's very sick. You can't move him without a doctor's orders; he's a stroke patient."

I yelled again for the kid to get out of the way, this time angrily enough that he backed against the windows. I doubted he'd bought the police stuff for a second—no way a legitimate cop would drag a critically ill patient out of a hospital room. He'd be on the phone to O'Brien before I got down the hallway. In fact, he decided not to wait; he rushed me, yelling for help.

I had to give Goodell credit for having a dedicated staff. I don't know if the assistant was aiming to knock me over or just to get away. But I didn't wait to figure it out.

I turned away from Benchley, spun to face the boy, and slugged him right in the stomach. He folded like a tent. As he doubled over, I caught him on the left side of the head with my forearm. He went down, holding his belly and gasping for breath. This wouldn't stop him, but it would slow him down for a few seconds. Another thing I'd learned in the Army.

I'd shocked myself. I wasn't the type to punch out an innocent, hardworking kid. But Benchley had to be sprung by any means possible. I'd diddled around too long already.

I grabbed the wheelchair and dashed toward the door. Benchley was still out of it, his head wobbling over to one side. "Benchley, can you hear me? You okay? It's Kit. We're getting you out of here. To a hospital."

I heard a grunt behind me and started to turn, but too late. The kid had gotten off the floor and was hurling himself toward me. He landed hard and my leg, which was already hurting from the "accident," buckled beneath me. The two of us went down, knocking over a tray table. Willie could probably hear the crash outside, as could the guard.

I couldn't get up. The kid was thin but strong and determined, and he was whacking me with the metal tray. The pain in my head was searing. We both obviously thought we were fighting for Benchley's life.

Suddenly, the pressure lifted from my back. The boy seemed to rise in the air; I heard the door to the bathroom open. Somebody was behind the kid, prying him off me and tossing him into the bathroom.

It was Luis. He slammed the bathroom door and jammed a chair under the handle.

A voice came over the intercom. "Jay, did you call? Is everything okay?"

Luis gave me the thumbs-up and darted out of the room.

I flung the wheelchair into the hallway and, in what must have looked like a scene from a horror movie, ran for the exit, limping, bleeding, ripped and dirty clothes flapping, pushing the unconscious form of Benchley Carrolton in front of me.

There were shouts behind me, but the electric exit doors popped open. "Willie. Go!" I shouted. He broke off his conversation and leaped for the Volvo outside; I pushed the wheelchair through the doors.

Guard Blank, trotting alongside, looked astonished. "Hey, what the . . . ?"

"Mr. Carrolton has been released," I said, rushing past him. Blank put his hand on his holster. I couldn't imagine what he made of this sight: the man he'd just seen hit by a car pushing an unconscious elderly man out the door. Robbery? Kidnapping? Terrorism? Some completely unfathomable act of madness?

I lifted Benchley into my arms and held him against me. "Go ahead and shoot an old stroke victim if you want, Officer Blank. But I don't think that's what they had in mind when they gave you that gun." I was gasping for breath. My head throbbed, as did my hand, from slugging the technician, and everything else, just about. I heard running feet behind me and sirens somewhere off in the distance.

The Volvo screeched up between the paralyzed guard and Benchley and me. Willie jumped out and opened the back door; I unceremoniously backed in, pulling Benchley with me. He was muttering something, but his eyes were glazed and unfocused. "Kit?" he whispered. "Kit? I can't go. I've got to . . ."

But Willie slammed the door and jumped into the driver's seat. "Go," I yelled. Behind us the doors burst open and Nurse O'Brien ran out, followed by Luis, the battered technician, and three or four orderlies.

"Stop!" yelled Blank, collecting himself and pulling out his gun. But what was he supposed to do, shoot a patient? He fired a shot in the air as the Volvo lurched out of the driveway and, veering onto the lawn, evaded the gate at the guardhouse. J. Blank would be in the unemployment line by morning, poor kid.

We careened down the street, made a few two-wheeled turns, and found the entrance to the Garden State Parkway South. Behind us we could see several Clifton police cars with lights flashing, rushing toward Elston Manor. I was sure the guard, along with half the staff, had memorized my license place, so this hardly qualified as a miraculous getaway. I dialed the Rochambeau Police Department, told the dispatcher who I was, and asked to be patched through to Chief Leeming.

Benchley's head was on my shoulder. I pulled the blanket more snugly around him. "Benchley, it's me. It's Kit. You're out of there. I'm taking you to the hospital."

Benchley's arm shot out and his hand grabbed my wrist with more strength than I would have thought he could muster. "No," he rasped. "No."

"No? But you need . . ."

"Home," he said hoarsely. "Take me home." His eyes, clearer now, looked almost fierce. The plea in his expression was palpable. I felt, as Luis had, that I understood exactly what Benchley was trying to tell me.

"Drive to the Garden Center, Willie," I said.

"Shouldn't we get Benchley to a hospital, boss?"

"No," I said. "The Garden Center. Now."

Chief Leeming's voice came over the cell phone. "I'm in a movie theater, Deleeuw. This better be good."

"It is, Chief. You probably already got a call charging me with trespassing, assault, and kidnapping. I wanted to check in so I didn't get shot."

He whistled. "Out investigating again, Deleeuw? Jeez. Who's going to call me? Is this a joke?"

"You haven't been called?"

"You're the only call I got tonight. I just talked to the desk sergeant a half hour ago and he said it's quiet as Christmas morning in Rochambeau. What's this about? Do I get to lock you up?"

Hell, what did it take for the Clifton PD to put out an APB? All I'd done was trespass, bust into Elston Manor, assault a medical technician, grab a patient and hustle him out, not to mention damaging some property in the process. How could the police not be looking for me?

I told Leeming that something was going on but I couldn't talk about it now; I'd call him back.

"What the hell? You call me up, tell me some bullshit about assault and kidnapping, then you're going to call me back? This is nuts, even for you, Deleeuw." I apologized and said I would explain.

"Make it soon," Leeming said. "Because if some other department calls with a beef about you, I'm going to come and personally arrest your ass."

I couldn't figure it out, but we were pulling up to the Garden Center. Willie hopped out and unhooked the chain across the driveway. Benchley's eyes were open, and to an amateur his pulse felt solid. He wasn't feverish, either. He did look ghostly pale, though. I prayed I'd done the right thing. I decided not to tell him about Rose Klock, not until later.

I'd called Benchley's doctor, John Morrison; his service had paged him. He was shocked to hear Benchley would be coming home, but agreed to come over. Maybe he could have a look at me, too: A large lump was rising on my temple, and my left knee was in agony.

My cell phone beeped. I realized the Clifton police could trace cell calls but flicked it open anyway. It was Luis. He'd managed to get the tech off my back—literally—without revealing his identity. "Pretty impressive moves, podnah," I said.

"I was pleased to be of service," he said, taking a sort of verbal bow. "But Kit, a strange thing occured. Miss O'Brien, the head nurse, made a phone call or two, and then announced that the management had decided not to press charges or pursue it further. That the staff would get in touch with Benchley in the morning, to be sure he was all right and to handle the situation. She even told the young technician that he could be in legal trouble for attacking you, that it would be best if he kept quiet about the whole thing. He said he was just worried about the patient, and she said he could keep his job, but she didn't want to hear another word about it."

"So no one called the police?" I couldn't believe it.

"Someone did, but when they arrived Nurse O'Brien told them it had all been a misunderstanding. She met with them privately, then they left. She met with the security guard also. Then everybody went back to work. It doesn't seem they reported this incident, Kit. She may have called one of her bosses, though."

"I can guess who. I don't suppose this is the kind of publicity Senator Goodell wants. You better get out of there, Luis."

"I can't, Kit. I promised Benchley I would keep an eye on his friend. And we may need to know more. How is he?"

"He's alert. The doctor's on his way." To know more, that would be helpful. "Are there visitors' logs, Luis?"

"Yes, on the receptionist's desk."

"Will you try to get copies? I want to check the names."

"Of course."

"You saved my hide, Luis."

"My pleasure," he said.

Benchley's head was still cradled on my shoulder as we pulled up to the sprawling clapboard house that had been his home all his life.

"Kit," he said in a slow croak. "I can talk a little now."

"I hear, Benchley. It's okay, we're home. You don't have to be there anymore."

"It . . . was . . . awful . . . Kit."

I told him to be quiet until the doctor came. We sat in silence as Willie tried the door of the house, found it locked, noodled around the back a bit. He must have found a window that opened, because in a minute a light clicked on inside.

My cell phone rang again. I recognized the senator's voice, taut with barely suppressed rage.

"Deleeuw, can you give me one good reason why I shouldn't have your license yanked tonight and see your ass in jail?"

"Only that it wouldn't look good in the papers, Senator."

"What the hell are you doing? Why shouldn't I call the cops?"

"Why didn't you?"

"Because it would, in fact, look awful in the papers. I know you're a friend of Benchley's, but he shouldn't be out on the street; he's a sick man. I can't let you carry off a very ill patient and not do a thing about it."

"Give me until morning, Goodell," I said. "I need to check out a few things you may or may not know about. You can claim you were unreachable till morning. Benchley wanted out. He's out. He'll be under a doctor's care. If the doctor advises, I'll take him to a hospital. But lay off till tomorrow. Something smells in your company. I'm giving you the benefit of the doubt, for the moment, assuming you don't know what it is. But don't push me anymore right now, or you'll be getting more bad publicity than you can imagine." I turned off my own phone.

Willie and I carried Benchley up to his bedroom and eased him into bed. He gave a deep sigh, then closed his eyes. Dr. Morrison's Mercedes pulled in seconds later. He was delighted to see Benchley, his patient and friend for decades, but bewildered by this sudden turn of events.

"Why isn't Benchley in the nursing home?" he said, pulling a stethoscope out of the bag he'd probably carried for thirty years.

"He really wanted out," I said.

"I'm not sure I can countenance that. Go outside and give me a few minutes here."

Willie and I sat on the doorstep of the old farmhouse, taking in the spring night. Willie offered me a smoke. I took it, the first cigarette I'd had in fifteen years.

"Nice job running me over."

"Anytime, boss. Will Benchley be okay here?"

"We'll see to it." I got my phone from the car and called Johnny "Two Dogs" Melmano. I didn't really know if Two Dogs was a Mob wiseguy or not, but he acted the part expertly. He had been recommended by several local PIs as reliable "muscle," rentable if I was closing in on an especially belligerent Deadbeat Dad or had some rough evildoer to confront.

Two Dogs had a couple of Rottweilers he adored. They were as sweet as kittens, but nobody except Johnny and a few friends knew that. They were enormous, and he had trained them to snarl and bark ferociously on command. He took them along wherever he went.

I decided it would be wise to bring Two Dogs and his two dogs in, lest somebody decide Benchley belonged in the nursing home after all.

Johnny was at home watching wrestling on pay-per-view. He said he'd be at the Garden Center in fifteen minutes. That would give Benchley's Quaker friends something to talk about.

Dr. Morrison came out and joined us on the front stoop. "Benchley would be better off in a hospital," he said.

"He doesn't want to go," I said.

"I know, he said the same thing to me. I suppose I have to respect that. But he's very weak, Kit. I'm disturbed by his symptoms."

"What symptoms?"

"His heart rate's slowing down and speeding up. His eyes look glassy. He's in and out, alert, then dropping off. I have a blood sample. I'm going to drop it off at the hospital and have it tested."

"It's not just the stroke?"

"Could be a drug overdose," Morrison said. "I can't believe that would happen, but it's possible. I'll call you when I know more."

Morrison said he'd called a private nursing service; they'd send an RN over soon. "You could probably persuade Benchley to go to a hospital," he told me, not sounding all that hopeful. "You could plead with him." I said I couldn't.

I left Willie on the stoop and went inside, to wait in a rocking chair in Benchley's room until the nurse arrived. Generations of Carroltons had lived in this old house. That cross-stitched sampler on the wall—probably some great-aunt or grandmother had embroidered it. The quilt we'd pulled over Benchley was no doubt an heirloom.

He stirred in the bed a bit, opened his eyes, looked at me, and let his gaze travel the room. Looking into Benchley's eyes, I understood that he needed to come home. And I think I understood why.

fifteen

ONCE THE NURSE had arrived and Johnny Two Dogs showed up with his sidekicks, Willie and I went home.

I warned Johnny to keep Sammy and Greta away from Benchley's plants, and to try not to scare the hell out of any early morning strollers who might come by the Garden Center. No problem, said Two Dogs.

Everyone was asleep when I got home. I took Percentage for a quick walk, then sat down to examine my wounds. I held an ice pack on my temple to try to reduce the swelling. My knee ached badly, but I could move it in all directions. I seemed to be sore and bruised, but whole. I guess I was lucky the security guard hadn't shot me.

The answering machine was blinking with a message from Luis, telling me he'd gone home. He said the staff was suspicious, they figured somebody inside might have helped me, but they didn't know who.

But in the hubbub, Luis had been able to copy the visitors' log for the past two months. He said he'd call in the morning; we would figure out what to do. He wanted to know right away if there was any deterioration in Benchley's condition, he added.

Dr. Morrison's words nagged at me. Say he was right, and Benchley had been given an overdose? Who would benefit from that? The Quaker Meeting would get money if Benchley died, but its members hardly seemed the sort to hasten an inheritance.

I went up to my computer and logged onto the Web. The PI conference I was heading for had been launched two years back. Five hundred private investigators from all over the country had chipped in to start a Web site to locate and share information.

PI Web sites had changed investigations dramatically. This was no substitute for old-fashioned legwork, for meeting somebody, looking him in the eye, gauging his integrity. But it was a useful addition to our arsenal.

We'd hired research techs for the site to be on call twenty-four hours a day. Each participating PI was allowed so many hours of research a month; after that we paid $40 an hour for their help, usually a billable expense. It was generally Willie who used the site for Deleeuw Investigations. We'd located more than a few Deadbeat Dads this way; runaways too. And for my insurance fraud cases, the Web was a gold mine, spitting out litigants' past legal histories, patterns of fraudulent claims, and biographical histories.

This task wouldn't be so easy. I had upgraded Emily's old Mac, but it wasn't nearly as powerful as the Power Mac we used at the office. It would take forever to download the list and text I needed. But I e-mailed the help number and said I needed to know how to access wills filed with the Essex County probate office.

A message came back in a minute: "Need name, DOB (birth date), Social Security number, address." I had the information handy, so I typed it in. The computer froze three times; even when it was operational, it moved at its own torturous pace. It was 4 A.M. before I logged off. Benchley had made more complicated financial arrangements than even good Senator Goodell knew about.

I was surprised at the addendum I'd come across filed by Eric Levin a few weeks earlier. I was surprised at the amount, too.

Benchley's forebears were wealthy Pennsylvania Quakers. I knew he had money only because he gave so much of it away; otherwise he never spoke of it. But if you spent fifteen minutes with him at the Garden Center, you knew he was in business for love, not cash.

For all that, the Center was profitable. Long lines snaked around the cash registers most of the year, except in the dead of winter. On busy spring weekends, off-duty Rochambeau cops were hired to direct traffic; the Center was that busy. In the fall, Benchley stocked mounds of pumpkins, jugs of cider, acres of mums. He sold exotic varieties of manure, expensive imported bulbs, all sorts of tools and accessories.

So in addition to his family money, Benchley had apparently made a good bit himself. His wife had died years earlier, and they had no children. I'd been wondering who'd inherit his wealth and property, aside from the modest amounts that Levin had told the Meeting about.

On-line I discovered the answer: In a codicil filed in the County Probate Court two months before his stroke, he'd left two million to the Wellspring Foundation of Middletown, Connecticut.

As Goodell had noted, Benchley never talked about his good works; this one was evidently unknown to anyone but his lawyer. I'd never heard of this foundation.

Wellspring's own Web site described it as a research and charitable foundation devoted to the needs of elderly Americans. It funded medical research into strokes, Alzheimer's, and Parkinson's disease. It paid for nursing care for the indigent elderly and funded assisted care institutions who took in the needy. It endowed several gerontology research chairs at medical schools.

It seemed Wellspring didn't run institutions itself, but awarded money to researchers and teachers, and subsidized people at facilities like Elston Manor. Perhaps that amounted to propping up struggling facilities attempting to care for those other than the affluent elderly. It was a classic Benchley endeavor and, on top of the arrangements he'd made with Goodell, very generous. One odd note, though: Pleasant Hollow was listed among the facilities awarded grants for taking in the elderly poor.

The Web site didn't list any officers, only Wellspring's attorney, Peter Mackley, a name that rang a distant bell. I made a note to call him on Monday.

I allowed myself an hour's nap, a shower and change of clothing—the ones I'd been wearing were candidates for the ragbag—and a kiss for my sleeping family members. But I was back at Rochambeau Garden Center by 6 A.M. I'd assigned Willie to get the Elston Manor visitors' logs Luis had copied and smuggled out, to look for connections and leads we could pursue to answer the too many questions we still needed answered: Had Benchley been overdosed? With Hemavero? And if he had been, why and by whom? Was Goodell running a crooked operation? And could we prove it?

I expected things would heat up this morning. Goodell, crooked or straight, would have to do something. He couldn't just let people snatch patients out of his nursing home and slug his attendants. Especially not if he was straight.

When I pulled up, Johnny Two Dogs was sitting in a station wagon parked discreetly a few yards from the house and drinking coffee out of a thermos. Johnny's neck was about as wide as my chest. Even without his dogs, I wouldn't want to try getting past him.

"All quiet?" I asked Johnny. The vicious Rottweilers nuzzled my hand through the open window.

"Not a peep," he said. "The nurse just told me everything was fine. She gets relieved in a couple of hours."

I told Johnny to head home; I'd call if I needed him later. Sure thing, he said.

Inside, I walked quietly past the living room where Benchley and I had spent so many winter nights drinking mulled cider and talking, and climbed the stairs to his room.

Patricia, the nurse, in jeans and a sweatshirt beneath a white jacket, was trying to persuade Benchley to sip some water. He brightened when he saw me.

"How we doing?" I asked, with some of the fake cheerfulness of hospital visitors.

"Okay," he said softly.

"He's been asleep until a few minutes ago," Patricia said. "All the vitals are stable. He seems weak, but fine. I'm supposed to check in with Dr. Morrison now. Then I'll make a bit of tea and broth for breakfast. Do you mind sitting with Mr. Carrolton for a bit?"

I sat down opposite the bed as she left to make the call.

"Thanks for getting me out," Benchley said slowly, with obvious effort. "I can't think so clearly yet. I get confused . . ."

"Benchley, I hate to ask this now, but I want to go over a couple of things."

He nodded, still an arresting figure with his snowy hair and piercing blue eyes, but he looked gaunt and very fragile.

"You told Luis about some medication being used . . ."

"I can't recall exactly," he said. He spoke haltingly. "I remember someone talking about a medication, about how some 'witch' would be gone by morning. They were *expecting* her to die. And then, next morning, the nurses were telling each other that a woman *had* died. I believe they might have killed her. It happened before I saw you. I couldn't speak then. I'm worried about Elizabeth, from my Meeting."

"I'm sure she's okay, Benchley. We'll have Luis check on her today."

He was trailing off. His mind seemed clear, but he had little energy. I didn't want to push him.

"Benchley, do you know about the Wellspring Foundation?" He nodded. "Can you tell me about it?"

Benchley looked at me. He held his hand out. I clasped it. "I've given them nearly all my money . . ." He stopped, took a few deep breaths. I gave him a sip of water. "For the last few years, I've been involved in elder care. These nursing homes . . .

well, many of them are horrible. I've been giving money so people can get good care. Wellspring does that . . . not for me because I can afford good care, but . . ."

"For poor people," I interjected.

He nodded. "I wanted to arrange a venture between Transitions and Wellspring. To give money so that people who couldn't afford it, who were a burden to their children . . . could go to places like Elston. Get fine care. Help their families . . ."

He seemed to lose the thread. I decided not to push it any further. He was quiet for a while. I thought he was dropping off to sleep.

"Kit," he said suddenly. "You are like my son." At this my eyes welled. I had never dared articulate it so directly, but it was true. If I was like a son, he was like a father. We each had an opening for one.

I'd met Benchley when I was a Saturday Dad, home from Wall Street and eager to pick up some greenery to adorn the house I could afford at the time. We became friends in a casual way, but when my career blew up, I spent long nights in his greenhouse or living room, plotting my new life. It was Benchley who'd urged me to start my own business, work for myself. He loved the idea of my being a PI, especially one who tracked down Deadbeat Dads, located runaways, wrestled kids with drug problems into treatment. He even lent me the money for the first three months' rent on my office in the American Way, money it took me two years to pay back.

Benchley and I both knew just how thin the veneer of the American Dream was in towns like Rochambeau. Inside those carefully maintained Colonials and Victorians, with their polished brass door knockers, people sometimes suffered terribly. They struggled with affairs, divorces, layoffs, debts, drugs. My work took me into the dark side of suburban family life. Defining my work in this way allowed me some sense of idealism, along with the bread-and-butter insurance fraud that paid the bills.

"I'm so glad you're happy in your work," Benchley went on, his voice sandpapery. "And that Jane is a psychologist at last."

I squeezed his hand, not trusting my own voice. He looked puzzled now. "Have you seen Rose? I can't understand why she isn't here. The nurse doesn't know who she is."

I couldn't make myself lie to Benchley. "I'm so sorry, Benchley. She died last week. I think she was just lost without you. I think that was just the last straw."

He closed his eyes. "Poor woman," he said. "What a difficult life. She never had an easy day on the earth."

"Except for the years you gave her. She loved you very much."

Benchley smiled. "I've been so lucky, Kit," he said, forcing the words out. It seemed important to him to keep talking. "Loved so many people and been loved by so many. So lucky."

"And you'll continue to be. The thing is to get you back to health. Dr. Morrison begged me to get you into a hospital; he said it would be better. He was worried that you'd had a drug overdose. Do you recall taking anything?"

He shook his head. "A man came into my room once or twice, adjusted the IV . . ." He stopped to take a few breaths. He was speaking barely above a whisper now. "He looked like a doctor, but I hadn't seen him before. Didn't introduce himself. He just came into the room."

"Can you describe him, Benchley?"

"Thin. In his forties or early fifties. I couldn't see much more. He didn't look at me. He never said anything."

He was quiet again, while I tried to puzzle who that might have been in a facility where everyone wore name tags.

"I am so tired," he whispered after a while.

"No more questions, Benchley. How about I take you to Rochambeau Memorial? I promise I'll stay there with you."

He squeezed my hand. "No, Kit, no more hospitals. I thought I was doing the right thing by going to Elston Manor. To set an example. They agreed to make room for people from the Meeting, and others. But I want to be here. I feel it; it's where God wants me to be."

"Benchley," I said, quavering just a little. "I want you to know I love you. You're the best friend I've ever had." I didn't know what else to say, really.

His grip had weakened. I decided to leave him alone to rest, and slipped my hand from his. But he awakened. "Kit," he said, so softly. I had to bend to hear him. "We Quakers believe in silence, in its power to bring us closer to God. Let's pray together, like Quakers do, loudly, in silence."

Praying loudly in silence. I took Benchley's hand again and we both closed our eyes. His breathing was regular and even. Mine was labored and fitful.

He was right; he belonged here. He didn't belong in Elston Manor, whatever deal he'd made with Goodell. Perhaps it was a perfectly good place, an appropriate choice for many people, but not for Benchley. I couldn't tell you why.

Sometimes I tended to canonize Benchley. But he wasn't a saint. Benchley had money, which made good works easier. His good deeds came out of profound religious conviction, which didn't detract from them, but which put them in a particular context. He'd been taught to wake up every morning and do good. Most people were taught to mutter a few prayers and get on with making a living. The deeply religious can lose touch with the cynical, grinding-down quality of daily life; I felt that sometimes with Benchley.

And he knew it. Benchley was, at times, almost too good to be true. He didn't have the responsibility of juggling work that paid the bills. He didn't have to worry about a family. I told myself these things sometimes, not to knock my friend but to reduce him to human scale. Because it was hard not to feel inadequate around Benchley. He was warm, generous, wise, and even handsome. He was otherworldly. It would have been easy to resent him if I didn't love him. I was thinking these thoughts within the very silence Benchley loved so much, so they must be okay.

After ten minutes or so, it seemed clear that he had fallen asleep. Downstairs the nurse asked if there was anything else she should do before her replacement arrived. I asked her to tidy up downstairs a bit, open a few windows. Without Rose, the house felt musty.

I took a little stroll out back. I made a mental note to call the Friend who was caring for Melody, Benchley's golden retriever. She should be back here; dogs were great healers. Benchley needed a life that approached normalcy. I was sure some people from his Meeting would be delighted to come by for visits and daily prayer sessions now that he was back home.

The fresh air was pleasant and smelled of lilacs. Behind the house, in a grove of young trees still in their burlap, I came to the lounge chairs where Benchley and I had yakked about books and philosophy over iced tea. Usually, a steady stream of Benchley's friends trooped in and out of this sweet spot. I intended to wheel him out there in a day or two; that would be healing too. But I didn't want to leave him alone for long, so I went back upstairs.

The second I walked into the room I knew that Benchley wasn't breathing. His chest wasn't moving. I couldn't hear a sound. I held the back of my hand against his nose, as I'd been taught in the Army; there was no warmth, no movement of air.

I started to shout for the nurse, then stopped.

I thought of hurriedly starting CPR—perhaps Benchley had only stopped breathing a minute ago—but I didn't.

I reached for the phone to dial 911, then pulled back.

How many times had we discussed this very eventuality? Benchley was clear about not wanting to have his life prolonged by technology or machinery or heroics. And he had suffered enough. He had died in the silence, just as he would have wanted, just as he probably knew and intended he would when he suggested praying a few minutes ago.

So I sat down on the edge of the bed and resumed my silent prayer. Dear Supreme Being, if you're there, may Benchley's life and death be cause for joyful celebration, not grief. May he live on forever in all the good works he did, all the friends he made, all the trees he planted. May he be an inspiration to all of us who are less gifted and blessed. May I never let a day go by without thinking of his love and friendship. Amen.

sixteen

THE MEMORIAL SERVICE was in the Quaker tradition: lots of silence, a song, close friends reading from Benchley's favorite poems and books. Then, people who knew Benchley got up and talked about him: They told jokes, made fun of his quirks, said how lucky they felt to have known him. The small Meeting House was packed, but the windows were flung open so that people outside on the lawn could hear.

There were older people in wheelchairs, town yuppies whose gardens he had helped build, kids, friends, historic preservationists, all kinds of people I had never seen before.

I sat with Ben and Em on one side of me, Jane on the other. At moments like this, even adolescents transcend their normal roles in life. Em might have still thought me dumb and annoying, but her grip on my arm steadied me. "You okay, Dad?" Ben, sensing the loss, had stunned me that morning by giving me a hug. I couldn't remember the last one. Evelyn sat behind us in a black suit that had probably seen a lot of service in the last few years. I often suspected she'd had a serious crush on Benchley.

As Benchley would have wanted, the tone was light, celebratory, and often very funny. One woman talked about sitting in her front lawn chair years ago when Benchley had pulled up in his beat-up old pickup and said he couldn't help noticing a wonderful spot for a small pin oak right in front of her house. Would she mind?

You mean for free? she'd asked incredulously.

Not exactly, Benchley had said. You'll have to prune it once a year and water it twice a week. The tree now towered over her front lawn, providing luxurious shade when she sat in that very same chair. It was the perfect Benchley story.

People told tales of how Benchley had planted other trees around town, like some white-haired Johnny Appleseed. How they'd called him at odd hours of the day and night with aphid and wilt emergencies. There was the sense of a life well and fully lived and of a person widely beloved.

But we left after thirty minutes. Quaker tradition notwithstanding, Benchley's death had left a gaping hole in my life. I couldn't imagine it without him. And I didn't want to try, not at that moment. I didn't have the Quaker knack for skipping grief. I was nearly overwhelmed by it.

We slipped out the side door, Evelyn nodding sadly at me. Luis caught up with us as we headed for the Volvo. He looked himself again in an elegant navy linen suit and silk tie. He took my hand in both of his, in wordless sympathy.

"Let's meet at the Lightning Burger this afternoon at three, okay?" I said.

"Of course," he said. "Of course. I am terribly sorry, Kit. I know what Benchley meant to you." Those weren't empty words; Luis did know.

Dr. Morrison called soon after we got home. He said he was obliged to report to the Rochambeau PD his suspected diagnosis of a drug overdose. "I'm so puzzled by this, Kit. I called Elston Manor to report the death and the nurse said they could take no responsibility, as Benchley had been removed forcefully and against their wishes. I'm just stunned. Is this so?"

"It's so, Dr. Morrison. Benchley was removed according to his own wishes and my belief that he was in danger."

There was a shocked silence. And then, "Danger? What kind of danger?"

"Well, in particular, danger of a drug overdose. Elston Manor and at least one of the other assisted care facilities in this chain may have a history of overprescribing a drug called Hemavero."

"Kit, this is a very serious charge. Are you suggesting that Benchley's death was induced?" Morrison took a deep breath. "Because if you are, I have to call the police right now."

"You just said you thought Benchley might have suffered from an overdose, didn't you?"

"But it didn't dawn on me that it wasn't accidental," Morrison sputtered. "I . . ."

"I don't know for certain if it was accidental or not, but I mean to find out. Doctor, you know what Benchley meant to me, to the whole town. If you call the police, cops will be swarming all over Elston Manor; everybody will hire a lawyer; we'll never know what happened to Benchley. I think I can find out. I want to." I didn't need Chief Leeming and the Rochambeau PD to come crashing into this case, not at this point. "Can you wait a day or two?" I was begging for time a lot lately.

He considered. "I sent the medical examiner over to the Garden Center yesterday, after the nurse called to report Benchley's death," Morrison said slowly, thinking aloud. "It's routine when old people die at home—the ME stops by, checks for signs of foul play, takes small blood and tissue samples. Avoids the delay and trauma of removing the body or doing an autopsy." He considered some more. "So I suppose I might wait for his findings. Shouldn't be more than a day or so."

I said I would be grateful.

"But we never had this conversation, right? I have no concrete evidence of foul play, just a concern."

"Right. You're clear."

The shocked and unhappy doctor hung up. He knew how

close Benchley and I had been, which was probably the only thing keeping him from dialing 911 then and there.

I wandered around the house awhile, feeling emptiness and sadness in equal parts. Luis was my closest friend now, next to Jane. But I could never drop in at his house unannounced, the way I could pop in on Benchley. I didn't even know where Luis's house was.

I had told myself it would be wrong to work today. But, of course, the case had now become a full-fledged obsession. I had to solve it; it would be wrong *not* to work today.

I went to my office in the American Way. Willie was holed up in his office; I could hear his keyboard clacking. I knocked a couple of times to let him know I was there.

I called the Wellspring Foundation in Connecticut, but got a recording. My telephone CD-ROM supplied a home number for Peter Mackley, the Foundation's attorney, in Southampton, Connecticut. Southampton? That's where Bill Hamilton lived.

That got me focused. Could there be a connection? I buzzed Willie. "Hey, Will. What are you doing?"

"I'm checking through insurance records for Benchley," he said. "Sorry I didn't make it to the funeral, Chief. I'm not good at those things."

"No sweat," I said. "Benchley wasn't into guilt; neither am I." Especially with Willie. Among the few personal things I'd learned about him was that both his parents had been killed in a plane crash and he'd been adopted. Which might explain his aversion to funerals.

"Will, can you get me the name of the lawyer who represented William Hamilton in his court case against Puritan Homes?"

"Sure, hold on," he said. More clacking. Willie held on to everything he'd ever learned in his voluminous electronic files. "Peter Mackley," he said. "M-A-C-K-L-E-Y. Southampton, Connecticut." He gave me the same address and phone number I'd just found myself.

I told the housekeeper who answered the phone that my business was urgent.

A minute later, a gruff, businesslike, and slightly annoyed voice picked up the telephone. "I have only a moment," he barked.

"I'll only take a moment. I understand you're the attorney for the Wellspring Foundation?"

"Yes."

"And also the attorney who handled Bill Hamilton's lawsuit against Transitions, Inc."

A brief pause. "Yes. What's this about?"

"Are you familiar with the bequest Benchley Carrolton of Rochambeau left to the Wellspring Foundation?"

"Yes, I am. I can't discuss the details, of course . . ."

"Most of the details are on the World Wide Web, sir," I said.

He sighed, as if the world was taking turns he didn't like. "I can't say I use computers very frequently. Still, how does this interest you, Mr. . . . ?"

"Deleeuw," I said. "I'm a close friend of Mr. Carrolton. I don't know whether you're aware of this or not, and I'm sorry to be bringing you this news, but Mr. Carrolton passed away yesterday."

"Oh, dear," he said. "I didn't know; I am sorry to hear it. But I still can't talk about his bequests to the Foundation. Is that why you're calling?" There was a marked caution in his voice; he was still waiting to hear what I wanted.

I kept my voice neutral and dispassionate, which was difficult. "I'm calling as a private investigator, Mr. Mackley. I've been retained to investigate the circumstances surrounding Mr. Carrolton's death."

"Is there something out of the ordinary about Mr. Carrolton's death?" I suppose he was thinking, Something that would affect our two million bucks? He added, as an afterthought, "May I ask who retained you?"

"No, sir, I'm afraid not," I said, very politely. "Mr. Carrolton's death is complicated. He left a series of bequests involving the elderly, amounting to several million dollars. And there have been some irregularities . . ."

"Such as?"

"Such as the fact that the drug Hemavero keeps popping up everywhere I go in this case. Sort of a common link. For instance, you're Wellspring's attorney, and Wellspring is getting two million dollars from Mr. Carrolton, who was in Elston Manor, and you also are Mr. Hamilton's attorney, and Mr. Hamilton got an undisclosed sum of money from Puritan Homes, and Hemavero seems rather freely dispensed in both facilities."

Silence for a good five seconds. "Suggesting?"

"Suggesting that perhaps you can help me out here. Whatever is going on, an investigation into Wellspring by the police wouldn't advance the cause of the needy elderly."

"And what precisely would the police be investigating?"

"Hardly matters. You know the media, they're not into nuance. They never give the fact that nothing is going on as much attention as the fact that something might be; don't you agree?"

Mackley cleared his throat and made pompous lawyerly noises. "This sounds very much like a threat to me," he said. "I have nothing further to say. If I read a word of any such investigation in the media I will hold you personally and legally liable. Is that clear?"

I was already talking to a dial tone.

Willie came popping out of his office holding some computer printouts. "Chief," he said. "Score."

"What kind?"

"The National Legal Resource Medical Center Library lists nine lawsuits involving Hemavero in the past year. Every one was settled out of court."

"Names? Details?"

"I'm working on it."

"Willie, can you find out who makes Hemavero?"

"That I know," he said. "It's Mayraud Pharmaceuticals, New York. A French company moving into the U.S. big time."

"Thanks, Willie. Get those details, please. Pronto."

He vanished back into his office and I went down to the mall to meet with Luis.

The Cicchelli's Furniture Store mannequins were already in shorts, sporting tennis rackets, ready to take on springtime in suburbia. I didn't quite get a full look, though. My way was blocked by two burly young men in shiny suits, flashing State Police IDs. Not another Goodell-prompted hassle, I groaned.

"Mr. Deleeuw, you are under arrest," said one, pulling out a pair of handcuffs. I didn't exactly focus on the rights he recited. The mall dwellers were gathering in knots, pointing and murmuring. Murray Grobstein bolted from behind the cash register at Shoe World and headed for Luis and the Lightning Burger.

"What's the charge?" I managed to ask.

"Criminal trespass. Assault. Among other things."

The other cop reached into my jacket pocket and pulled out my PI shield. "We'll be holding this for a while. We're taking you to Rochambeau police headquarters for booking."

seventeen

SITTING IN THE holding cell at Rochambeau police
headquarters, the license that allowed me to work
seized by state authorities, I had ample time to brood.

Not only had I lost my dear friend and emotional anchor, I
was about to lose the new career he'd helped me build. I had no
more careers up my sleeve, other than going to Essex County
Vocational School and taking up TV repair. And if the state
moved on Jane and *her* license, I wouldn't even be able to pay
for the course.

Probably the most frightening part of all this was that I had
actually done all the ghastly things they were undoubtedly about
to accuse me of. I had, in fact, illegally entered Elston Manor.
I'd assaulted a technician, damaged equipment. I'd dragged a
terminally ill person out of a hospital bed without proper medical supervision, and I didn't even want to approach the lurking
nightmare that doing so had contributed to his death. I was open
to criminal prosecution and probably a civil suit as well.

And why had I done all this? Because I thought a confused,
elderly man was sending me an SOS via finger tap. An ambitious

DA or venal plaintiff's lawyer would have fun with that on the stand. Meanwhile, I had learned in recent days that Benchley had entered into an agreement to go to Elston Manor of his own free will, that Goodell's part of the bargain was more than generous. I didn't have a shred of proof that anybody intended to harm Benchley, or had, in fact, harmed him at all. Yet I'd yanked him out of the facility and dragged him home, ignoring the pleas of his doctor to take him to a hospital.

And I expected that somebody who'd done all that was going to keep his PI shield? I'd be lucky to stay out of jail.

On top of which, as the cell door clanked open, here was Rochambeau PD Chief Frank Leeming lumbering in to gloat at my predicament. A beefy man who favored checked sports jackets and shiny black pants, whose demeanor announced that he'd seen it all—and he had, in fact, seen most of it during his years as a Brooklyn cop and precinct commander—Leeming always looked exhausted when he saw me.

I never meant to cause him problems, but my very existence never meant anything but trouble for him. He hated the whole idea of a PI running around in a town like Rochambeau. "Why don't you do what all the other Wall Street losers do, Deleeuw, and go open a bagel store or something?"

Leeming had taken the job here, he was fond of telling me, because he had seen enough of the real world in Brooklyn. With two daughters heading for college, he couldn't exactly retire. But he figured the Rochambeau PD would be the next best thing: a quiet gig where bicycle theft constituted major crime. He thought he could put in five or ten years, pocket a pension, then head for the Florida Keys to fish. Things hadn't turned out that way.

Our first case together was a spectacular murder with links to the town's forgotten past. I had solved it; and he hadn't. Our second case involved a deranged person who liked to shatter families. I'd closed that one, too. Then there was the housewife charged with murdering a high school principal.

I'd lucked out, with the help of the American Way Irregulars.

I got admiring publicity; Leeming got a red face. I wasn't a tenth the cop that he was, but I knew suburban culture from the inside out, while Leeming was something of an alien. Had I been in Brooklyn, I'm sure it would have been just the opposite.

Aside from Luis, Benchley, and Willie, I had the eyes and ears and fine mind of my wife, who, as a shrink, was well wired into the dark side of town. And I could call on an unofficial but devastatingly effective network of coaches, merchants, parents, and teachers who could peek under every rock. I had even formed a unit called the Rochambeau Harpies, a collection of diverse women—careerists, homemakers, den mothers, activists, lesbians, blacks, whites, Pakistanis—who could spit out the intimate lives of every family in town if necessary. Sometimes it was.

My career was launched, and Leeming had had little choice but to put up with me. Now, he might not have to endure me much longer.

He wasn't a mean cop. He just didn't want trouble, and my presence always suggested there would be some.

We had come to a sort of uneasy accommodation, trying to stay out of each other's way. Leeming was fair, but a tough cookie and an old-fashioned stickler for the rules. There was never any doubt whose side he'd be on if I broke the law or screwed up in a major way.

Now, I'd broken a whole bunch of laws. Leeming wouldn't go out of his way to crush me, but he wouldn't throw himself in front of the train either. The State of New Jersey was notoriously touchy when people it had licensed went around slugging people, breaking into buildings, and abducting sick people. I can't say at this point I disagreed.

I felt bereaved, stupid, and vulnerable. Apart from my own career, Evelyn and Willie could lose their jobs. There was a threat hovering over Jane, and we still didn't know if it was connected to my problems or not. We might have to leave Rochambeau. The kids might wind up working their way through vocational school with me.

Leeming sat down on the bench opposite me, clutching a Styrofoam cup of coffee in one hand, offering me one with the other. I recognized the acrid smell of the motor oil that flowed from the Rochambeau PD coffee machine. No amount of sugar or powdered creamer could disguise it. I have to say, it did wake you up.

"Sorry about Benchley," he said. "I know you guys were tight. He was a good man." Benchley had warmed even Leeming's tough heart, donating the bulbs and shrubs and turf that landscaped police headquarters.

He kneaded his forehead with his thumb and forefinger. Pleasantries were over. He was, after all, the law, and I was a lawbreaker.

"Deleeuw, you're in such deep shit I can hardly believe it. You always tended to the reckless side, but this stuff is crazy. It doesn't make any sense. We've got several felony charges here. The state Licensing Office is going to melt your shield down and make Parkway tokens out of it. And I'm sitting here wondering just what the fuck you thought you were doing, busting into a private medical facility, roughing up a nurse—"

"Technician," I corrected.

"Whatever. Then hauling Benchley, a dying stroke victim, out of there? Dragging him home without medical permission? Man, they could hit you with a manslaughter charge. And they just might. So this was the call you made the other night, the one you chickened out on? If I were you, I'd start talking long and loud."

The truth is, I didn't want to talk to him at all. I didn't want the cops stumbling around, spooking everybody, causing files to disappear and medical records to be altered. Whatever evidence there was could already be gone.

And to be candid about it, I didn't totally trust the Rochambeau PD either. Goodell was powerfully connected, and if he was the bad guy here, there would be plenty of reasons why the police would listen to him more than me. The state helped fund local police departments. It bought their equipment, trained their officers, investigated serious crimes.

It wasn't that Leeming was a crook. But he and his superiors had many more reasons to throw the book at me than to rap me on the knuckles. Nobody needed to tell Frank Leeming how the world worked. If he could be a nice guy, he was. If he couldn't be, too bad. I didn't know what role Goodell was playing in all this, but I did know that he was the most powerful politician in the state next to the governor, and that he and his nameless investors had millions tied up in these nursing homes.

But as Leeming glowered at me, as I listened to the depressing sounds of a jailhouse—the clanking, the jeering, the squawking radios—I had to be honest. The real reason I didn't feel like a heart-to-heart was personal, about as personal as you could get.

This case was mine to solve. Benchley had been my friend; he was my responsibility. I wasn't going to let anybody else run this investigation or muck it up. Maybe I was being willful and stubborn, as Jane said I had a tendency to be. But I wasn't inclined to give on this issue. So I told Leeming I wasn't prepared to discuss the charges yet.

Not surprisingly, he exploded. "Deleeuw, you dumb son of a bitch. You're in a world of trouble. You're facing actual jail time. You're sure to get sued. And you can kiss your license goodbye unless you start singing. I told you this was serious work; I told you detecting is for pros, not Wall Street whiz kids. But you got lucky and solved a few cases and then decided you were Sam Spade. Now look what's happened."

"Chief, I appreciate your concern, but I've made up my mind—"

The Chief was launching into another, even angrier rant when he was interrupted by the dignified arrival of Luis, flanked by a jailer and another man I didn't know, a stocky guy in his fifties wearing a rumpled gray suit. Luis was even more elegant than usual in a handsome navy poplin affair, crisp white shirt, and blood-red silk tie. He always looked more like an ambassador than a burger man, but this was a notch higher, a different image. This had to be the look he'd worn when he was Havana's most distinguished criminal lawyer. My guess was, the guy in the gray suit was a local attorney Luis had hired to handle the details, while he directed from behind the scene.

"Kit," said Luis, "you've just made bail."

Leeming stood up and eyed the two newcomers warily. He had encountered Luis on a couple of my past cases and wisely judged him responsible for some of the Rochambeau PD's embarrassments at my hands.

"Mr. Hebron. You've got to talk some sense into your lughead friend. This isn't mischief. We're talking felony charges and loss of license, at a minimum. He's got to talk to me."

Luis smiled and nodded, as if he revered the Chief and was thrilled to see him. "Chief Leeming, I am sure Kit appreciates your concern. I was wondering if I might have a word with him, along with his lawyer, of course, Mr. Bob Gerard."

The Chief softened a bit, sure that an actual lawyer would echo his advice, and turned to me. "Deleeuw, we've had our differences. I know you think I'm pissed because you've shown up the department a couple of times. Believe me, I can live with that. But this is serious. I want you to cooperate. If I have to go out of here and tell the Licensing Office that you're up on all these charges, facing lawsuits, being investigated, and on top of it all, that you're not cooperating, they are going to roast your ass, pal." He turned to Luis and Gerard. "I hope you can get that through his head." He waved disgustedly and walked out of the cell.

"I'll be in my office in the event somebody wants to talk some sense." He paused, then turned back. "And there's another thing, Deleeuw, and I take this personally. I care about the law here. You have no right to play vigilante, which is the only thing I can think of that makes any sense out of your bizarre behavior. If there's something illegal going on, you better bring it to law enforcement." He was almost breathing fire.

Leeming stalked off muttering. Escorted by a cop, Gerard, Luis, and I headed for the conference room where prisoners and their attorneys met to disuss their cases. They'd taken my belt, wallet, and shoes, so I shuffled along behind the dapper Luis in a pair of paper slippers, my pants held up by a narrow strand of what looked like yarn.

The three of us settled around a scarred table. Luis went out for a moment and came back with a Diet Coke. "Mr. Deleeuw," said Gerard. "I assume you're comfortable with my representing you. I am a friend of Luis's from . . . well, let's just say we're friends."

"If you're a friend of Luis, then you're my attorney," I said. "How much trouble am I in?"

"I don't know yet," said Gerard. "You'll be able to leave shortly, once the paperwork's completed. I've been busy in the meantime. I just got off the telephone with Senator Goodell, at Luis's suggestion."

"We didn't discuss your fee," I pointed out. "For that matter, I don't even know who the hell you are."

"Kit, I will speak for him. He is a top criminal lawyer in New York. You may not have heard of Mr. Gerard, but that is probably because he handles matters before they come to public attention."

I got it. A killer behind-the-scenes operative who specialized in triage rather than courtroom theatrics. I allowed myself a breath of hope.

"Then I'm a fortunate man. You've been talking to Goodell?"

Luis twinkled. He was careful never to play lawyer, especially in public places; it could get him in trouble. But he clearly played a role here. "Before Mr. Gerard explains, I have a report. I've just been to see the medical examiner. I know this is a difficult subject for you, Kit, but I'm sure you understand that this is no time for pleasantries. We have a great deal to do."

I nodded.

"Benchley was given an overdose."

I was half expecting that, but gasped anyway. "You mean he was killed?"

"I didn't say that, Kit. I don't know." Luis looked down at the floor. "But Benchley was administered an extremely high dose of Hemavero, at least twice the amount prescribed by the doctor that morning. It damaged his heart, weakened him. Given his stroke, there was nothing to be done. He only had a few hours to live. You not only weren't responsible for his death, you allowed him to die at home. For all we know, you may even have prolonged his life by getting him out of there before they could give him more medication."

I couldn't describe the relief I felt. Luis sensed it, smiling. "You were a good friend to him, Kit." I wiped my eyes. Gerard and Luis looked away for a few minutes, until I got myself under control.

Luis went on. "It appears somebody came into the hospital and either gave him Hemavero by injection or changed the dosage in his IV. There's no way to know when this happened. And I doubt he had any idea how it happened. But," he paused, "Benchley probably knew he was sinking."

I nodded. "From the look in his eyes when I drove him home, he certainly knew. That's why he wouldn't go to the hospital. He brushed off his doctor too. He just wanted to go home, to die at the Garden Center."

"Kit," said Luis, "the Hemavero might have hastened Benchley's death, but he died of heart failure and stroke, the medical examiner said. Benchley's death wasn't caused by Hemavero, even though his blood showed far higher levels of the drug than it should have."

"But I understand the Hemavero can aggravate the symptoms of heart disease and stroke if it's given in high doses. The ME might not be able to tell."

Gerard interrupted. "Well, he thinks he can tell. And he's a doctor, whereas you aren't." He didn't seem the sentimental type, which was probably good for me.

"Kit, I've got to be in New York in an hour, so I'll get to the point," he said. "About my talk with Senator Goodell. Luis called me day before yesterday, so I'd had an opportunity to strategize and prepare." Luis shrugged at my startled look. He was on the phone to a lawyer even before Benchley had died? He must have seen trouble coming. The training of a good lawyer, I suppose.

"Goodell had no choice but to file charges," Gerard went on, "if for no other reason than to protect himself. Not filing charges would send a powerful message under these circumstances. Somebody breaks into your hospital facility, roughs up a technician, causes damage"—here Gerard gave me a what-were-you-drinking look—"and you don't call the police? Why not?"

"So this is a defensive move?"

"Absolutely. Goodell doesn't know what you're up to. He strikes what appears to be a legitimate and mutually beneficial deal with Benchley Carrolton. He puts a lot of money into getting Benchley and some of his friends into the facility, thinking he's got this revered icon as a loss leader . . ." Gerard looked to see if that had offended me. It hadn't; it was an accurate description.

"Plus, Benchley gets to take care of his beloved Quaker Meeting House and know he's providing a nurturing environment for some needy elderly people. Next thing we know, you're nosing around, asking questions, frightening the staff, implying that Benchley is being mistreated. This rattles Goodell, he sends some muscle to test your resolve. You not only hang in there, but you pop up in his front yard." Here Luis looked surprised. "Then you break into an old age home, knock a medical technician on his ass, smash up some equipment, drag a very ill patient out of the place. Am I missing anything pertinent?"

I thought about mentioning Hamilton and the Hemavero lawsuit, plus what Dr. Bennett had told me, but I decided to wait. "A few things, but we can catch up later," I said. "There's a big drug scandal involved in there somewhere. I don't know if Goodell is in on it or not."

"You're referring to the Hemavero stuff?"

Now it was my turn to blink.

"We have computers too, Mr. Deleeuw," he said. "William Hamilton's lawsuit, you mean. And Dr. Bennett's firing?"

I nodded.

"Hamilton?" said Luis, frowning. "Did you say Hamilton?"

"The Connecticut man," I reminded him. "Filed a suit claiming his father was killed by an overdose of Hemavero. Remember?"

Luis nodded, but I could tell something was bothering him.

"Anyway," Gerard said. "I called Senator Goodell, whom I know. We golf together and have the occasional lunch in town. I wouldn't say he's an intimate, but we are acquainted."

Gerard may have been the hardest-headed, most no-nonsense person I had met in years. He was all business, without a wasted word or gesture.

"I told him we were preparing to file a major lawsuit against him and the State of New Jersey, seeking one hundred million in damages for the death of Benchley Carrolton, plus the unlawful and unwarranted harassment of you and your wife . . ."

"Jane . . . I don't know if I want her . . ."

"Please, Mr. Deleeuw," said Gerard, looking at me cooly and firmly. "This is a conversation I had with Senator Goodell; it's not necessarily what's going to happen." Luis held up his hand, then put his forefinger to his lips, a gentle way of telling me to shut up.

"I told him our suit would ask that all facilities owned by Transitions, Inc., be closed and all patients evacuated until investigators could determine the cause of a number of safety and health problems, the most serious of which was the systematic overprescribing of drugs that had led to at least two deaths and probably more. We would also seek forty million in punitive damages for harassment of my client and his family . . ." I whistled, feeling the need to comment in some way.

Gerard had further informed his sometime golf partner that he knew about the Hamilton lawsuit and the Bennett firing, both of which could keep the media busy for weeks. He'd even faxed Goodell some potential headlines: "Jersey Pol Caught Running Death Row for the Elderly." Gerard chuckled for the first time. He'd clearly enjoyed the call.

"You're a *friend* of this guy?" I asked, dumbfounded now.

"It's business," he said. "Nothing personal. Like the Mob. Besides, I owe Luis, big time." What could he possibly owe Luis for? Would I ever know?"

"It goes back a way," said Luis, chuckling too. "A Cuban connection. Let's just say we have been helpful to one another."

"I'm sure Goodell loved this."

"Kit, I don't wish to disclose too much," Luis said, leaning forward. "Just in case we are being monitored. But it is my belief and Bob's—he knows Senator Goodell fairly well—that whatever is happening is not something the senator knows about or is responsible for, at least not directly."

Gerard jumped in. "That's right. I've tangled with this guy. He's a cold-blooded, pragmatic politician. He's not getting any younger, he's not going any higher. He's a reasonable, honest fellow, and he's tired of being broke, especially as his kids head for college. This sort of guy, well, he doesn't have to kill people, do you know what I mean? He's smarter and better situated than that. He has other options."

"Right," I said. "Like building fancy assisted care facilities the boomers won't feel guilty putting their parents in, and using his muscle to make them work."

"Exactly," Gerard said. "There are so many state dollars flowing into those homes already, through various welfare and social service budgets and grants, it would take you years to trace it all. But he runs good places, is the word. Not as good as he'd have you believe, maybe, but quality care. I can't see Goodell as somebody who would, for any reason, countenance any kind of grossly criminal behavior, if that's what you're getting at with your investigation—which, frankly, I'm eager to hear about."

I sipped from my Diet Coke. Luis looked eager to hear as well.

"I'm not positive what I'm getting at. Benchley signaled me very clearly that he was frightened, that he'd seen something."

"He indicated the same thing to me," Luis added. "Even more explicitly. He said it. He said he was frightened, and that he'd overheard people talking about getting rid of patients."

Gerard looked skeptical. "I'm sure nursing home staffs talk about their patients in lots of unflattering, even frightening ways. You change people's bedpans all day, you can come to resent them. So you banter and chatter and mouth off. It isn't uplifting work all the time; the people who do the menial work in these institutions could easily resent their lot in life. I'm not condoning that, just trying to think like a jury."

He didn't say so, but the clear implication was that he was thinking like a juror who might be hearing my case.

"Plus, you're talking about a man—a beloved man, to be sure, but a man who's just suffered a serious stroke and might not be all that clear about what he heard. You are convinced he was frightened, Kit, but that doesn't mean he was clearheaded about what frightened him. See what I mean?"

I saw what he meant.

"So here's what I'm getting around to. I have to be as blunt with you as I was with Goodell. You don't have squat on these people. You have a settled lawsuit, a fired doctor—maybe enough for a state fine. In the doctor's case, Goodell is covered. He unloaded the guy and, bad news for you, he even reported him to the Medical Licensing Board."

Ouch. I grimaced.

"That's right. Which is more than you did, Kit. He went to the state authorities with his problem and did the paperwork. You turned into the Equalizer. Goodell said he did you a favor by not filing charges against that kid you work with too. What's his name, Willie?"

I waited.

"So here's my pitch. What Goodell wants isn't vengeance. Or justice, either. What he wants is for you to go away. He is willing to honor his bargain with Benchley. To give money to the Quaker Meeting, to give those people free medical care, all in Benchley's name. And he's willing to drop all charges against you, right now."

"And all I have to do?"

"Is sign this," said Gerard, putting a piece of paper in front of me. "It says that you will drop this case, go away, never again investigate Transitions, Inc., or generate any unfavorable comment or publicity, and leave Mr. Goodell and his assisted care facilities alone. That means no Web searching, no phone calls, no inquiries or interviews, nothing. If you sign, he will help in any way possible with the Licensing Office inquiry into your investigative ethics."

"I see. And my wife?"

"He denies any involvement in any difficulties she might be having. I believe him; it's not his style. He doesn't need to go after her; he's got you firmly and tightly by the balls."

"Are you recommending that I sign this?"

"I'm not your conscience, Kit. I'm just relaying the deal. You've made bail; you can walk out of here either way. I'll be happy to defend you in court if you choose to slug it out. But I have to tell you, it's hard to imagine an effective defense in this case. In fact, a smart prosecutor could convince a jury you had endangered Benchley Carrolton's life, along with everything else."

I looked at Luis, but he was stone-faced. "Do what you think is best, Kit. You have to live comfortably with yourself."

I wasn't sure that was possible, at least not at the moment. "No deal," I said. "Though I appreciate your efforts. I've got to get out of here. I've got a case to investigate, and a client to represent."

"And that would be?" asked Gerard, startled.

"That would be Benchley Carrolton," I said. "Somebody killed Benchley. I've got to find out who. If I messed up, it was in not getting him out of that place sooner. I'm not going to fail him again."

eighteen

WITH LUIS posting my bond and Gerard glowering at the Chief and muttering about lawsuits, I got dressed, recovered my shoes and belt, and walked out into the parking lot a free man—for now. We agreed that Luis would report back to work at Elston Manor.

I worried a bit that he might be compromised if Goodell or his security people began checking into the staff in the wake of what had happened, but Luis brushed me off. "They don't see immigrants as people," he said. "Not those of us who mop the floors and clean the bedpans. The staff is invisible to them. I'll look in on Benchley's friend, Mrs. Keyes. Then I'll check in with you. I won't leave before we talk."

"Luis," I said, as he turned toward his car. "You looked odd when William Hamilton's name came up in there. Why?"

He hesitated before answering. "I don't like to speculate, Kit. I can get someone excited, especially someone who wants to avenge a lost friend. But Hamilton's name was among those in the visitors' log the night Benchley died."

"He visited Benchley?" I was shocked.

"I don't know. The log shows who enters Elston Manor; it doesn't specify who was being visited. But I believe I've seen that name elsewhere, too, in logs for other days. I'll talk to you later, Kit." He climbed into his big Buick, waved, drove off.

What possible business could William Hamilton have had at Elston Manor? Maybe there was some other Hamilton; it wasn't exactly a rare name.

Frustrated and pissed off and frightened all at once, all I could think to do was to keep moving, keep following the few connections we'd made, keep at it. If I slowed or stopped, grief or fear might overcome me altogether.

I called Jane, who I had insisted skip the jailhouse visit, to tell her I was out, fine, and on the move.

Em answered the phone. Maybe absence had made her heart grow fonder. "Dad, are you okay? Where have you been?" It almost sounded as if she missed me, uncool moron that I was. I felt a stab of guilt. "Mom is driving Ben to basketball. She said to say hello and to wish you luck."

"Thanks, sweetie. I miss you. Maybe next weekend we can do something fun together, okay? Maybe we could go to the zoo; we haven't been there in a while."

"The *zoo*?" I could almost hear her recoil; did I think she was *six* or something? I had blown my big chance.

"Or a movie or something," I tried, treading water. Too late. We said lame goodbyes.

Then I called New Jersey State Police Lieutenant Tagg, a source to whom I'd handed over half a dozen drug rings and who owed me, at least up to the point of not jeopardizing his own ass.

I asked Tagg to meet me at the American Way in three hours. In exchange for the information I thought he'd be interested in, I asked him to bring along the source of the complaint that Jane had overcharged and violated confidentiality. "I'll meet you, Deleeuw," he rumbled. "But this other thing, if it's political, I'm not getting into it. Clear?"

"Clear," I said. I understood the rules. There were some things a cop couldn't do.

I was beginning to spin a pretty big web here. I'd better snare something in it before I was the one who got caught and devoured.

Even with all the information in the world available in minutes via keyboard, what is unchanged for a PI is reliance on feelings, a sense of where to go. However meticulous you are about gathering information, at some point you have to let your instincts take over.

Willie was a brilliant data wrangler; Luis had proved a master strategist. But my own instincts had grown stronger in the past few years, and I was beginning to trust them. When I'd driven Emily and her pals to see the newly rereleased *Star Wars*, thoughtfully sitting many rows away so as to avoid mortifying her, I'd chuckled at some of the clunky costumes, the heavy-handed mythology. But I didn't laugh at the Force.

I drove to the American Way, where I hoped I could sit and think for a few hours, putting together what we knew, casting about for leads. Nobody was there. Willie was working at home. Evelyn had taken the rest of the day off. Benchley's death had hit her hard, too.

I sat in our empty office, looking out at the traffic on Route 6, mulling.

One theme that ran through this whole case was Hemavero, apparently present at every turn. Was that a happenstance—such a drug would naturally be used in facilities for the elderly—or something more?

William Hamilton had turned up in a couple of different contexts. His father had been killed by Hemavero. He'd hired Peter Mackley to sue Transitions, Inc.

"Silly" Bennett had also popped up here and there. He had access to Hemavero, and a motive for hating Goodell and his nursing homes—might he even want to sabotage them?

On impulse, I phoned Information in Connecticut, then placed a call.

"Puritan Homes," said a warm voice.

"Hey there, can you connect me to the nurse's station, please?"

"Certainly, sir."

It took just seconds. "Third floor nursing. Mrs. Canty. Can I help you?"

"Hey, I'm looking for Dr. Stillwell Bennett. Is he around? This is Buzzy, his college roommate—Dr. Buzz Leeming. If he's not saving someone's life, that is."

The nurse laughed. "Well, he might be, but he isn't here. Dr. Bennett isn't on staff."

"What? He told me at a conversation to call him if I ever got to Connecticut. Said the local golf courses were superb!"

"My husband thinks so too. Sorry, Dr. Leeming. Dr. Bennett hasn't been on staff for several months; I believe he has a practice in New Jersey now."

"Are you certain, Mrs. Canty? I believe I talked to him there a few weeks ago."

Her tone got a bit firmer. "I'm quite sure, Doctor. Perhaps you called on a Thursday. Like several other geriatric specialists, he still comes in to check on his patients. He's here on Tuesdays, very early in the morning, and on Thursdays. But he's no longer a staff physician. He left to run his own facility. We gave him quite a going-away party. He was a lot of fun."

I'll bet. I thanked Mrs. Canty and rang off.

So Bennett wasn't just a casual visitor to Puritan Homes. He still had access to patients there.

Just for the hell of it, I called Peter Mackley's home too. Maybe I'd luck out again.

The rattled housekeeper put him right on the line.

"I'm calling from the Morris County Prosecutor's Office in New Jersey, counselor," I said gruffly. "I'm Assistant District Attorney Jimmy Pearson."

"New Jersey?"

"Yes. I'm calling about one of your clients, a Dr. Bennett."

"Stillwell Bennett? Is he in some sort of difficulty?"

"Maybe," I said, enjoying the anxiety in his voice. "I'm just confirming that you are his attorney."

"Who is this? What's this about?"

I cleared my throat, stalling for time. I hadn't planned this far ahead. "Um, there's a question of some outstanding parking violations . . ." I should have done better, but the truth is, that was the only explanation that flew into my head.

"Hold it." The voice on the phone was turning chilly. "What's your name again?"

"Pearson."

"Pearson. Do you think I'm an idiot? You're calling me because Stillwell Bennett forgot about a few parking tickets? And why would a county prosecutor's investigator care about such minutiae anyway?"

"You obviously don't know squat about New Jersey law, counselor," I blustered back. "I don't have to take this crap from some stuffed-shirt attorney, especially from out of state. I've approved a standing warrant. Tell your client that the next time he's pulled over, he'll spend the night in the can, okay? He *is* your client, I believe . . ." He hadn't quite come out and said it, though he couldn't have come much closer.

"Our relationship is none of your business. If he's going to be arrested, then . . . then . . ." Mackley didn't know what to say. I left him sputtering and hung up.

If Bennett actually had any unpaid parking tickets, he'd wet his pants. And that was the least of his problems. Not only had he lied about his connection to Puritan Homes, he had this other strange connection. The attorney representing the man who sued Transitions, Inc., for killing his father with too much Hemavero also, it seemed, represented the doctor fired by that same company for taking kickbacks from the pharmaceutical firm that made the drug.

I didn't know what Mackley's definition of a conflict of interest was, but to my mind, that was a whopper.

As I was considering what this meant, Luis called, his voice taut. "Meet me as soon as possible," he said. "By the back door of Elston Manor. I'm carrying a heavy bundle of computer printouts, from an office I managed to spend some time in. But I can't take them with me when my shift is over; we are observed as we sign out. There's a lot of security outside, so be cautious, Kit."

"What's going on . . ."

"I can't talk now. If you see anything amiss, drive over to the Parkway entrance and wait; I'll try to meet you there. How long will it take you to get here?"

I told him I was about twenty minutes away. "But Luis, I might not be in the Volvo. Look for another car. I'll flash my lights or something."

My ancient station wagon was by now very well known to the Manor's staff and to the Rochambeau PD. It wasn't a car to be inconspicuous in. And I didn't want to draw attention to Willie by borrowing his VW. I needed another vehicle.

I left the office and drove home, put the Volvo in my garage, and scurried over to Harry Philby's house three doors from mine. Harry might have been the model for Ned Flanders on *The Simpsons*. He was sweet, trusting, religious, abstemious. He even said, "Howdy, neighbor," when I walked by with Percentage. He had three children who called me "Mr. Deleeuw" and who never seemed to shout or get dirty. They went to church *en famille* every Sunday, and even appeared to look forward to it.

I'd once caught Philby on his hands and knees, snipping dead blades of grass from his lawn with a tiny scissor-like tool. I'd pictured a horror chamber of cleanliness and order inside.

It was beneath me to dis Harry, who defined Salt of the Earth. I guess I resented how easily he and his family conformed the mainstream of suburban life, and how far I and mine had drifted from it. I rarely walked down the block when Harry and Bess weren't heading out for a backyard barbecue or an athletic awards banquet or something equally heartwarming.

Yet Harry always beamed when he saw me, as if I was the one person in the world he had been waiting to cross paths with. Over the years, he'd genially offered me every conceivable good service, from baby-sitting to mowing my lawn when I was away to lending me his tools, his car, his grill. I had never taken him up on any of it, but this was his night to do a good turn for society.

Tonight, with the Philby house lit up like a cruise ship, the whole gang was probably playing Monopoly. I had a lengthy emergency list on my refrigerator from Harry, including the location (with map) of the birdbath in his backyard under which his house keys were hidden and the third flagstone of his front walk under which he stashed his spare car keys.

His Mazda was, blessedly, parked out front. I hoped Harry wasn't planning to go out; I didn't need a stolen car report filed. But family togetherness would probably keep him at home, at least long enough for my purposes.

I unearthed the keys, opened the Mazda's front door, released the parking brake, and pushed it down a few yards before jumping in and driving off. My first car theft. I'd be careful. I'd stay under the speed limit and avoid wheelies and, if things went according to plan, be back in a half hour.

Security had clearly increased at Elston Manor. Two police cars and a private security van were arrayed along the building entrance. I didn't even slow. I swung around in a wide two-block arc and came up behind the building, by the tall fence that bounded the deserted yard. There were no cop cars back here. No need, I thought, remembering the sensors sunk in the lawn.

I flashed my lights as I drove up, then slowed, noticing shadows off to my right. I couldn't imagine how Luis planned to get past this fence—it was a good eight feet high, and I didn't see a gate.

I saw a light or two pop on inside the building and wondered if flashing my lights had been a smart idea. Behind me the Parkway hummed and roared, inviting in its anonymity. Up ahead, I saw a car cruising around the other end of the block.

Then the shadows moved, and suddenly the lawn was lit up like noon. Sirens sounded, lights flashed; Luis had tripped the sensors. He hurled a canvas satchel over the fence. Then I watched, amazed, as Luis clambered swiftly up the chain link like a cat, pausing at the top to swivel his leg cleanly over the barbed wire coils, and vaulted like a gymnast to the other side. On the way down, he managed to grip the fence to slow his fall, then drop to the ground with astonishing agility. Luis was trim and fit for a middle-aged man, but this was commando stuff, not usually in the repertoire of fast-food managers.

As he sprinted for the car, I heard shouts from the rear of Elston Manor. The car coming down the block suddenly came alive, its dome lights flashing, its engine gunning. Luis bounded to the passenger door and leaped inside. I hit the gas.

The police car was racing right at me. I swerved to the left, as if I was going to make a U-turn; the cops sped up in pursuit. Then I jammed the accelerator and shot off to the right, rushing toward the police. The driver sped past me—his only other choice was to plow headlong into me. Luis gripped the door handle with one hand and the dashboard with the other. I hoped he was praying; I was.

In my rearview mirror I saw another police car, lights flashing, rush up behind me. I shot ahead, swerved to the right, and shuttled down a narrow alley. The car behind me couldn't turn quite as tightly as Harry's Mazda. By the time he could back up and straighten out, I was zipping down a side street two blocks away.

I didn't dare head for the Parkway; the entrance was too easy to block off. So I drove to Broad and cruised into Rochambeau on local streets. It didn't even strike me as particularly odd that I was eluding the police. I was already in trouble up to my neck.

I had never taken chances like this before. But then, I'd never been this obsessed by a case.

"My Lord," said Luis after a few minutes. "That was some driving, Kit."

"And that was some climbing. Anything you want to tell me?"

He patted his brow with a cotton hankie. For the first time, I noticed that he was clutching the satchel he'd tossed over the fence. "How do you think I left Cuba, Kit? I was persona non grata. And Fidel didn't call me a taxi."

We glanced at each other. I'd learned more about Luis's past this week than he'd told me in five years. So in addition to being a lawyer, he had some sort of political history, as I'd suspected. Maybe in another five years, I'd know what it was.

"Mrs. Keyes?"

Luis shook his head. "I'm so sorry, Kit. She passed away a few hours ago. I was in her room. She seemed unwell; her pulse was faint. I was thinking how I might rescue her with all these private guards around when a nurse came in. Perhaps she was responding to an alarm from the monitor."

"Did the nurse report you to security?" God, I thought, I didn't want Luis facing charges too.

"No, Kit," he said. "She stopped and looked at me. Her name is Rosalita. I'd spoken with her a few times in the last few days; she is also from Cuba, more recently than I. She said to me, 'You're not really a janitor, are you?'

"I said no. I said I couldn't say who I was but I was a friend of Benchley Carrolton, and he'd asked me to look after Mrs. Keyes. I told her I feared something terrible might be happening in Elston Manor. She nodded, said she thought so, too. I said I was there to do good, not harm.

"Mrs. Keyes was breathing heavily right next to us; she opened her eyes once, smiled at us, then closed them again. She didn't speak. I saw the lines on the monitor go flat. Rosalita turned off the machine and took Mrs. Keyes's hand. It was a beautiful moment at a strange time, Kit. Rosalita knelt down and prayed for the woman; I prayed with her. Afterward, I told her I might need her help. She said she badly needed this job, but yes, she would try to help if she could. That the Lord Jesus would take care of her if she told the truth. I said the Lord Jesus had always taken care of me as well."

We rode in silence for a few blocks. There was nothing in the rear mirror to suggest anybody was following me.

I liked Harry's peppy little Mazda. It moved a lot more smartly than my creaky Volvo, and I was grateful I hadn't plowed it into a police car.

With just a bit of luck, we'd have it back where it belonged in a few minutes. I called Willie and told him to meet me at the American Way. If I wasn't there in half an hour, he should call Bob Gerard, my new lawyer.

"Dare I ask what you're doing, Chief?"

"No," I said. If Willie wasn't in the loop, he couldn't get into trouble.

"Well, be careful. I thought you were the mild-mannered professor when I sighed up. Now I see you're Steven Seagal."

Steven Seagal, that was rich. If I was really an action hero, I would have burst right through the walls of Elston Manor the first night and gotten my buddy out.

"Kit, these documents are crucial. Let's hide them for a while. Just in case."

It was a good idea. I stopped at Rochambeau Municipal Park. We both looked around. A man was walking a collie along one path, and we waited for him to drift away. Then Luis ran off into the shrubbery and vanished for a second.

"I put the satchel in a thick azalea to the right of the World War I statue," he said when he returned. "If we get stopped, they'll have no proof of anything."

"And if that nurse stays quiet, the only thing they have on you is leaving ahead of your shift."

"Yes. Although I fear my days of working in health care are ended. I never even got my first paycheck."

Back on my block, Harry's house looked exactly as I'd left it. I'd only been gone half an hour; if he hadn't looked, he would have no reason even to notice that the car was missing. But overnight street parking was illegal in our town; at some point, Harry would have to come out to move his car into the garage. With luck, that was hours away. Right about now, Harry was probably putting his third house on Park Place.

I flicked off the lights, glided the car to a stop, turned off the engine. Luis and I tiptoed out like cat burglars moving down the block. I thought Luis might want to change at my house; maybe even say hello to my family, if they were home. But halfway there, I saw three police cars. Even in the dark, I recognized the markings—two Clifton patrol cars, one from Rochambeau, pulling over in front of Philby's.

"They must have gotten the plates," said Luis. We ducked into my garage and hopped into the Volvo. As we drove away, none of the cops even glancing in our direction, I saw five or six uniformed officers converge on the Philbys'. They'd never have another Monopoly game like this one.

I felt bad, I did. But Harry had plenty of alibis—his whole sweet brood—and would emerge with some rich stories to tell in church the next Sunday. I'd never meant to cause him embarrassment, but the truth was, it couldn't have happened to a nicer guy.

"What are they doing?" asked Luis, wondering for the first time about the Mazda.

"You don't want to know," I said.

Thinking how wise Luis was to have hidden the printouts, we drove back to Rochambeau Park, now completely deserted. Past 9 P.M., nobody walked in the park except kids swapping six-packs and joints.

I saw in the Volvo with the lights on and the engine idling, as Luis went to retrieve his loot. Suddenly, I heard running sounds. In a flash, Luis was back yelling, "Kit, go! Go!" He didn't have the canvas bag with him.

I lurched away from the curb, flabbergasted. This *was* getting to be a Steven Seagal sort of evening. I was not enjoying it.

"Down, Kit!" Luis shouted suddenly, grabbing me by the hair and pulling me sideways on the seat. I heard a pop or two behind me, and my side-view mirror on the driver's side exploded. The car continued to race forward; I popped my head up and swerved, steering without thinking, turning up one block, down another.

"Jesus," I said. "Were they shooting at us? You okay? Am *I* okay?" Neither of us had been hit, but the mirror casing had been shot right off the car.

Luis shook his head and crossed himself. I sped toward Route 6 and the mall.

Once safely in traffic, I could breathe again. "What happened?" I asked. "This has turned into a shooting war."

Luis looked grimmer than I could even remember seeing him. "It becomes a shooting war when the stakes get high," he said.

"What about the bag you hid?"

"I had left a string—three shoelaces I'd tied together, from the uniform closet at the Manor—across the front of the bush where I hid the documents. When I saw it on the ground, I turned back. And I heard somebody running after me. We were evidently followed before . . ."

"I looked in the mirror, Luis; I didn't see anybody."

Luis smiled. "You don't see professionals, Kit. So they didn't get us, but they obviously got the printouts. I wonder if Rosalita . . ." He left the thought unspoken.

"If she turned you in?"

"Not exactly. I gave Rosalita a few of the more important papers and asked her to fax them to you from the office. About twenty pages, I believe. If she's honest, and lucky, she's done that. If she's not . . ."

"Or they might be on to her, too . . ." I interrupted. He nodded.

I called Willie at the mall; he picked up on the second ring.

"He says the fax machine has been spewing," I reported. Luis breathed deeply.

My hands were shaking on the steering wheel. Watching my mirror get blown away, knowing that but for a few feet, it could have been my head or Luis's, tended toward the unsettling.

And there was something else on my mind. "Luis? Were you really a lawyer?"

"Of course. Why?"

"You know how to do some scary stuff."

"I've been trained to do some scary stuff," he said quietly.

"That's all you're going to say?"

"That's all I can say," he replied. "Others depend on my discretion."

I nodded. I could be discreet, too.

Harry Philby right about now was being grilled by Chief Leeming, who was no dummy and would shortly determine that Philby was my neighbor and would put it all together. But that was a far cry from proving any lawbreaking. By the time he could do that, perhaps we'd know who'd done what to whom.

I leaned over and squeezed Luis on the shoulder. He patted my hand. The sign that announced the American Way gleamed ahead of us in the darkness.

nineteen

SATURDAY NIGHT was a twilight time at the Amway. Since we didn't boast a movie multiplex, people who shopped on Saturday night tended to come with kids and to come early. By mid-evening, we were down to a few teenagers who would soon be shooed away by mall security.

Luis and I had calmed down. Actually, *I* had calmed down. This was a lot of action for me, a long way from tracking Deadbeat Dads. Luis already seemed at ease, if a bit grimmer than usual.

He was right; people shot at you when something big was at stake. But if they'd really wanted to kill us, we'd probably have lost more than a rearview mirror. Either they were serious but they weren't pros, or they were pros who had decided to let us live.

But we had to be getting close. The trick was to stay alive and out of jail long enough to figure out who They were.

Who was the bad guy, or combination of bad guys? Goodell had millions at stake. If he was tainted or his homes tarnished by any serious scandal, his lucrative sale would fall apart. But politicians like Goodell didn't have to shoot people to succeed, as Gerard had pointed out. They had other, safer ways.

I had a hard time seeing Silly Bennett as a criminal mastermind. He was a pathetic drunk, trying to squeeze money out of a ratty nursing home.

Mackley definitely was connected to this, and he would hardly be the first lawyer to play one end against the other. But I doubted he'd been cruising Rochambeau with a shotgun, or dirtied his hands by hiring thugs who had. Nor did Bill Hamilton, the smug and prissy squash player, have the stomach for something like this.

Nurse O'Brien? Plenty mean and smart, but not powerful enough.

I was looking for somebody who took a broad view of aging, geriatric medicine, boomer guilt and anxiety. But what was the scam? Selling Hemavero? Or something else?

Plain James, our transplanted transvestite buddy, was sitting by his CD cart, headphones on, eyes closed, lost no doubt in some R&B memories. I decided not to bother him. James was in his Saturday-in-the-city finery: a flowing blond wig, purple velour dress, glitter-spiked heels. He'd be back Monday with deliciously decadent tales to share over coffee at the Lightning Burger.

Luis waved to his employees, who seemed startled to see him in his janitor's jumpsuit. Luis had lost a touch of his gracious veneer. He walked purposefully. I could tell he was furious. Enraged about Benchley. Angry about Mrs. Keyes. Seething at whoever shot at us.

I supposed he'd been involved in some heavy-duty political operations in Cuba. How else to explain such feats as barbed-wire fence-hopping, strung-together shoelaces, and coolly adept bullet-dodging? Might he have been involved in the Bay of Pigs? Or was he too young? Would I ever know?

We walked past Murray Grobstein's Shoe World, where the special of the week, helium-powered rocket sneaks, were reduced to just $90—lucky parents. We laughed and took the stairs up.

I was surprised to see Evelyn sitting purposefully at her desk, her gray bun swept up at the back of her head, her buttoned-up blouse giving her a formal, schoolmarm air. She gave Luis and me appraising stares. "Willie's in his office," she said. "I'm working this case, too, until whoever harmed Benchley is caught. I won't be shoved into the background. I can be useful."

"I'm glad you're here," I said. No way I was going to argue with Evelyn. Although somewhere around seventy, she was energetic, tough, too determined to be stopped.

Willie wafted out in a Wallflowers T-shirt, jeans, and decaying sneakers, looking drawn. He must've been at the keyboard for hours.

He was carrying faxes, which he added to those already on Evelyn's desk. "I'm sorry, Kit; this fax transmission is so poor. Can't read much of it. What's up with you?"

That wasn't good news. "Not much except we got chased by cop cars and shot at by who-knows-who."

Evelyn's eyebrows rose at that.

"If the Rochambeau PD calls here, tell them I went out of town. Keep them away if you can, okay?"

Evelyn looked uncomfortable—she hated being asked to lie— but she nodded. "We've been busy too," she said.

Luis went downstairs and returned in a few minutes with cups of strong, black coffee for everyone. We pulled out chairs and sat down to confer.

"What do these documents that we can't read show?"

"They show purchase orders for a significant amount of Hemavero," Luis said. "And they also include visitors' logs, showing regular visits by both Peter Mackley and William Hamilton."

Hmmm. "Hamilton may be the person Benchley heard talking shortly after he first entered Elston Manor," Luis went on. "The one who spoke of people being glad to get rid of burdens. We can't prove that, of course, but the logs show that he was there the day Benchley arrived. Why would Hamilton have driven here from Connecticut? He had no family in Elston Manor. These logs also recorded regular visits by Dr. Bennett. I counted nine visits from Dr. Bennett in the past three months. And five visits from Mr. Mackley. On different days, with Mackley always shortly before Bennett."

Willie shuffled through some papers. "There's lots of money in these drugs, Chief. That's our strongest motive so far." I nodded vaguely. I could think of another, but it was too horrifying and far out for me to even raise. It wasn't possible, not in the '90s, not in New Jersey. I shook it off.

Odd that Bennett was still around. I would have imagined he'd stay well away, yet he hadn't entered surreptitiously. Maybe kickbacks weren't considered germaine to medical practice. Maybe he had a right to keep visiting his patients. Maybe Goodell didn't give a shit.

And what was Mackley doing there at all? He didn't have any business at Elston Manor that I knew of.

Willie ahemmed. "Kit, Evelyn and I have been studying death certificates in the counties where Transitions has facilities. Puritan and Elston Manor show up in twenty-two deaths in the last six months, which I don't think is unusual. Eight give cancer as the cause of death, three from pneumonia, the rest heart failure and strokes. I went on a geriatrics medical conference and asked some of the docs if these figures were out of order. I said I was working on a research project for medical school. They all said there were no red flags. One doc said, people go there to die; the only question is when and why."

We all sipped our coffee and looked at each other. What to do with all this information?

I asked Willie to go wake up Plain James and ask him to come join us. Everybody blinked. James had popped in to say hello now and again, but nobody in the room seemed to have a clue as to why I would bring him into this.

Three minutes later, James, resplendent in his Saturday glamour gear, sauntered in. He was a knockout as a woman; I wondered what he looked like as a man.

Looking puzzled, James sat down on the edge of Evelyn's desk, crossing his long legs. He nodded at everybody, tossed his long blond wig, waited.

"Evelyn, how old are you?" I asked.

"Sixty-eight," she said. Evelyn was formidable; she took no guff from anybody. In addition to organizing the chaotic nightmare that was my office, she'd even worked on one or two cases— there was no better undercover operative than an elderly woman with a bun—and pestered me constantly to do more. I was ready to give her a chance.

Before I could elaborate, Lieutenant Tagg knocked once, loudly, and walked in. His eyes lighted on Plain James, then on me. "This is important, right?"

"Right," I said. "Let me explain what I have in mind. It involves our friend Plain James here, a fresh face in this drama. It involves Evelyn, if she's game. It involves a major case for the New Jersey State Police, one that could garner tons of publicity for you and your worthy colleagues. And it involves justice for the killers of Benchley Carrolton. It might even save some lives, though I'm not really sure."

Tagg took a coffee cup from the tray, and leaned against the bookcase. "You've got my attention, Deleeuw. Though I'm not completely comfortable doing business with somebody who doesn't even have a license to practice."

"I'm not practicing, just hatching a plan," I said. "If you like it, I hope you'll call Chief Leeming and brief him on your idea . . ." I saw Luis grin at this ". . . and help me execute it. Making use of some equipment you might be able to borrow from your world-famous laboratory in Trenton."

My colleagues were looking at me oddly—this was the first they'd heard of any plan. But then, it had only occurred to me in the past half hour. There was really only one way to figure out what was going on in these facilities, what had happened to Benchley; I think I knew what that way was.

"Evelyn, I'm sorry to speak of personal things, but you have a heart condition, am I right?"

"I'm on medication, yes. And I have high blood pressure."

"Good. Okay. James, nobody involved in this case has ever seen you. And the fact that you're . . . let's say flamboyant . . . can help us here. Nobody would confuse you with the police, know what I mean?"

He laughed, tossed an amused glance at Tagg—who was goggle-eyed—and agreed. "I know what you mean."

"Thanks to Luis's undercover work, we have connected several people to trouble at Elston Manor, and perhaps elsewhere. We have a bead on a lawyer, a crooked doctor, and a troubled son who made money on his father's death. Benchley tipped us off that something was wrong, but he couldn't tell us what; perhaps he didn't really know. But he clearly sensed something was wrong. So do we; tonight, somebody shot at Luis and me."

Tagg leaned forward at this. "Was this reported?"

"No," I said. "And it's not going to be, unless someone else saw it."

"Deleeuw," he said, "this puts me in a strange position."

"We're all in strange positions, Lieutenant. But I think I've got a way of breaking this. We have less than a day to get ready. A few hours for you to get some equipment here and teach us how to use it. A morning for James, if he's willing to participate, and Evelyn, if she is, to rehearse. To learn about acting infirm. To learn how to impersonate James's aging and disoriented aunt."

Jaws were dropping all over the room, but I could see Luis got the drift right away. "Can you drool?" he asked Evelyn mischievously.

I called Jane and told her she wouldn't see me until Monday at the earliest. "But when you do, I hope to hand you Benchley's killer on a platter. Love to the kids."

"Hey, Emily even says she misses you," she reported.

"Great, let her tell me herself."

There was a brief consultation. "Forget it," Jane said. "Em

says no chance. As for Ben, he's too immersed in the NBA play-offs to speak to anyone."

"What about you?"

"I love you and miss you. But I have ten reports to write, and I want to get them written before they yank my license." She sounded breezy, but I knew better.

"Sweetie, I'm going to nail this thing down. And the part of it that involves you as well. I want you to trust me."

"I do, Kit. But don't go making promises you might not be able to keep, okay? We don't know if your troubles and mine are even related. And it sounds like you've got your plate full. This is the toughest thing you've ever been through. I want you to know that I'm fine, the kids are fine. We'll get through. If we have to move to Maine and make beeswax candles, we'll do it. Your whole life is not in their hands."

I wasn't sure this was true, but let it pass. "I'm hitting the mattresses here tonight, honey," I said. "We had some trouble earlier . . ."

Silence.

"I can't go into it now. But I want you to button up the house pretty tight, okay? I need to hole up here."

"Would this trouble have anything to do with Harry Philby?"

"Come again?"

"I just wondered if the trouble was related to a whole flock of cops showing up tonight and hauling him off in handcuffs. All the Philbys were hysterical. It brought the whole neighborhood out. Something about his almost ramming a police car, or something crazy like that. It happened up in Clifton."

"In Clifton?"

"Yeah, Kit, right near that nursing home you're investigating."

"Imagine that."

"And this trouble wouldn't have anything to do with reports of shots being fired in Rochambeau Park? Two of the cops were talking about it at the Philbys'."

I whistled. "Shots being fired in Rochambeau? What are the suburbs coming to?"

"Oh, Kit, are you okay?"

"Yes."

"Promise?"

I promised, and we said goodbye.

More coffee arrived from the Lightning Burger. As I outlined my plan, every face in front of me registered either shock or anguish.

Tagg called Leeming. Evelyn went home to rest. Plain James went to his apartment for the clothes he would need. Luis said he wanted to stop in Jersey City to freshen up.

Willie and I were poring over the documents Rosalita had faxed; they stopped abruptly after page 16. Luis said he might stop by her apartment, not far from his, to make sure she was okay.

"Leeming is furious," Tagg reported. "He'll go along with the plan only because he doesn't have much choice. As a state cop I supersede him. But he wants to kill you. Something about setting up some schmuck who lives on your block, and trying to kill some Clifton cop. Deleeuw, what the fuck is going on?"

I snorted. Why get into it all? "The Chief must've sustained brain damage back in Brooklyn. I was with Luis all night having dinner."

"That's true, Lieutenant," Luis put in. "We were eating at a Cuban restaurant on Poplar Avenue in Jersey City. One of my favorite places. If you have any questions, call Hector. He is the manager there on weekends. He will be happy to confirm our presence."

Tagg smiled briefly, but he turned to me with a look of something close to genuine concern. "You should have come to me sooner, Deleeuw. I don't know if anybody can save you now. The Clifton PD and Leeming are hot on your ass, and you've given the state folks a dozen reasons more than they need to yank your shield. It's not like the old days, you know. I can't pull strings. I just want to prepare you."

I nodded. "I appreciate your candor. I guess this means you can't enlighten me on that other matter, then. These supposed allegations about my wife the shrink?"

"I'm working on it," he said, sounding glum. Perhaps he missed the old days himself.

So. We'd meet at 8 A.M. We'd plan and rehearse all morning, meet with the State Police technicians at noon. Then at 2 P.M. Operation Benchley, as Luis called it, would be under way. It might very well be my last, now that I'd broken all the rules.

Luis left for home. Willie went into his lair to sleep. I tried to sleep on the couch in the waiting room, my knees up against my chin.

An hour later, I was still listening to the trucks heading west on Route 6, bound for Pennsylvania and New York. At night they rode by in a steady hum, almost a reassuring sound. There was something surreal about sleeping, or trying to, in an invisible alcove above a mall alongside a busy Jersey highway.

All I could really think of was Benchley. And my faltering dad. And of Elizabeth Keyes, dying alone in a room at Elston Manor with two strangers praying for her. If watching people get old was this rough, what would aging itself be like?

twenty

LYING AWAKE through the night, staring at the ceiling, listening to trucks and thinking of Benchley, I understood that this wasn't really a plan. It was a giant crapshoot, with my career, my reputation, and my family's financial security riding on the outcome.

Were it not for Benchley, I can't imagine behaving so recklessly or betting so much on a single case. But there would be no peace, no normalcy, until I had dealt with this.

Chief Leeming was the first of our commandos to arrive in the morning. He was on board but, as Tagg had warned, angrily and reluctantly. Leeming took his police duties seriously, and he knew I had been involved in eluding and nearly ramming police cars, setting my neighbor up, even some gunplay.

We both knew the rules: He would help me so long as I didn't cross the line. I had not only crossed it, but obliterated it. Only the chilling implications of my theory about what was going on at Elston Manor had caused him to put his fury on hold.

"But Deleeuw," he told me as his crew trickled in, "however this turns out, the state will have your ass, and I'll get the rest.

Start thinking about finding other work, after you've served your sentence."

Okay. I knew it wasn't personal, and I knew he meant every word. I had committed crimes on his turf, brought trouble, even gunfire into his kingdom.

I did manage to elicit from the Chief the happy news that Harry Philby had spent only a couple of hours at police headquarters. But poor Harry was utterly flummoxed by the whole affair. When this was over, assuming I was still a free man, I'd stop by and straighten things out with him.

There was lots to do first, though. I was scared to death. We had assembled a sophisticated police operation. Two FBI agents were present as observers, since the case could potentially cross state lines, but for now, Tagg was hanging on to jurisdictional control like a bulldog.

At noon, the state and federal lab technicians arrived at my office. Since none of the adjacent offices were open on Sunday, we had converted the hallway into a work area. A startling number of men and women piled in, carrying cases of equipment. Meanwhile, scout teams had quickly located and encamped in an empty apartment two blocks from Elston Manor. We'd move our command post there at 2 P.M.

Evelyn looked brave and purposeful. For a sixty-eight-year-old woman who, just a few years back, had been filing cards in the pre-Internet days of the Rochambeau Public Library, this was quite a scene. She was in a bathrobe, female techs wiring her with a tiny earpiece. Since she would be checking into Elston Manor as a patient, she couldn't conceal a wire anywhere else, but Luis said that residents kept their hearing aids.

"It feels strange," she told the tech. "I can't hear anything in it."

"You're not supposed to," the policewoman answered. "It's a microphone with a range of a quarter mile. We'll be hearing what *you're* hearing, and saying."

Plain James, dressed in a somber navy blue suit and low heels, his wig a more businesslike brunette than he usually favored, arrived breathlessly. Three technicians swarmed over him, and he shrieked in mock outrage as they began unbuttoning his blouse.

"Don't be surprised, my dears," he yelped. "You might not find what you expect!"

But the techs had been briefed about James and, in any case, didn't seem the excitable sort.

"How did it go?" I asked, as Tagg and Leeming listened.

"Great, I think," James said, beaming. "This is *very* exciting. Just when I thought I'd spend the rest of my life selling rhythm and blues to uncaring suburbanites in northern New Jersey, this has given me a whole new lease on life. Kit, you *have* to promise me that I'll get to work on other cases. Promise?"

"Let's just see how things go with your debut," I said. It actually wasn't a bad idea.

"So here's what happened," he recounted, enjoying our attention. "I went home like you said. I called Elston Manor this morning and said I had a great-aunt living with me who I just couldn't care for any longer. That I was driven to distraction by the burden. I said she had some insurance that would cover nursing care, at least for a time. They said I'd have to meet with Mary O'Brien, the head nurse, and she wouldn't be in until Monday. Just like you told me, Kit, I said my Great-Aunt Evelyn had lost consciousness and was drifting in and out of reality for the umpteenth time, and I was going mad."

James paused and asked for a drink, and then theatrically resumed. He was loving this. "Did they peg you as a cross-dresser?" I asked. I'd asked James to be obvious.

"Oh, I swished right over the phone," he said. "They pegged me as unsavory and strange, at the least. A natural role for me." He laughed.

"So I told them I'd either go to an assisted care facility or to a hospital emergency room, because I was at my wit's end. I said I'd seen ads for Elston Manor and driven by, that it looked great and I had to make a decision because this was so very, very *painful* for me. I couldn't care for Evelyn anymore. She'd been with me for two years, and I was losing my sanity. So they called me back and said Ms. O'Brien could meet me this afternoon, since it was an emergency.

"Then Ms. O'Brien called me—which was a surprise—and said there were complex legal ramifications involved. I told her I was on the edge, and just about broke, and she said she understood; that's why Elston Manor was there. Did I have an attorney? I said no. You thought they'd ask me at the nursing home, Kit, but she didn't seem willing to wait. I said I'd be ever so grateful if she could refer me to someone. She gave me a name— Peter Mackley—and said he lived in Connecticut but was licensed to practice in New Jersey and could come down this afternoon if I needed him. I said I'd think about it, and then rushed in here. Did I do it right, Kit?"

"You did great," said Tagg. "Here, let's get James wired up and on a telephone right away."

Five minutes later, tape machines twirling, James dialed Mackley's number. He was so histrionic as to be nearly over the top; he sounded like Nathan Lane in *The Birdcage*. But that was his role; I'd wanted him to sound outrageous and desperate.

Mackley had clearly been waiting for his call. "Nurse O'Brien told me about your aunt," Mackley said without preamble or warmth. "Can I be of service?"

"She said you could help me with the legal arrangements," James said, dithering wildly. "Oh, Mr. Mackley, I just can't do this any longer. I'm broke and exhausted . . ."

"I understand," Mackley said. "You're not alone. Tell me, what are the insurance arrangements?"

"Oh, I've read the policy so often I know it by heart," James keened. "She has ninety days of nursing home benefits, just three months. That's why I've waited this long, because she has a terrible heart and I've saved the care for what seems to be the end, but . . ."

"And she has a life insurance policy?" Mackley interrupted.

"Yes, three hundred thousand dollars. I'm the beneficiary."

"I see." He sounded as though he was making calculations.

"I'm at my wit's end," repeated James. "I love my aunt, but I love the person she was, not this, this . . ." I waved to him to cool down a bit. James was not having trouble with the spotlight. He took a breath. "Having Aunt Evelyn living with me—the rest of my family has all passed—has been a terrible strain. It's ruined me financially," James went on. "To be honest with you, your being my lawyer and all, I am not an entirely conventional person . . ."

"That's of no consequence," said Mackley, not wishing to delve much further.

"But my point," said James, "is that I don't have a lot of money to pay you."

"That's all right," Mackley said. "You don't have to pay anything at this point."

"Nothing?" James gasped.

"Not now. I am expensive, as I'll explain, but we should have this conversation in person. I can help you, but let's sit down face-to-face. I'll bring an associate along, Mr. Hamilton."

Mackley agreed to meet James at Elston Manor at three. He was due to bring Aunt Evelyn in at two.

If James was relishing his role, Evelyn was even more enthusiastic. She practiced letting her head loll, ignoring questions, slurring her words. She had snipped and snarled her steely hair so that it looked unkempt. Her clothes had been carefully stained. When she slumped back in her chair, she looked at death's door.

Maybe it was time to expand Deleeuw Investigations and bring Evelyn and James into our little band—if Deleeuw Investigations survived the next twenty-four hours.

Tagg called me aside and handed me a slip of paper. "I ran a check on the complainant against your wife," he said. "Someone who's had some minor brushes with the law. Here's her name and address; that's all I can do. You can check her out. No intimidation of any sort, though, or I'll bust you myself."

I thanked Tagg and stuffed the paper in my pocket without even looking at it. The complainant would have to wait.

At one-thirty we were ready: Tagg, four State Police detectives, a pair of federal agents, Leeming and a small flotilla of uniformed officers from the Rochambeau PD, James, Evelyn, Luis, Willie, the technicians, and me. We piled into four dark vans. Behind us, a yellow school bus carried State Police SWAT team members, maybe twenty of them.

"They'll be nearby," Tagg said, noticing my gaze. "Unlike you amateurs, our motto is be prepared. Fewer screwups that way."

Had I set all this in motion? I swallowed hard.

It took us twenty minutes to get to Clifton. A detective stood waiting by the open back door of a three-story wood frame house. We all marched up the back stairs, except for James and Evelyn, who got into a small blue Geo—James's car, I gathered. The techs fussed with their gear—Evelyn had the earpiece, James was wired around his groin and chest. Then the technicians climbed into the van, which was one listening post. The other was upstairs in the two-bedroom apartment, empty except for some tables and chairs the state cops had set up.

The troopers knew what they were doing. The bay window in front of the apartment was angled so that if you looked to the right, you had a clear view of Elston Manor's entrance two blocks away. But nobody from the Manor could see into the apartment, or would even think to try.

I trailed along behind the bustling Tagg, who went back downstairs. Leeming was testing the earphones along with Luis, who seemed to know a lot about gear like this. Willie had set up his wireless-modem-equipped laptop and was sniffing around somewhere on the Web. He kept a pair of binoculars nearby as well.

Somebody had hooked up a TV monitor that showed the Elston Manor entrance and security gate. The two federal agents, who had barely said a word, made calls on their cell phones.

Out back, I leaned over the Geo and shook James's hand. "You don't have to do this, James," I said. "It could be dangerous. Somebody shot at Luis and me the other night . . ."

"That's the third time you've told me that, Kit. I get it, I get it," he said. "This is wild. I wouldn't miss it." He paused and looked me in the eye. He had poured on the makeup—the eyeliner was a good half-inch wide—for what he clearly saw as a command performance.

"Here's a chance for me to help out you folks who were helpful to me. Lots of people don't care to inconvenience themselves for some trash-and-flash transvestite," he said firmly. "A chance to help nab bad guys who are preying on helpless old people. I get to be a hero for once. So we don't need to talk about this anymore, okay?" he said. "I'm here because I want to be."

Right. I leaned over toward Evelyn, who was limp in the backseat, "getting into character," as she put it. I didn't even get to clear my throat. "Don't even bother to patronize me," she snapped. "I don't need any warnings. You know I loved that man. Now go away. I have to prepare myself to play a drooling, ill-tempered old bat."

"I don't see that as a stretch," I cracked, retreating under Evelyn's fierce gaze. She had made herself look old, vulnerable, and out of it. It made me feel both sad—I didn't want to lose anybody else—and fearful. Could I really justify sending her into that place?

Tagg tapped on the roof, and the Geo sailed out onto the street.

"You sure they're safe?"

Tagg shrugged. "Anybody who makes guarantees in my line of work isn't a truthful person," he said. "But Leeming and I talked about this last night. I think your idea of bringing this James weirdo in was pretty smart. They'll think of him as crazy and desperate; they'll feel safe running their scams on him. And they're not going to shoot Evelyn, right? So I think we're cool. And if we hear anything we don't like," he tapped his inside jacket pocket, "I've got a warrant in here and a small army out there. We can be inside that facility in a flash."

We headed for the stairs. I begged someone—God, fate, karma—for good fortune. I wasn't particularly religious, but at times like this, you want to cover your bets. If there was a God, I wanted Him on our side. But then again, I thought, if there was a God, wouldn't He have been on Benchley's?

Upstairs among the troops, I poured myself a cup of nasty coffee. I thought of my father, whom I doubted I would recognize if I met him on the street. I could hardly bear the thought of going to see him. But this week had made me realize that time had a way of running out abruptly.

"They're past security," said a technician.

twenty-one

ON THE MONITOR in our dingy hideout, we watched the Geo wind up toward the driveway.

A radio crackled. "They got security out back, Lieutenant. A guy walking a Doberman." They were obviously anxious to avoid a repeat of Luis's fence-vaulting.

The FBI agents, still silent, moved closer to the monitor. The techs sat in a row, fiddling with the dials on their recorders and cameras and radios. Leeming, stationed at the window, watched through his binoculars until the Geo had passed under the canopy that shielded arriving ambulances and patients too ill to walk from the lot. He was like a dog on the scent—focused, tense, oblivious to everything else. I wouldn't want him on my trail. Though I guess he was on my trail.

"They're inside," Tagg said. We heard somebody welcoming James, heard his shrill answering hello. Evelyn muttered something incomprehensible.

"I can't tell you how glad I am to see you," James chattered. "She is not in good shape. She needs care and attention. I am overwhelmed." Easy, easy, I thought. They don't give out

Oscars for this. But the other voice sounded sympathetic and understanding, even though I couldn't make out the words. There were more muttered sounds from several voices. The techs looked at each other.

"This isn't very clear," Tagg barked.

"I know, Lieutenant. But it doesn't work all that great when there are two or three people talking at once. It should clear up."

"It better," he said, echoing my thoughts.

James was invited to fill out some forms. I heard the cool, tough voice of Mary O'Brien inquiring about Evelyn's medical history. Mostly, James said he didn't know much. He gave Dr. Morrison, Benchley's physician, as Evelyn's, but we had already called Morrison and asked him to be unavailable to Elston Manor until Monday. The Chief himself had to get on the phone and assure Morrison it was all in the service of justice.

James and Evelyn were in different rooms, it seemed. I could hear James's pen scratching on some forms. I heard an attendant speaking soothingly to Evelyn about changing her clothes, about the view, about the nice roommate who would be arriving the next day. The attendant seemed genuine and warm. "Why not rest now," she said to Evelyn, and then seemed to leave the room.

"I'm going to pretend to take a nap" came Evelyn's voice, in a whisper.

"Jeez, didn't we tell her not to do that?" Leeming fussed. "She shouldn't be talking to the mike. She doesn't know if somebody's listening in on her or not."

As a matter of fact, none of us had thought to warn her about that. I hoped she would just lie quietly.

"The bad guys are coming in," said Tagg.

The monitor showed a Lincoln Town Car pulling up at the security gate. "That's Mackley; we know his license plate," said one of the FBI agents; evidently they'd been doing some homework. "And that's Hamilton next to him, I bet," I said, though all we could see was the backs of two heads.

Mackley and Hamilton gave their names to the guards and were quickly ushered through.

"That guy a doctor?" one of the guards asked afterward.

"Hey," I said, surprised. "How can we hear the guards? They're not miked!"

Tagg smiled smugly. "Oh, yes, they are. We don't want reinforcements getting called in without our knowing about it, do we? There's a directional mike pointed at the booth from an unmarked van across the street."

Sometimes I underestimated cops. They could be pretty impressive.

Meanwhile, Mary O'Brien had begun working on James. "This must be hard on you, Miss, uh, James," she said soothingly. She'd probably never met a relative quite like this one. In our apartment, the digital recorders were lit up.

James launched into a wrenching lament about his life, the cost of caring for his aunt, his fatigue. "I'm desperate," he said. "Desperate. The hard thing is that we never got along that well. I mean, naturally I love Evelyn. But she disapproved of my, um, lifestyle, sometimes harshly. Now I'm supposed to sacrifice my whole life. I've run through my savings. I can't bring anyone to the apartment. She yells and thrashes around half the night. God, I think I'm going to lose my mind."

O'Brien said she'd be right back. She returned with some herbal tea. "I think we can help you, Miss James. I'm glad you hired Peter Mackley. He's a highly effective attorney. But he's not cheap," she added. "I have to warn you about that. Still, you can have your life back, be freed of this crushing responsibility. It's a shame, a young . . . person . . . like you, Miss James."

"Just call me James," he said airily. "We don't have to pretend, do we?" James *should* get an Oscar for this; it was almost disturbing how comfortable he was. "I'd be so grateful for some assistance. I'd do anything."

A door opened; we heard Mackley and Hamilton introduce themselves.

"Good to see you," said Mackley, whose voice was deeper and

more resonant than Hamilton's, and who apparently didn't waste a nanosecond on niceties. "I've made a few phone calls, hope you don't mind. Checked out a few financial details. I see you have gone through your savings; at least, you don't have much in your accounts . . ."

"I've got nothing left," said James bleakly.

"And I've checked out Mrs. De La Cretaz's financial history and insurance policies, too," Mackley said.

Willie threw Tagg a look of relief. With the police blessings— unusual in his life as a hacker—Willie had been up until 2 A.M. creating a false financial history for Evelyn on the giant insurance Web site maintained for hospital administrators and health care operators. Well known in the insurance industry, the site provided round the clock information for emergency room staffs, insurance investigators, people who need to know who had which policies. Mackley was a member, according to the site administrator.

Tagg had quickly wrangled higher-ups' permission to "alter" Evelyn's policies. And Mackley had taken the bait. We'd made it a sweet pot.

There followed some pro forma chitchat about grief and aging and responsibility. Then it was Hamilton who spoke up. "My dear James," he said—the condescension in these guys' voices was nauseating—"I want you to know that I've been there. I've been through this. Mr. Mackley thought it might be helpful if we talked privately."

Yes, said Mackley. Why didn't he and Nurse O'Brien go and get a cup of coffee.

"Hmm," Luis murmured. "So Hamilton is a shill. A tester. He will insure that James is willing to play along, then bring Mackley back. If James seems uncomfortable or grows outraged, then they will simply abort. It is a shrewd approach. Mackley maintains deniability and, in any contest, it will be Hamilton's word against James's. And who would believe James?"

Hamilton and James were left alone. We also heard a cough or two from Evelyn's microphone, then a whispered "Hello, I'm still resting."

Luis groaned. "Fortunately," he said, "she is a woman of few words."

Hamilton sounded as though he'd moved closer. "James, can we speak frankly? You're the only living relative, correct?"

"Yes," said James. "It's all on me. It has been for two years."

"Yes," said Hamilton. "We checked the chart on your aunt when we came in. The initial exam said she was weak and disoriented . . ."

"And incontinent. Did they mention incontinent?"

"No," said Hamilton. "That hasn't come up. Not yet." There was some silence.

"Who are you?" asked James, startling all of us with the suddenly suspicious tone in his voice. "I'm not stupid. You all want something. What? You can talk openly to me; I've been very open with you."

Hamilton sounded a little rattled. "Are you having second thoughts? Are you . . ."

"No," said James impatiently. "I'm just not dumb. Ever since I talked to Mr. Mackley and he assured me there was a way out of this, I knew there was something going on. And that it wasn't pretty. That's why I'm here, goddammit, not to have a tea party. Look at me, for chrissake, can't you see that this is driving me out of my mind! I don't lead a conventional lifestyle. Now, I can't go out, I can't have friends or lovers come by, I'm bankrupt and changing diapers in the middle of the night!" He actually began to sob. "What can you do for me? That's all I care about. I don't have to know more . . ."

I couldn't believe my ears; James could hardly have been more convincing. But Tagg shifted nervously, and Luis also looked worried. "Careful," Leeming advised, as if James could hear. "He's got to say it. Don't tell him you don't want to know."

"My father was sick like this," Hamilton commiserated. "He

was incontinent. He didn't know me. He couldn't eat unassisted. I was burning through my life's savings. I know what you're going through, believe me. I made an arrangement with Mackley . . ."

"How much?" asked James coldly, abruptly.

A longer silence. "Half of the insurance. You get relieved of the responsibility. You get relieved of the monthly costs, which, as I well know, Medicare and insurance don't entirely cover. And you still get one hundred and fifty thousand dollars as the beneficiary . . ."

James gasped. "One hundred and fifty thousand dollars. Oh my. And Mackley gets half? What does he do for half?"

"I don't know; you don't want to know," said Hamilton, in a whisper. "He just takes care of it. Nurse O'Brien explained it to me; I'm explaining it to you. If you wait, borrow on her insurance to pay the bills, you're exhausted and she dies and there's nothing left. This way, you have a little nest egg, a way to rejoin life, a small reward for all your sacrifice."

James sat quietly for about a minute or two. "What happened to your father?"

"He died. About a day after I hired Mr. Mackley as my attorney. My father had a severe heart condition. He was given some medication improperly. I sued, you know."

"And how much will you get out of this?" James asked.

"Just twenty-five thousand this time. And a trip to Hawaii. I didn't take a vacation for years; I was with my dad all the time . . ."

"I know," said James, sounding sympathetic. "You mustn't feel bad. You did the right thing, believe me."

"Thanks," Hamilton sniffled. "You are very kind. And easy to talk with. I'm gay, I don't know if you could tell . . ."

"Why, no, I couldn't," said James.

"I just feel you understand."

"I do. I do. Now, please, go get Mr. Mackley. Let's take care of this. I want to get it over with. Then we'll go and have dinner together, shall we?"

"I can't," Hamilton said. "I have to go back to Connecticut with Mackley. He wouldn't like our having dinner. But you can call me. Here's my card . . ."

"Here's a break," said Leeming. "He relates to Plain James! That's a small fan club, I bet." Luis and I gave him a warning look, and he shut up.

Inside Elston Manor, Hamilton had exited; Mackley and O'Brien returned. "Mr. Hamilton tells me you want to retain me. You understand my fee . . ."

"Yes, yes, half of Aunt Evelyn's insurance. Please, Mr. Mackley, I don't want to discuss this. I just want to proceed."

I couldn't speak. I wanted some sense of triumph, or at least satisfaction, but all I felt was weary and a little sick.

Willie tossed a computer disk across the room. "The fuckers," he said quietly.

Tagg was shaken too. "God, you were right, Deleeuw. I can't believe this. It's the most horrible thing I've ever heard. They kill these people! Prey on their exhausted and bankrupt relatives and then go kill them, don't they? Bastards . . ."

"Easy," said Leeming. "Let's stay very cool."

Tagg was normally the most businesslike, least emotional person I've ever dealt with. Now, his face was purple. The detectives and techs looked sickened.

Mackley had some forms ready and James was signing them. It took perhaps two minutes.

"Who will care for my aunt?" he asked, finally, sounding as if he was fighting back tears.

"The doctor is with her now," said O'Brien.

Evelyn's microphone came to life. "Hello, hello? Mrs. De La Cretaz? I'm Dr. Bennett. Dr. Stillwell Bennett."

Luis, Tagg, Leeming, and I all exchanged panicked glances. "He's in there already?" shouted Luis.

"He didn't come through security."

"What the fuck?" Leeming bellowed.

The voice, unctuous and creepy, continued. "I guess you can't hear me. Let me feel your pulse and check your heart," he said. "Oh, yes. Hold still now. This won't hurt . . ."

I couldn't hear the rest of the sentence. Tagg was screaming "Go! Go! Go!" into a radio transmitter. I heard the school bus outside roar to life. We were all scrambling down the back stairs.

twenty-two

THE COOL SCENE in the apartment had degenerated into mayhem. The bus was maneuvering to get through the narrow alley entrance onto the street. The rest of us were piling willy-nilly into the vans out back. Only the techs remained behind to keep the tapes rolling.

I grabbed Tagg's walkie-talkie: "This is Kit Deleeuw. When you get inside, get to admitting and find Evelyn De La Cretaz's room. There's a Dr. Stillwell Bennett who might be giving her a shot or putting in an IV line. Keep him away from her. He's dangerous."

Tagg grabbed the walkie-talkie back. "This is Tagg. Confirm that. Team A, arrest O'Brien. Team B, your target is Mackley. Team C, William Hamilton. Everybody else, right into De La Cretaz's room; get her out of there. Detain Dr. Bennett. Operations, call an ambulance; she might need one."

What was scaring the hell out of me—and all of us—was that we hadn't heard a sound from Evelyn since Bennett had promised that something wouldn't hurt. Why hadn't she struggled, or said something to let us know if she was okay or needed help? Could she have lost consciousness already? Or worse?

Tagg wound up in the van's front seat with a driver in a black SWAT uniform. Leeming and I were in the back, with four other heavily armed troopers. I couldn't imagine there'd be a gun battle in a nursing home, but these people were ready for one.

Luis was in the second van, along with the FBI agents, who, I'd noticed, seemed curious to know who he was. Maybe they'd have better luck than I'd had. Willie had stayed behind with the techs.

"Light 'em up," said Tagg into his radio. Sirens and lights switched on all around us. We bolted out of the lot and bore down on Elston Manor in the Sunday quiet. Kids froze in their front yards and bewildered adults came outside to gawk at the armada howling past.

The two security guards came running out of their booth, but a sedan drove up onto the lawn and three troopers jumped out, flashed their badges, and corralled them. The bus shot down the driveway; its doors popped open, disgorging a stream of black-uniformed officers in flak vests and helmets, toting automatic rifles as they charged through the main entrance.

"Be careful," said Tagg. "You've got old people in there who've already had heart attacks and strokes. Don't scare everybody to death." A bit late for that caution. Anybody sitting in a wheelchair inside was about to get the shock of his life.

We pulled up behind the bus, were all out and running. A trooper tried to hand me a vest, but I brushed it off; I wasn't about to stop and pull it on.

"Follow me," Luis snapped. "I know where Evelyn will be." Tagg paused. "Mackley and Hamilton," I said. "Don't let them get away." Tagg charged down the hallway toward the main nursing station, a squadron of clanking troopers—radios squawking, keys jangling, guns clanking and clicking—behind him.

Leeming and I—plus four troopers and two FBI agents—

raced off to the right after Luis, who sprinted down the hallway beneath a sign that said "Ward A: Admitting, Visitors." We plowed through the swinging doors, slowing to avoid crashing into three patients sitting in wheelchairs in the hallway. Two seemed not to notice us; the third smiled and waved. We dashed right, then right again.

Luis kicked open one door, then backed away and kicked open another. We all held back. He kicked open a third door, then charged in. I followed, along with Leeming.

We heard a curse and a grunt, then saw a large body fly halfway across the room and plow into the far wall, pulling down the IV stand next to the bed with a crash.

"What the hell . . ." said the body, which slumped to the floor and groaned. Evelyn lay in the bed, her eyes closed. I saw the hearing-aid transmitter on the tray table next to the bed; Bennett must have removed it. The troopers landed on Bennett, flipped him over adroitly, pulled him to his feet, and slapped on the cuffs.

"Bennett," I cried, my voice shaking. "This woman works for me. She dies and it's murder one for you. What did you give her? What?"

"A hundred milligrams of Hemavero," he said, without hesitation. "Digitalis will counteract it. But do it soon."

Two paramedics came rushing into the room; two other troopers grabbed Evelyn's bed and started to roll her out. Bennett yelled instructions to the paramedics, who got on their radios immediately for authorization to give her the digitalis. Seconds later, she was gone, in an ambulance racing toward the Hackensack Hospital Center.

Bennett, looking wretched and defeated, was read his rights and marched out. "Jeez," he said to Luis, "you didn't have to drop-kick me like that. I'm sorry, I'm . . ."

"Save it for court," Leeming snarled, nudging him out.

Luis, white-faced and trembling with rage, walked out after them. The two FBI agents moved out of his way with admiring looks.

And here came Tagg, escorting Mackley and Hamilton and Mary O'Brien in a procession toward the entrance. They were in handcuffs, each flanked by two state troopers. "Twenty-two years in police work," he was proclaiming. Their faces were impassive. "And this is the happiest arrest I've ever made."

The astonished staff of Elston Manor stood back against the walls. A few had the presence of mind to move the patients inside their rooms. "We've got people to take care of here," one nurse announced coolly. "The circus is over." She eyed Luis curiously, but let him pass without greeting or comment.

"I've got Senator Goodell on the telephone," another nurse said, walking over to Tagg. "He isn't happy. He wants to talk to the person in charge."

Tagg stuffed his revolver back in its shoulder holster. "Tell him to call the governor," he said, heading for the door.

twenty-three

BY THE TIME we got to the hospital, a shaken but restored Evelyn was sitting up on a gurney in the Emergency Room, surrounded by a gaggle of SWAT troopers. The digitalis, administered en route by the paramedics, was magic stuff, it seemed.

"I'm fine, Kit, just fine," she said hastily as I came crashing in with Tagg. We exchanged the first hug of our years together. She was full of justifiable pride; I was nearly limp with relief. I squeezed her hand, told her what a terrific job she'd done. She groused about the annoying doctors and their insistence that she remain overnight "for observation."

Then, promising a full briefing as soon as she was released, I gave her a peck on the cheek and left the ER. We all boarded the vans for the State Police outpost on the Garden State Parkway.

Tagg had taken over a big meeting room there. The first reporters were starting to call, and Tagg was setting up a press conference with his supervisors. He asked me if I wanted in, but I shook my head no.

Luis had gotten a lift home with his admirers from the FBI. I wondered if they knew more about him than I did. My favorite theory was that Luis had helped the feds battle Castro in one way or another. Perhaps that explained his hurried departure from Cuba, his being cut off from his family, and his reluctance to take up work that might call attention to himself. Maybe someday I'd know. Willie had left with Luis, which surprised me; maybe he was shy about the press.

At the postmortem, attended by perhaps thirty state and local cops, there was a lot of back-patting and high-fiving. Tagg took the podium and declared Operation Benchley "an unqualified success." There was scattered applause.

"I'd like to say that I especially appreciate the cooperation and assistance provided by Kit Deleeuw, who as you know is a private investigator." More applause, along with a few puzzled looks.

"And we have to give special thanks," he added, looking both embarrassed and uncomfortable, "to James Del Riccio, better known as Plain James . . ." James mock-curtsied and blew Tagg a kiss; the lieutenant turned a striking purple, as the detectives and SWAT team members hooted and cheered. James announced dramatically that he was off to New York City to resume an interrupted rendezvous, and waltzed out the back door, pausing to wave at me.

"Here's what we've got," Tagg proceeded, leafing through his notes. "The arrested parties are attorney Peter Mackley; Head Nurse of Elston Manor Mary O'Brien; businessman and investor William Hamilton of Southampton, Connecticut; and Dr. Stillwell Bennett of Burlington County, New Jersey. All charged with capital murder."

Some murmuring from the troops. In New Jersey, that made the death penalty a possibility. "State monitors have assumed operation of the Elston Manor Rehabilitation Facility. As of this briefing, the FBI and the Connecticut and New York State Police are making cautionary inspections of the other facilities owned by Transitions, Inc., although we don't know of any crimes being committed there." Tagg loosened his tie. "Let me commend you on the professional and disciplined way this very delicate operation was conducted. Our raid took place among some very elderly, infirm residents. People could have been roughed up, injured, scared to death. But that didn't occur. Good work, men and women; I'm proud of you."

Okay, enough plaudits, I thought, as Tagg relished his moment in the spotlight. We all knew the spotlight would move on as soon as his bosses arrived from Trenton to talk to the press waiting outside.

"I'm glad I can now tell you what this is about. What we have here is an organized ring of cold-blooded murderers. They took advantage of the elderly and their families by seeking out people who were staggering under the burden of caring for their aging relatives. They worked out an insurance-fraud scheme to split life insurance benefits with surviving family members, who had often been driven to financial ruin by caring for these people. Then they made sure the insurance payments arrived in a timely fashion by administering overdoses of a drug called Hemavero to nursing home patients who'd suffered heart attacks and strokes. Hemavero is difficult to detect in autopsies . . ."

I interrupted. "Which are rarely conducted on those in their eighties and nineties who die in nursing homes anyway."

"Right," Tagg said, startled by my interjection. "Their death certificates were signed by Dr. Stillwell Bennett, the same doctor who oversaw or administered the drug overdose."

Tagg's voice became a drone. I didn't need to listen; I knew it all. Bennett had gotten in trouble initially because one of Elston Manor's other attending physicians had noticed that he was prescribing high drug doses and called the nursing home administrator, who uncovered the kickback scheme that led to Bennett's firing. The whistle-blower had lost his contract to care for people at the Manor, of course. But then, neither he nor the administrator imagined that Bennett was killing people.

I supposed it was Bennett and O'Brien whom Benchley had overheard talking about killing a patient just before my visit, when he'd frantically tried to signal me. He couldn't be more precise and even I had doubted what he remembered. But he had known, even in his diminished state, that something was terribly wrong.

In fact, Willie had uncovered the deaths of eleven of Stillwell Bennett's patients, all of whose relatives were represented by Peter Mackley. I didn't know for sure yet, but I suspected the scheme really took off when Mackley represented Hamilton in his lawsuit. Mackley had also represented Bennett in several scrapes and probably saw his scheme taking shape: the sympathetic shill to lure in despairing relatives, and the embittered, alcoholic physician who could prescribe the murderous medication and foreclose any investigation by signing the death certificates.

When somebody in James's situation appeared at a Transitions facility, Mackley—alerted by someone like the vigilant O'Brien—checked him out as a possible mark. Caring for the aging had become so expensive and terrifying, especially in cases like the fake one we'd presented, that his approach stood a good chance of success.

You took an exhausted, broke, perhaps distant family member. You looked for an incapacitated, terminally ill old person who hadn't yet borrowed away all the value of his life insurance policy. You had Hamilton approach to gauge the level of desperation, then moved in for the kill.

It was understood that the relative would pass away quickly, before running up too high a tab, and that the insurance would be split. You didn't want to know any more than that, as James had declared. You couldn't really feel conscience-stricken about what you didn't know.

It was a tragic mishap that Benchley had innocently stumbled into this horrid gang. He thought he was offering himself as a sort of role model, entering an assisted care facility—something I think he didn't really want to do—so that a bunch of other, less fortunate people would be assured high-quality care. He was a sucker for that kind of approach, as Goodell had no doubt understood. But Bennett and O'Brien may have realized that he wasn't as out of it as he first seemed, that he knew something evil was going on and was somehow communicating with people on the outside. On the other hand, his doctor had said that the stroke had caused so much damage that he wouldn't have lived long in any case. But he'd been alert enough to grasp something of what was going on around him.

I walked out of the briefing, though Tagg was just warming up, and sat for a moment in the old Volvo, suddenly feeling tired. My work was done. I didn't want there to be any more. I wasn't even in a hurry to learn who'd shot at me; it didn't seem to matter much. Driving home on a sweet spring afternoon, careful to avoid runners, cyclists, dog walkers, and street hockey games, I was eager to be someplace where no one was over fifty yet.

Jane and Ben were waiting for me; Emily was upstairs, but came running down and actually threw herself into my arms. Nothing like nearly being killed to upgrade your stature in the family. I knew I had only a few hours to enjoy this respite; by breakfast, I'd be the Big Goofus again.

"Congratulations, Dad," she said. "Maybe you're not such a dummy, after all."

"Why, thanks, Em," I said. "I'm going to get all misty."

Ben rolled his eyes. "Never mind the applause, Dad. What happened? We heard the news about Elston Manor on the TV. You've already had some calls from reporters."

"I took a message from the *New York Times*. And CNN!" Emily announced importantly. And added, puzzled, "They want to interview you." It seemed nearly incomprehensible.

"I'm not talking to any reporters," I said, sitting down at the kitchen table. Jane made me some tea. Percentage came hobbling over to present me with his stuffed toy beaver, Bucky, a high honor. But then, Percentage always rejoiced in my accomplishments, like getting up in the morning and shaving.

More unusual was the fact that my family, who normally broke out in yawns when I discoursed about detecting, this time were all ears.

Ben took the chair across from me and waited; Emily boosted herself onto the countertop. They looked expectant; Jane looked grim.

"So, these people killed sick old people for their insurance?" Ben asked. For the first time, I noticed a second earring, a small silver stud, glittering in his right ear. We'd said yes to the first, but this one seemed to have materialized unnoticed by his doting parents.

"They murdered Benchley, too?" Jane asked sadly.

"I don't really know, to be honest. It's unclear. But he knew that others were being killed; he tried to tell us. I can't imagine the horror of his realizing that the arrangement that he'd made for so many people might be a death trap."

"This aging thing," Jane said. "It comes up in my practice all the time. It's barbaric."

I nodded, leaning over to scratch the dog. "I saw Pleasant Hollow, Stillwell's place. I wouldn't put Percentage in there. And it still cost a fortune. You have a lethal combination here, unscrupulous lawyers, a drunken wreck of a doctor, desperate relatives, and people very close to death, unable to protect themselves. They got greedy, of course, and it was dumb of Mackley to be representing everybody. He muttered to one of the detectives that he was just a couple of weeks away from moving to the Caribbean. I don't know if we'll find more cases or not, but from the ones we do know about, he pocketed over two million bucks."

Ben whistled. "Unbelievable."

"My friend Plain James will admire your earring," I added.

Ben grinned and sipped from his Diet Coke. "Sorry, Dad. Just was in a weird mood."

I smiled back. I was happy to be at home with my family.

"So, Goodell?" Jane asked.

"Didn't know about any of this, I don't think," I said. "He tolerated Bennett because Bennett brought him a lot of business. The state will probably go after Goodell for not banning Bennett completely after his kickback problems. Goodell will be ruined. Transitions, Inc., isn't going to fetch the hefty price he expected. It's probably not saleable at all. And his political standing will be shot, for sure."

Ben looked closely at me. "What about you, Dad? Are they going to yank your license?"

"I don't know, Ben. And we still have to figure out what's going on with Mom."

"Mom's just fine," Jane put in. "A Mrs. Barrett Wallowby called an hour ago. She said she'd just had a visit from two associates of my husband's, a handsome young blond man and a middle-aged Spanish gentleman. It seems they had uncovered some information about her past that they thought she'd be interested in learning. And she said she would withdraw the complaint first thing Monday morning. I remember her vaguely. She came to see me, but I referred her to someone else . . ."

"What did she come to see you about?" I asked.

Jane shook her head. "She might be crooked, but she still gets therapist-client privilege."

So that was where Luis and Willie had gone. I'd bet this woman had a long insurance-fraud record or something equally unsavory, and Willie had dug it out. Then, with the address Tagg supplied, the two of them had paid a personal call to persuade her it would be wise to bow out of this case.

"What about the arrangements Benchley made for other old people?" Jane asked. "Are they null and void?"

"I don't know," I said. "If Elston Manor stays open, I don't see why they would be. But enough shoptalk. I've had it. I'm tired and sad. I want to do what Benchley told us—to get on with life. I want to take my daughter, son, and wife out for ice cream cones. Two scoops each. Crushed Oreos on top. The works. Life is short."

epilogue

JAMES GOODELL resigned from the State Senate. One of his last official acts was to write the state Licensing Office urging leniency for my "perhaps overzealous" investigation of his nursing homes. He quit the assisted care business too, and ascended to politician's heaven: a powerful and high-paying Trenton law firm that lobbied his former colleagues in the legislature.

"Two of the least gratifying businesses in the world these days are politics and nursing home care," he told me in a farewell phone call. "I'm getting out of them both. I'm going to spend a lot more time on the links." And, I suspected, in court. At least eight families were suing Transitions, Inc., for the wrongful deaths of relatives who'd gotten high doses of Hemavero.

The Food and Drug Administration even suspended use of the drug pending an inquiry. But I gathered from the state cops that this was routine. "The drug is fine," said one of the doctors working with the State Police as an expert witness. "It just depends on how you use it."

Plain James and Evelyn received awards for heroism from the

governor, who was happy to place the medal around Evelyn's neck with a kiss but kept at arm's length from James, who got only a quick handshake. The medal graced his cart at the American Way, anyway.

The Licensing Office suspended my PI license for a month and put me on probation for two years. Chief Leeming testified against me, arguing that I had put myself and others in danger. But after the hearing, he came up and offered his hand. And I happily shook it. No hard feelings.

"I know you were just acting out of friendship with Benchley," he said. "But my job is to protect the town. You behaved irresponsibly. I think your punishment should have been more severe than this wrist tap, but, hey, that's the law."

"And you get paid to uphold the law."

"Right," he said.

Dr. Bennett was the first of those arrested to turn state's evidence; there was intense plea bargaining going on. The county prosecutor declined to seek the death penalty, which I personally found to be a relief. I didn't relish being responsible for anybody's execution.

The truth was, this wasn't an issue anybody wanted to focus on for too long. "The very aged and infirm have no real constituency," said Jane. "There are plenty of dedicated health care professionals busting their butts to take care of these people. But for God's sake, this is a society that doesn't even want to take care of its *children* let alone it's elderly. Nobody really wants to deal with this. Nobody has the money to pay for proper care. Nobody wants to think about it in advance, either. So this sort of stuff will happen again."

I understood perfectly; I didn't want to think about it either.

A few weeks after the showdown and arrests, Jane, Emily, Ben, Luis, Willie, Benchley's dog Melody, and I gathered for a private memorial behind his house at the Garden Center.

In keeping with Benchley's religious beliefs, it was mostly silent.

"So long, dude," said Willie.

"Benchley," I said. "You had a genius for encouragement."

"And for nurturing," Jane added. "There are things growing all over town, some of them will live on for a hundred years, because you planted them."

We had scattered his ashes among the hills overlooking his old house, following his instructions. Rose Klock hadn't left any instructions, but we did the same for her. We suspected she'd died of a broken heart. Benchley was the last thing in the world she had to love, and when it was clear he had moved permanently to someone else's care, she no longer had any reason to endure loneliness and loss.

The Garden Center itself was in some peril. Three developers had already expressed interest in carving condos out of it. One even proposed calling the development Carrolton Gardens.

Over my dead body. I had already organized a citizens' committee to preserve most of the acreage as open space, with a permanent park in Benchley's honor. We were prepared to resort to any tactics up to and including terrorism to keep this place from being consumed by Jersey sprawl. It might take that much.

So, as Benchley had said a zillion times, life goes on. You can't sit around mourning what's past; you have to get on with the business of living.

A sympathetic Emily decided for a couple of days that I wasn't all that repulsive. She even allowed me to take her to the movies—and sit next to her, sharing popcorn. But the impulse soon passed. It's what we wanted, isn't it? For her to be independent? So, no whining when she is. The afternoon after my licensing hearing, I made the foolish mistake of asking how her day had gone, and she accused me of wantonly invading her privacy and trampling her sensitivity.

Other things had likewise reverted to normalcy. Luis was overseeing his corps of surly teenagers in a vain effort to force them to be courteous. Willie was back in his darkened office all day, tracking down people and records via the Web. Evelyn, fully recovered and quite full of herself, made it clear that she

intended to do more investigating; she threatened an age dis-
crimination suit if I balked.

But I wouldn't. Evelyn was a lethal undercover operative. I
pictured a grandma-grandson team, pursuing cases. Nobody
would ever suspect a thing.

For several weeks, I had put off the unfinished business of my
own that I knew had to be dealt with. But early in June, I did
it. I drove to the American Way on a Saturday morning, filled
with resolve and dread. I waved to the Cicchelli mannequins,
sporting their new spring polo shirts and plaid Bermuda shorts.
I saw Murray Grobstein's latest find—sneakers with high-inten-
sity safety lights for night running—in the window of Shoe
World.

Luis wasn't at the Lightning Burger. I felt a rush of affection
and gratitude for him anyway, as loyal, dependable, and un-
knowable a friend as I could imagine.

Plain James waved cheerily to me from his cart in the atrium.
I walked over. His wig was askew, his makeup smeared, his linen
dress rumpled.

"Rough night?" I asked. He nodded. I heard Etta James coming through his earphones, squeezed his shoulder. Then I
crossed over to the Lightning Burger and brought him a cup of
black coffee. He blew me a kiss.

I went up to my empty suite and locked myself in my office.
Opening the safe where I stored my unused gun, I found a piece
of paper I had stashed there two years ago.

A feeble but still gruff voice answered my call.

"Yeah."

"Jack Deleeuw?"

"Yeah. Who's this?"

"This is your son."

There was a long pause at the other end. "Kit. This is Kit?"

"Yes. This is Kit."

More silence. "Why are you calling me?"

"I'm coming to see you."

"Why? To put me in a home?"

"Maybe."

"Well, come on then. We'll see what we'll see." He hung up.

I took a long, shaky breath. And another. Then I called and made reservations on a flight to Chicago, open return.